INSIDE THE STRING

A Sam the Seeker Novel

J. LEIGH BROWN

Inside the String is published by
8 Finch Productions

PO Box 2015
Helena, Montana, US 59624

www.8finchproductions@gmail.com

Cover Design by Milan Jovanovic

Ordering Information:
For details, contact: J Leigh Brown
8finchproductions@gmail.com

Library of Congress Control Number: 2020916172

print ISBN: 978-1-09831-773-7
ebook ISBN: 978-1-09831-774-4

Printed in the United States of America

First Edition

This book is dedicated to my courageous tribe:

Barbara G. Crocker

Robin Ann Hutton

Sherrie B. Chenovick

Yvonne C. Foy

'Man follows earth. Earth follows heaven.
And sometimes things are ahead,
and sometimes they are behind.'

Chapter 1-
WILDERNESS SURPRISE

Rex Higley stands in front of the hotel's bathroom mirror. It takes nearly an hour to perfect his Camo FX face paint design. The slick, mid-twenties Southerner checks his Camouflage Falcon watch. It's 4:00 A.M.

Trophy pursuits take considerable time, money, and planning. A white face easily noticed against the murky ravine's backdrop might betray his entire scheme. Hunter's face paint and camouflage reinforces Rex's ability to disappear, but also validates his self-image as a trophy hunter.

The plush gully inside Montana's Bob Marshall Wilderness provides the perfect resting place for elk, deer, and bear. This robust ecosystem promises a hassle-free pursuit. Rex planted a salt lick in the valley two days prior to fortify his triumphant expedition.

The trophy hunter uses the early morning hour to cover his movements. It's fair to say this depraved, out-of-season foray is criminal. That's why the sham huntsman parks his truck five miles from the ravine.

Rex pre-loaded his Polaris four-wheeler for prompt access to the intended hunt. This off-road vehicle will eliminate the drudgery of a strenuous haul. The headdress on a trophy elk is weighty enough to slow a grown man down on a short trek, never mind five miles. Rex isn't concerned about the carcass. He'll leave that behind, but the carriage of a flawless trophy rack with its combination of long beams, points, mass, and wide- spread requires an intricate conveyance.

Fragments of low-lying fog lace themselves in and around the undergrowth. Residual mist from a colder-than-usual night hovers above the gully. A prevailing tension augmented by the ghostly hour infects Rex's every move. This thrilling edginess is the reason he hunts.

Concealed downwind on the edge of the gulch, the hunter is further disguised by thick branches and heavily laden trees. It amply veils Rex's presence, or so he thinks.

Eagerly, he lifts his Rem Mod 700 rifle with high-powered scope to appraise the area. Sweeping right to left, he inspects the ravine, searching for the kill. Nothing. Not a single offering. Skeptical, he takes another, much slower swing around the gully. Something unexpected emerges inside the scope's lens. Rex adjusts the scope's power ring for better magnification.

A petite woman masked in bird plumage stares back with revulsion and then vaporizes into the morning mist. An instant twinge of anxiety invades Rex. Twigs snap from behind. The coward overreacts, shooting at a shadowy nonentity.

Rex's hunt is in ruins, but another has begun. He slinks back to his four-wheeler, but it's not where he parked it. Instead, keys dangle from a string tied just out of reach. The retreating hunter's heart pounds as it competes with the blistering pace needed to reach safety. The sinister manifestation haunts him across the rugged terrain.

"You know the difference between a natural predator and a trophy hunter?" asks the ghost, as if she's telling a bedtime story.

Rex stops just long enough to determine a way to bypass the banshee. Omnipresent, the female voice persists.

"A trophy hunter targets the strongest of animals. All that remains are weaklings — scrawny, more vulnerable animals derived from an exhausted gene pool. The treasured headdress, developed genetically over generations, vanishes."

An arrow lands a half-inch from Rex's right foot. The trophy hunter wets himself. Ghouls fill the forest now. Every shadow, every sound terrorizes the gutless hunter.

Two hours into Rex's race for safety, the landscape is washed in an eerie morning light. He stops to catch his breath.

"Why don't you drop the rifle? It makes it easier to escape," shouts the aberration from somewhere he can't trace.

Frozen in place, Rex senses that the suggestion isn't a request. He drops the rifle and dashes on in horrified frenzy. The truck is visible, just ahead, within reach. Relief engulfs the hunted. Moving forward, the exhausted man searches his camo vest for keys. The persistent ghost awaits her trophy from the opposite side of the truck. Rex freezes focused solely on the aberration.

"I've been waiting for you," snarls the ghost.

A strong thump echoes off canyon walls as the trophy hunter falls to the ground, insensible. The behindhand blow is sudden.

Hours later, the county sheriff stands beneath the netted man-animal dangling twelve feet in the air from a giant fir. Law enforcement received a poaching tip, complete with coordinates. Apparently, the netted ass was hunting out of season.

Sheriff Drake Stoltz, a tall redhead with a kind smile, tells his undersheriff to cut the rope and carefully lower the nude man to the ground. A combination of urine and sweat permeates the ensnared beast.

Rex Higley, conscious but confused, spent an anxious day suspended in the sweltering sun. When the sheriff tries to question the man, he mumbles something about being chased by a feathered ghost.

Higley's truck bed holds a four-wheeler and foolproof evidence of a trophy hunt. Spent bullet cartridges, salt lick, and a rifle broken into multiple pieces are lined out as testimony of the trophy hunter's illicit intentions.

Stoltz tries not to laugh but can't help appreciating the irony of the stark-naked man's fretful testimony — tracked, chased, and hung in a tree just like a trophy animal. The only missing article is a decapitated headdress.

The disgusted undersheriff throws an orange jail suit at the bewildered captive. Nervous jitters make it difficult for Rex to find its pantlegs. The undersheriff shoots a sideways glance at his boss as he loads a cuffed Rex Higley into the back of the patrol vehicle. It will be a long ride to lockup in the company of this fetid fool.

Stoltz stays behind to investigate the crime scene. He grins with sheer pleasure, adjusting his cowboy hat before surveying the immediate area. A variety of footprints are present, along with a single feather.

Expanding the five-foot search to ten, he shouts, "I'll be damned if Higley's head didn't run into a coup stick. He could've been seriously hurt or even killed. Plus, that Southerner is barbequed to a crisp, hung naked in the sun all day. I imagine he'll tolerate the pain all right. The sheriff's department is mighty grateful for the tip."

The only response comes from a growing breeze. A solitary feather stands upright, centered between a formation made of tiny, pearl-shaped river rocks. Stoltz uses his sizeable boot to wipe out the small insignia. A ceaseless grin on the sheriff's face widens before he heads back to headquarters.

Chapter 2-

COOPER'S DYNASTY

The room designed like a NASA control center is lit in a bluish glow. Multiple figures flash on mega-sized screens suspended from the ceiling. They display a mix of geological maps and latitudinal and longitudinal coordinates, as well as Fish, Wildlife and Parks and Department of Natural Resources Trust Land Management economic statistics, all referencing the great state of Montana.

Tall chairs on casters fit snugly under a huge, lit glass table in the center of the room. Closets line the exterior walls filled with wigs, makeup, and a variety of apparel to outfit all sizes and genders. A false front covers one wall that folds inward, concealing numerous weapons. An eye scan is the only way to gain access to the inner chamber.

A small bathroom with a shower sits on the far side, beside an interior office that is much smaller, elegantly decorated with little clutter. One oversized leather chair with an ottoman sits under a micro-sun lamp in the corner, beside a shaded exterior window.

A ringtone plays a soundbite of a disco-era song. Cooper, a handsome young man, well-dressed and finely groomed, answers in a very professional voice.

"Good morning, sir! Yes, the Gulf Stream is an hour out. I agree. The Yellowstone trip was very successful — one less rogue on the loose," reports Cooper in a decorous voice.

"We can close the books on the notorious Yellowstone trophy poacher. Thank you, sir. I'm grateful that my research played a role.

"Yes, we've placed Painted Rock on hold, primarily based on the evening's news coverage. My guess is Sam already knows, sir. We've been working Finch888 for roughly three weeks. Betty is in place and will be glad to hear the case is now a priority."

The United States' secretary of the interior laughs into the phone's earpiece. Mac enjoys the conversation, declaring, "Betty must be somewhat of a standout. I'm not an expert, but there probably aren't many mulattoes in Montana, except perhaps at the Air Force base in Great Falls."

"She has mentioned it's a rather odd sensation," remarks Cooper. "Betty looks at it as a disorder and has even given it a name: 'foreign planet syndrome.'"

"That's hilarious. Please ask Sam to give me a call as soon as possible. We're to meet with the president in the morning. A very incensed Tully Neff is flying back now, and I'd better have some idea how to proceed," reports Mac.

"Yes, sir, we have an eye on the headlines and understand their importance. If you'd like, you can reach Sam on the plane, sir," conveys Cooper.

"No, that won't be necessary," replies the secretary. "Just have the Seeker call back ASAP."

An hour and twenty minutes later, Sam strolls into the undercover unit, "reeking," as Cooper describes it. Dressed in full camouflage, Sam the Seeker lapses into an invariable ritual. She stores her weapons and then falls into the precisely placed chair fronted by the shaded window. Next is the slow consumption of her favorite blended coffee and then a luxuriously hot shower.

"Why don't you go home to clean up?" asks Cooper, as he does with each homecoming.

"I don't want to deny you the odiferous pleasure of my return," replies the Seeker.

"You're filthy. Please stand exactly where you are. The least you could do is strip off those soiled clothes," snipes Cooper, returning with a second mug of steaming coffee.

The nearly nude Seeker sits back in the comfort of the over-stuffed chair and inhales the scent of cinnamon before sipping the hot brew. Sam smiles broadly at Cooper in a show of genuine appreciation.

Casually, the Seeker asks, "How many times did he call?"

An extra-white cotton laundry bag and a brand-new set of rubber gloves appear with Cooper.

"Your superior called once. He knew you were probably sleep-ing and didn't want to bother you during the flight home. Why don't you like him?" asks a smitten Cooper.

"I needn't probe into your motives, as they are rather discernable."

The satiated coffee drinker stretches like a wild cat and then casually strides towards the shower. Cooper continues to pack dirty odds and ends into the laundry bag.

In third person, Sam mocks, "The secretary is intimidated by the Seeker, wouldn't you agree?"

"Your intimidation tactics are nothing more than a weak form of control; at the very least, one should not gloat. I admit that Mr. Reilly Geo Mac fills out his three-piece suit in a way only few can, but if you think his graying temples are the only things I appreciate, you're quite mistaken. The man inspires. He values our work."

Sam's large, tiled, walk-in shower echoes with the retort. "Crush on the new guy, huh? That's unique, Cooper."

The Seeker slides into a bathrobe and then towel-dries her thick blonde hair. Slightly muffled from under the towel, she comments, "For the record, I'm neither an enthusiast nor a detractor, and do you know why?" asks Sam. "Because he's the new guy! I'll proceed much as I did with the last appointee, slowly and with caution. Let me advise you to do the same."

Cooper works around Sam, amassing the soiled garments from the Yellowstone operation into a nearby hamper before turning to his computer.

"Well, I've taken the liberty to check into Secretary Reilly Geo Mac," responds Cooper. "It appears he and the president are trusted friends. DOI's new director has a significant military past. So far, with help from the Center for Military History database, I've traced Mac's namesake as far back as the United States Cavalry.

"There are three generations of Reilly Geo Macs. The current rendition is an accomplished military man in his own right. With the help of the ROTC program, the secretary acquired a degree from Montana State University. He served three tours of duty, one in Iraq and two in Afghanistan.

"Our new boss has a rather substantial inventory of accommodations and certificates of honor to his credit, not to mention the fact that Mac holds a Ph.D. in Environmental Science from Berkley. It's said he shuns all recognition. I guess we can insert this rare modesty to his list of outstanding personal character traits. Shall I go on?" asks the information technology and research specialist.

With no response from the bathroom, he continues.

"I think you'll find this tidbit of history interesting: It appears Reilly Geo Mac's great-grandfather shares a past with the Ink Prayer Indians. I think this a curious coincidence, don't you?

"The Wildbird clan are prominent members of the Ink Prayer tribe. In fact, our primary suspect, Henry Wildbird's clan, can be directly linked to Private Reilly Geo Mac during his years as a Cavalry soldier.

"An Englishman named Sir George Gore built Fort Gore, where present-day Miles City, Montana sits. This Gore was a rich slob who hunted for the thrill of the kill. Historians heavily document his wanton waste. It appears he was ushered out of what is now Montana by that era's version of homeland security: Native Americans."

A fully clothed Sam Cherchez joins Cooper in front of the large screen for more details.

"Gore's recorded kills are committed out of true conceit. From 1854 to '57, this English nobleman slaughtered an estimated ten thousand animals, including bison, bear, antelope, elk, deer, and birds."

Sam looks at Cooper, and in unison, the two pretend to spit on the nearby floor.

Enthralled, the Seeker asks, "Have you found an outright connection?"

"Mac's cavalry unit was forced to escort Gore out of Indian territory. It makes sense that if two families are in such proximity, there's a link," replies Cooper.

And sometimes, things are ahead,

Chapter 3-
THE NEAR FUTURE

This is the third time the young woman makes the hike to Bandy Hawk Lake. Tee Fairfax's rookie status means she's charged with this assignment by default. The truth is no one at the historical society thinks this ethnic record is obtainable, but Tee can't shake the importance of the testimony.

The hike isn't easy. The trail to the cabin is shrouded in nature's grandeur. Distractions are plentiful, as are the enormous granite boulders littering the pathway all the way to the mountain's crest.

The gangly journalist's straw-blonde hair is secured by a bandana, but she's still forced to tuck errant strands behind her ears. Tee stops abruptly, smelling a fetid danger.

Sunlight and shadows mask the gap between bear and hiker. One minute, the animal is five hundred yards off, and the next, it evaporates entirely from sight. The journalist ignores the wilderness rule to freeze; instead, the hiker's pace quickens. Tee's mindset declares the risk of movement gives her the best chance to survive.

With renewed speed, the historical society's young reporter is forced to take a break two-thirds of the way up the mountainside. The bear's stench is still detectable. She stops a second time to look around, but the wild creature is nowhere to be seen.

The trekker presses on with two concerns and ruminates over both. *First, bears have been known to maul people to death, and secondly, the Ink Prayer's story will be lost forever.* Her frantic tempo suddenly turns into a mad dash.

———————◆•———————

Mattie opens the door to a spent, frenzied traveler. It isn't until the two women relax before the fireplace that the younger woman's pounding heart finds renewed regularity.

Settled now, Tee reveals an honest concern. "I think a bear was stalking me in the canyon."

The medicine woman casually confirms Tee's suspicions. "Oh, yes. I trust Black Bear was good company?" replies the elder woman matter-of-factly.

"My totem has great influence. The added protection in such a remote area is a good thing."

Tee's disbelief goes unnoticed.

Pain has taken a discernable toll on the tribal elder; her eyes are singed with discomfort. Mattie has aged since Tee's last visit. The two women settle into the task of recording the Ink Prayer oral history. Mattie Wildbird begins without fanfare.

"Nearly everyone I know is dead."

The tribal elder wastes no time.

"It cannot hurt to speak of their brave deeds now. We, devotees of the String saved the deer, the bighorn sheep, elk, cougar, and mountain lion. Our anarchistic approach can be scrutinized, but not our yield. The wildlife corridor is a proven ecological coup. My grandmother's greatest ambition is now reality."

Mattie looks purposefully at Tee and then adds, "A good hunter is invaluable. The true sportsman doesn't intrude on nature, but rather views wildlife as a part of the community. Nature's old friend, Jim Posewitz, wrote a wonderful handbook called *Beyond Fair Chase*. As a lifelong biologist, he maintains that hunting is a privilege, and primary to any hunt is ethical behavior. The early 1900s are proof of his insight. Biologists, farmers, ranchers, and ethical hunters all worked to protect multiple wildlife species near extinction. With the help from the government, those dedicated and thoughtful people triumphed. All we had to do was follow, but years later, our fight was complicated by endless urban sprawl and human populations that grew like cancer."

Mattie stands to look out the giant windows facing the lake. Her withered frame betrays a once rock-solid athleticism. What remains is a hint of grace. A half-light fills the old medicine woman's aging eyes as she remembers.

"Congress was at odds with the president, and this legislative impotence placed enormous strain on the middle class. A rumble of discontent threatened humanity, spilling over into everyday life. Gun violence tore gaping holes in our communities."

Tee looks up to witness an edginess swallow the old woman's body as she struggles to spill her personal history.

"My own family was victim to this brand of brutality. Tree and Isabelle Wildbird, my father and mother, were shot down in cold blood. Profound despair nearly consumed what family remained, and would have, if not for the String."

Mattie's age-old body cannot tolerate standing for long. She finds herself back in the rocking chair. Stilted seconds pass before the elderly woman finds a way to speak of the past.

"My parents' sudden demise became our incentive. Would my Grandmother Hinmah, a small but powerful tribal medicine woman, and her giant deaf-mute husband have lived life with less distinction? Perhaps the maladies that besieged us were essential to the task.

"I swore not to speak of the Ink Prayer riders, or the String until Delahunt left the office. I have kept this promise."

Tee's eyes widen with recognition. Mattie modestly continues as if such a conversation about a United States president is commonplace.

"It's without guilt that I tell this true story, and promise to do so, without aberration."

The old woman bears an honest look that warms the room. "Before we start, let's have a cup of tea."

The longstanding mistress of the house shuffles down the hall. Not wanting to miss a word, Tee trails behind, juggling a backpack and handheld recorder. The Historical Society's neophyte reporter catches Mattie in the kitchen; her tiny frame is entirely hidden behind the refrigerator door. She resurfaces with creamer in hand. Before the awkward young woman can object, Mattie adds a sampling to both cups, then settles back into a living room chair. Two large apertures frame the lake's breathtaking panorama.

"I've never gotten over this view," says the room's elder stateswoman.

Tee Fairfax finds her way into a chair beside Mattie's, and out of courtesy, takes a sip of tea. The historian's eyes widen.

Mattie cajoles, "I like to add a little something to make my tea palatable."

Both women settle in, as the tale is expected to run well into the evening.

Mattie graciously asks, "Should we begin?"

Chapter 4-
FOURTEEN

"Violent change is perpetual. At fourteen, life should be fanciful, exhilarating, and generous. For me, it wasn't any of those things.

"I witnessed my mother, Isabelle, run to hold back the flow of red from her lover's wound. She couldn't suppress her sentiments as they poured out, like the blood from her husband's chest.

"That crazed day at White Earth obliterated whatever whimsical hopes seize a teenage girl. I watched as a megalomaniac drunk delivered the shot that killed my father.

"Frozen, a bystander, I stood perched on the edge of Bandy Hawk Lake's slender shore and watched as that same drunk leveled his gun upon Isabelle Wildbird's head. The last words she spoke were, 'RUN, MATTIE!' as she crumpled upon my father's motionless body.

"If that wasn't enough, the same intoxicated madman and his inebriated friends hunted my brother and me down like wild dogs. I didn't hear the shot that took my left arm at the elbow but felt a pain different from the loss I'd just witnessed. Today, this fake appendage is a reminder of both heartbreaks."

Mattie thrusts her severed arm in the air as a testament. "I barely survived the shock of my wounds and wouldn't have if my twin brother Henry hadn't pulled me to the bottom of the cold lake. His pride would not let us die at the hands of such wretchedness; if nothing else, he'd choose how we two would perish. Dragging his unconscious twin into the depths of Bandy Hawk was that choice.

"I eventually returned to this world inside the warmth of my grandmother's cabin — this very cabin — exactly where we now sit. For two nights, Grandmother used her powers and knowledge of medicine to heal my wounds.

"It was not until the third day that I returned from a place shared with my parents, so peaceful I almost chose to stay. In the end, they encouraged my otherworldly departure, so I drifted back to the source of my deepest anguish, forced to contend with all the intricacies of sorrow.

"Damaged by our shared loss, those of us left behind grasped for sanity and understanding anywhere we could. Thank God for the String."

Mattie pensively sips her cup of tea and then continues. "My grandparents were vibrant, intellectual people. Life's harsh reality took more than one swing at them. Their vitality and intelligence pulled us through so many challenges.

"While I regained strength, Hinmah plotted the family's future with a frantic passion. She admitted later that she did so as a madwoman. I could see an evident lunacy in the hollowness of her eyes. Who could blame Grandmother, after burying her only son?"

Sadness creeps across Mattie's wizened face. Tee sits paralyzed, frightened that the slightest interruption might interfere with this in-depth narration.

Churning painfully through the past, Mattie reminisces. "What was born of insanity became a systematic plan for our future. In the end, it might even be considered brilliant. As a tribal leader, Hinmah was no stranger to veneration. She maintained a level of respect few enjoyed. It was easy for her to guide my family to a new-found conviction honoring our lost loved ones.

"You see, my parents, Tree and Isabelle Wildbird, dedicated themselves to the conservation of wildlife. Dad did so each day as a warden for the state of Montana's Fish, Wildlife and Parks. My mother handled legal matters for that same department as chief legal counsel."

Tee timidly pushes her glasses into place, daring to ask, "Did both your parents share the aspiration to create this passageway?"

The historian's prompt brings Mattie back from a dark remembrance.

"Yes, but my mother took the lead to create a legislative template that earmarked a small share of FWP's resources for the development of a wildlife corridor. This shared idea, based on a then-new and very accurate scientific model known as island biogeography, became the basis of my grandmother's pledged objective.

"Hinmah aimed to construct a wildlife passageway that would connect national parks, state parks, and wetlands throughout the Rocky Mountain West. All of it was meant to honor Tree and Isabelle Wildbird.

"This corridor would allow wildlife populations threatened with extinction a greater means to contend with urbanization and human sprawl. Ultimately, it became Hinmah's unique tincture to ward off sorrow. She couldn't tolerate the thought that her children's demise meant all their good deeds died with them. From pain came enlightenment."

Tee's laptop slides awkwardly against the armrest of her chair. Whatever was added to the tea takes effect. This slight unevenness is lost on the young woman, but Mattie recognizes the signs of her potent tonic. In frustration, the ham-fisted historian makes a slight adjustment, unperceived by her interviewee. Mattie's revival continues, despite the journalist's clumsiness.

"Grandmother's simple plan to regenerate my parents' ecological aspirations required the implementation of three basic military tactics. She and her band of followers would become experts in misdirection, diversion, and distraction, all familiar tools utilized by her ancestors.

"With each raid on an illicit hunting camp, the Ink Prayer riders applied creative responses to evade impending law enforcement and military tactical responses. These incursions acted as a distraction from the primary goal, the construction of the String. All that required exceptional organizational skills, to be sure."

Mattie stops to make a minor physical adjustment to relieve her achiness. She slightly shifts her undersized frame and begins again.

"We, the Wildbirds, pledged ourselves to what was christened 'Mattie's String of Pearls.' Our priority was the purchase of integral fragments of land that formed our safeguarded passageway. Of course, our means to achieve this task is subject to much criticism.

"Say what they might, today, the String runs from the northernmost tip of Glacier Park down the entire eastern front of the Rocky Mountains, acting as a geographical conduit to and from Yellowstone Park."

Tee is amazed by this revelation.

"I've heard of this, but it's considered an urban legend. Are you telling me that the Ink Prayer are responsible for the Delahunt Wildlife Corridor?"

"Believe me, there is always a price, and in the end, the String's name is of trivial consequence. Dismiss ego. The corridor is intact and deftly accomplishes its mission.

Multiple species utilize the String. Today, video footage verifies that wildlife by the thousands trek back and forth along the passageway," modestly declares Mattie.

"To accomplish this goal, my grandmother worked to build a network with others who aspired to conserve wildlife habitats. Around this scheme, Hinmah advanced designs for everything, to include her grandchildren's education.

"Logical time frames were cultivated for the accomplishment of each objective. What at first was a crazed woman's fledgling philosophy turned to religion and finally conviction, all to absorb our fundamental pain.

"Make no mistake, the String became fanaticism. We would accomplish this ecological miracle by any means possible. What happened over the next decade is a tale to be retold by fervent eco-advocates, far and wide."

Mattie's expression deepens as the story reveals itself. Tee Fairfax sits amazed as the construction of the String is disclosed. As the early evening presses forward, a detailed oral record falls into the young historian's lap.

Several hours pass before nature's clock brings the old woman back to the present. A late evening sun throws slanted shadows against the lake's cliff harbors. The tribal medicine woman unfolds herself from the rocking chair as Tee concedes to Mattie's advanced age.

"That's enough for today, child. I kept you too late. You should stay the night. The spare room is ready. Please, make yourself at home and eat what you want. I will rest now."

With that, the old woman retires without a backward glance.

Chapter 5-
BYGONE CACHE

Left to wander, Tee Fairfax does so. She examines each photograph standing guard on the old cabin walls. She trails her fingertips along countless books that line numerous shelves — unusual reads such as the *U.S. Army Counterinsurgency Field Manual* and *Island Biogeography: Theory and Experiment*.

The pensive young historian is left to discover the hidden treasures of generations with no one to stop her. A native American flute key sits beside a handsome man's picture. Michael Haykin's original oil, "String Theory," is centered atop the fireplace mantle. A pearl necklace hangs encased in glass alongside multiple poetry books by Tyler Knot Gregson.

Inadvertently, Tee trips over an expanding file tucked under the table, neatly labeled but exposed. It tugs hard at the journalist's inquisitiveness. The multi-colored folders reveal a variety of tagged records, news clippings, and personal memoirs.

Tee can't resist. She takes a quick look around to confirm she's alone before prying further. There are multiple files, but the first to catch her eye are two intriguing names. Former Montana Lieutenant Governor Greyson Chance and a high-ranking retired military officer, Bridgette "Gig" Robbins. Tee pulls the file and settles in at the kitchen table.

There are several historical artifacts: a photo of Chance and Governor Crebo Lund shaking hands on their inauguration day followed by *Independent Record* and *Great Falls Tribune* newspaper clippings about governmental legislation. Chance's military record is attached along with an aerial photo of some monument inside the Bob Marshall Wilderness.

Tee can't believe her luck. Mattie's plan to provide this conclusive documentation bolsters the oral history's standing. The young researcher sips at a second cup of tea before curiosity demands she look deeper in the file.

A large manila envelope holds newspaper clippings from the *Mile City Star*, documenting a standout athlete and scholar named Bridgette "Gig" Robbins. Turned brown with age, but still legible, the newsprint details Gig's winning competitions and academic achievements.

Last, there is a handwritten statement from Gig Robbins protected inside a plastic sleeve. She declares herself a proud member of the String's inner circle and does so with honor and gratification. These final artifacts are labeled the property of the late Greyson Chance and are attached with these last words:

"Gig and I grew up in Miles City, Montana. It's a beautiful burg in the middle of the country so enormous it scares most city folk. Only the bold, resourceful, and strong-willed can tolerate such immenseness. Common among the population of my hometown is pride in family and community.

People hold children in great esteem and support them in ways rare for this day and age. My adopted parents were no exception.

Years passed, but each time I visited these well-established folks, the town rolled out the red carpet. I was lucky Mr. and Mrs. Robbins shared their home with me, but the greatest gift was their only daughter Gig.

"You see, Bridgette 'Gig' Robbins was an 'A' student and a superior basketball and track athlete. Ranked nationally, she still holds the 110-yard hurdle record, a feat that makes the old man beam when raised in conversation over a cup of coffee downtown at the 600 Cafe.

"In short, Bridgette 'Gig' Robbins made her folks proud. After high school, the slender, nimbly built Gig gained entrance into the United States Air Force Academy, but not without heartbreak.

———————◦♦◦———————

"Two houses down, on Main Street, in the Pine Hill School for Boys lived a sad, alcoholic man who lost his wife prematurely in an auto accident. This loss stripped him of tolerance for the living, even though she left behind a boy child.

"Before long, that boy became a mainstay in the Robbins household, often taking meals and doing homework with Gig at the kitchen table. As the days passed into years, Gig's parents accepted me as one of their own. Somehow, the Robbins found the compassion to understand that I had little control over my wretched circumstances.

"Gig and I were inseparable and mimicked one another in all things. Age carved its predetermined path forward. It was no surprise that a lover's eye shadowed us until the very day it came to our attention. After an uncomfortable first kiss, Gig and I grew so close that we couldn't imagine life without one another. The only real difference between us was an indeterminate future.

"My drunk of a father couldn't bear the idea of an added loss. After more than one argument, I joined the service without his consent. It was the only way I could pay for college. I never told Dad about the ROTC. It helped to defray Yale's costs. The old man, lost in sorrow, never asked me where I went every fourth weekend.

"Life finally caught up to Gig and me. Eventually, we two were forced to kiss one another goodbye under Miles City's autumn foliage. I realize now the pain of separation was more mine than hers. Someone like Gig couldn't be held back. She had too much to give to the world.

"A fearless decisiveness didn't make her life at the Air Force Academy easier. In fact, it brought the worst out of her male counterparts. It didn't help that women were new to the institution. Initially, I fretted over this.

"Gig had no idea she was beautiful, but her sculpted limbs, confident demeanor, and Mayan-blue eyes soothed even the most jealous. Over time, this powerful and decidedly gifted woman earned the respect of her classmates.

"Bridgette 'Gig' Robbins graduated with honors and served her country as one of the very first female F-16 pilots in the nation."

———•◆•———

"While Gig busted barriers at the academy, I managed to stay financially afloat at Yale. Between my caddie job, ROTC, and my studies, time hurried past with a pronounced haste. I lost contact with Gig as our individual commitments exacted a stalwart price. Our long-distance love dwindled over time.

"Gig's career superseded any personal life she might have once had. Our love letters became sporadic, as did our phone calls.

Eventually, we were forced to accept the revelation that things had changed.

"The state of Montana was proud to have a celebrated officer with Bridgette Robbins's experience and expertise. Its National Guard is notably small. My return to Montana made a Greyson Chance/Bridgette Robbins reunion inevitable; we both played an active role in the small ranks of these combined forces.

"Oddly, as life would have it, Gig and our mates developed a social connection, doing everything together. I guess you could say we found an acceptable means to perpetuate our love, and we often mocked this counterfeit sibling relationship.

"Gig eventually landed the job of Montana's joint chief of the armed forces, a privilege never held by a woman in the National Guard. Her understanding and access unlimited, Gig maintained a better overall knowledge of operations than ninety-nine percent of all ranking guardsmen."

Chapter 6-
A SECOND CHANCE

Tee admires the Greyson Chance revelation. She presses forward, warmed by the soldier's admission.

"Even now, my part in the String feels like a confession, but old age demands I set the record straight. Mattie Wildbird means to give the historical society a full account of what happened during that fateful period of our lives. She promised to present this account after her own death. All I need to do is make sure I beat the old medicine woman into the afterlife. That shouldn't be a problem; Mattie is much tougher than me.

"Joint Chief of Staff Bridgette 'Gig' Robbins is gone now, so my testimony can't hurt her or anyone she loved. I got her tangled up in this thing we all came to know as the String. The blame is mine. Gig was my first love and the one person I could always count on, so I eventually asked her for help. She didn't flinch, and that kind of loyalty is rare.

"The joint chief managed to leave a few words of her own behind. I'll pass on her contribution to Mattie for the historical society. You can trust Bridgette Robbins's words. That woman was as reliable as the sunrise.

"My share of this yarn isn't flattering, but it feels right to set the record straight, so here goes.

"This morning, like so many, I watch the sun rise above the secluded 16th hole of the Hidden Links Golf Course. My wife Danielle and I built a modern ranch just off the east edge of the fairway on the far side of the Ten Mile Creek decades ago. Hot steam rises off my cup of freshly made coffee as a whitetail deer forages just off the rim of green. Hoof marks are the only imprints disturbing the fairway's morning dew. I'm sure this gracefully mystical animal comes to chasten me, a timeless reminder of the Bandy Hawk incident. I can't imagine ever again discharging a gun, given what happened that fall afternoon.

"Lund's hunting party was out of control by the time Warden Wildbird showed. Worse is the fact that Tree Wildbird was off duty. He and his family were innocently camped nearby for a weekend of fun. Fatally bad luck!

"Not one member of Crebo Lund's hunting party showed any restraint, including myself. Alcohol and its abuse were plainly factors. Between the guns and Lund's favorite bourbon, my famed reasoning vaporized. To make matters worse, that son of a bitch Lund completely avoided justice.

"These recollections always bring me back to another luckless encounter. I first meet Crebo Lund at Yale. Montana's future governor came from old money while I didn't have a dime. I worked my way through college with a combination of merit-based aid, odd jobs, and an ROTC scholarship.

"Lund and I are from an entirely different Montana. I'd run into Crebo at a variety of frat house poker games and played out of necessity. Crebo had a need too: unmitigated domination. We both acted with premeditated coolness. I was always the more victorious. Lund grudgingly admired this, so a relationship germinated from a less-than-friendly rivalry. Based on a profound antagonism, our camaraderie was peculiarly distinctive.

"I realize my relationship with Crebo Lund never really evolved. The consequence of this acquaintance was and will always be detrimental to me and those I love.

"Most glaring is the clear difference between our personalities. Lund's flamboyant, assertive manner still aggravates me in an indescribable way. I'm a trained military man who prefers a dutifully polite demeanor. This dissimilarity often caused trouble. Of course, Crebo Lund was always too self-absorbed to notice anyone else's discomfort.

"After college, I served with distinction in the United States Army as a fully commissioned officer. I saw action overseas before coming home to Montana with a master's in business.

"Afterwards, my Stanford girlfriend and I settled in for the long haul. As man and wife, we developed the Eagle Creek golf course with its surrounding property. The land sold quickly to homebuyers who wanted their own view of Montana's dramatic landscape.

"I love my wife Danielle, although she wasn't my first love. This old heart has always belonged to Bridgette Robbins.

"In hindsight, I think myself a fortunate man right up until Crebo Lund reappeared. When Montana's future governor approached me, I failed to recognize the full extent of his base malice.

"Old money, Yale, and family history play a role in what now feels like the inevitable. Lund showed up at the Eagle Creek land office and announced his political ambitions. He had plans for the governorship and then a quick advance into a U.S. senatorial seat.

"Crebo Lund rarely offered anyone anything free. I'd developed substantial connections within the military and business community. That meant I held renewed worth from Lund's Machiavellian perspective. He wanted to know if I would join his political ticket.

"I secretly hoped Danielle would object. It shocked the hell out of me when my single-minded wife pounced on the idea. 'You'd be a great public servant,' said the unflappable woman.

"Danielle sensed my hesitation from the start, but assumed it was because of a private nature. She encouraged the partnership,

"'We're every bit as much a part of the community as Crebo Lund.'

"But the differences between Lund and me were made profoundly clear that day at Bandy Hawk Lake. Callous murder isn't part of my constitution. Neither is the concealment of such a deed.

"It took years for Mattie Wildbird's family to prove that a very affluent Crebo Lund used his wealth to conceal the events at Bandy Hawk. Every hunter in the camp bolstered Lund's storyline — that is, everyone but me.

"Even now, I'm ghastly embarrassed to admit that I passed out after consuming too much bourbon. Unconscious, I didn't regain my senses until after the shootings.

"Rumor is that Lund had taken out extra insurance through remuneration. I couldn't prove it, but wealthy people often buy the law.

"One member of the ill-fated camp exchanged his immediate future for an undisclosed sum. Dennis Ciske made the decision to take the fall for manslaughter and did twenty-four months in the state penitentiary before being released on probation for an additional year.

"Everyone in the camp kept the story straight. The problem with a confession is its inevitable miscarriage to compensate damaged parties, particularly if the wounds are beyond healing.

"My attempt for personal redress came twenty-four hours after the shootings. A residual sense of decency took me to Hinmah and Delsin Wildbird's cabin. Guilt pressed me to check on the children and explain to the old woman what I thought happened.

"Fresh death hovered in the troposphere like an H-bomb. Hinmah told me that the giant of a boy had somehow managed to save his sister, but Mattie's wounds were substantial.

"Hunkered down in an obscure corner of the cabin, Henry Wildbird watched me as I lingered over his twin sister. I didn't see him until it was too late. The boy attacked with the fury of a feral beast and flattened me with one unexpected blow.

"When I came to, Henry's grandfather Delsin was physically dragging the young man outside. My ribs were broken and my left hand crushed. It felt like a semi hit me.

"Given the circumstances, Hinmah graciously intervened. The tribal medicine woman smiled compassionately as she wordlessly treated my wounds. All I could do was express my gratitude and explain what I thought happened at Bandy Hawk Lake.

"Once my version of the story had been disclosed, I watched the old woman's grief fade into something ill defined. Before I could get too carried away with my self-renewal, Hinmah gently stipulated her own plan for my salvation. That's how I fell into the String. My future was as unsettled as the Montana vista. No matter. Because of the String, I won't go down a coward.

———— ◆ ————

"The night Henry Wildbird whipped my ass, Gig found me cowering in the backside of Tony's Lounge. Distraught, I couldn't find the words. Still dressed in bloody desert camouflage, I cried alone in a dark corner. Gig did her best to calm me down, but I couldn't shake the guilt or embarrassment of what happened at White Earth.

"At first, I eluded her questions and begged for time to make sense of things. Bridgette Robbins looked deep into her first love's eyes before granting my request. I ran off before she could put the pieces together. She was forced to call Danielle to confirm my safe arrival home, but my wife was cryptically distant about whatever might have happened.

"'Anguish' best describes the days Gig spent in wonder. Later, headlines in the local paper partially resolved the mystery. One thing is certain: Gig's dedication and love would be tested. Later that week, I called for help, and that's how the National Guard's joint chief of staff became a member of the Ink Prayer's inner circle."

———◆———

Tee's admiration for the two small-town groundbreakers overwhelms. Love and loyalty merged; it's difficult to supress such powerful forces. The journalist is consumed by this poignant love story.

Chapter 7-

BREAKFAST FOR DINNER

Time and Hinmah's tea force the submerged writer to diagnose a deep rumble emanating from her stomach. A grudgeless Tee Fairfax makes a bargain with herself to set aside the many artifacts of history just long enough for dinner. Thinking of Mattie Wildbird and grateful for this rare and wondrous narrative, she'll cook for two.

A quick tour of the kitchen renders all the elements of a spinach omelet, rye toast, and bacon. Fairfax hopes the old woman likes breakfast for dinner.

Tucking stray hair behind her ears, Tee meticulously sets the table and then slips back towards Mattie Wildbird's nest. The shy woman pushes her retro Timothy-round glasses up the bridge of her jagged nose and knocks delicately. There's no response as the leggy woman presses against the door. It creaks as Tee enters.

The same remarkable landscape envelopes this room as seen from the living area. There before the lake sits Mattie, gracefully propped against the copious wings of an overstuffed chair. Tee calls to her host as she steps forward, only to find that the renowned healer has faded into the throes of history.

———◦ ◆ ◦———

She doesn't understand the complexity of her emotions. Tee's previous role as a journalist in the United States Army exposed her to a multitude of horrid deaths.

Dejected, the young woman cannot fathom why she's so affected by Mattie Wildbird. Peacefully departed, the old lady's passing triggers something deeper. The war-hardened Fairfax shudders with inexplicable grief.

The open bay doors flood the room in abject moonlight. The young woman leans in on the elder. She smells the forested freshness in the medicine woman's hair.

Still warm, Mattie's coiled fist easily surrenders the flower-embedded envelope clutched against her chest. Alone and jolted by this somber event, Tee Fairfax takes the dead woman's advice and contacts the name written on the outside of the envelope.

Chapter 8-
LUCE'S KITCHEN STORES

The acrid smell of freshly ground coffee hovers over the remodeled kitchen galley fitted with state-of-the-art appliances. The small pantry just off the kitchen looks as it did decades ago, with freshly painted wainscoting but otherwise unaltered. This is the only request Sam made of her son Atlas and his wife Amy. The homestead belongs to them now. Atlas's family kindly embraces Sam as extended family.

A small bedroom off the cozy store provides a perfect haven. Sam relishes the peace. This is still her favorite place to read about and ponder past and present. The elder takes the early hour call here in this place of solitude.

"You don't know me, but I didn't know what else to do." Weeping, Tee Fairfax can barely explain herself.

Enigmatic and firm, Sam recognizes the moment for what it is.

"I'm on my way. Get a hold of Mattie's son, Henry Junior. His number is underneath a magnetic strip labeled H.J. on the front of the refrigerator. Call him now; he'll handle everything."

The firm voice stiffens Tee's resolve.

"I will, but please, tell me, who are you?"

Stillness followed by mystification.

"You'll know soon enough. Tell Henry I'll be there by mid-afternoon tomorrow," declares a resolute Sam the Seeker.

The phone line goes dead, but Sam's vague response reignites the young journalist's curiosity.

Henry Junior Gray, proud son, unaccustomed to the binding tightness in his chest, falls to the floor in agony. His wife immediately recognizes the one thing that can take this robust man to his knees, the devasting loss of his beloved mother.

Sally Gray runs to H.J.'s side. She applies her trademark remedy, a resilient hug, but even within Sally's firm grasp, it takes her husband time to control his sobbing. Finally, in the wake of his tears, he looks at his loving partner.

"For all my considerable size, you'd think I'd be a little tougher," he said, managing a small laugh to regain his control.

Sally kisses the wetness from his face and helps the giant of a man to his feet. With innocent sentiment, death swallows Henry's immensity.

"I thought I'd prepared myself for the inevitable."

Sally holds her husband's hand.

"Tell me, who have you met that is ready?" Sally presses Henry's giant palm against her reddened cheek. "I'm here, Henry, to help you stand tall. It will take everything you've learned to fill Mattie's shoes. She depends on you to take care of her Ink Prayer."

Henry Jr. rallies with a silent nod, proudly accepting his mother's obligations. The solemn couple spends the remainder of the night notifying tribal members of Mattie's death.

Chapter 9

TREASURE HUNTING

Outside the cabin's expansive windows, the sound of quiet waters pushed to the brink of the lake's shores soothes the historian's panicked soul. She's left with Mattie's remains until morning.

Fairfax cannot pry her eyes away from Mattie, nor can she determine why this stranger draws such empathy. Admittedly, the two just met. Is it the story or the curiously inexplicable connection she felt in the presence of the kind medicine woman?

Adrenaline wanes as Tee fights off exhaustion and whatever concoction Mattie poured into her patented tea. Still spooked, Tee moves back into the kitchen to clear away the remains of the food she cooked earlier.

Forcing herself to stay busy, she's reminded of the file folder discovered earlier. Clues in connection to the mysterious Samantha Cherchez give her renewed purpose. The journalist pries deeper into Mattie's belongings. There it is. A file labeled "Sam the Seeker." Tee covets the file, moving quickly back to the dead woman's side.

"It's my honor to watch over you until H.J. arrives. I hope you don't mind that I've stumbled onto a few clues. Your files will act to collaborate the String's history. I hope you can forgive my inquisitiveness."

Tee detects a rocking chair tucked neatly against the bedroom wall. She grabs two blankets and pulls the chair close to Mattie. Then she covers the old medicine woman with respect, tucking the blanket around Mattie's remains before finding her own seat and blanket.

"I'll read to you. It may help me to stay awake."

Chapter 10-

OH, CANADA

Tending to the needs of eight children is difficult, to say the least. Store-bought goods were often unavailable inside the Shield. Wild game and canned goods saw the family through tough times. I can't remember my mother at rest, challenged by the onus of subsistence. Come hell or high water, Luce Cherchez made time to read to me, her only daughter.

Quarters inside the cabin were tight, but Mom and I found space in a cozy hideaway behind the stove, just beyond the cluttered food stores. It was there that she delivered stories that bolstered. This was her plan for my surviving seven older brothers under the vast and wild Canadian Shield.

Life inside this wilderness was challenging, but also extraordinary. The place demanded the faultless traits of independence and daring. Simultaneously, it extracted close-knit cooperation as I worked alongside my brothers to survive. Traits contingent on endurance became the flawless mechanisms used to raise eight self-sufficient children. Luce Cherchez relished the strength and personality each of her children discovered in the forest's depths.

During hunting season, competition was paramount. First, my seven brothers viewed me as a handicap. The responsibility of caring for a youngster was bothersome. They didn't cut me much slack. I was forced to learn quickly or suffer the ire of whichever sibling was made to tolerate the responsibility. This involuntarily influence forced me to develop an excellent sense of direction. I used this measure to cut down the forest's vastness. Eventually, my knowledge of the surroundings surpassed that of all seven Cherchez boys. The only one more familiar with the Chic-Choc Mountains was my beloved father, Jules.

From the start, I fancied exploring the Shield's vastness. In time, I became both the best shot and tracker in the bunch — that is, except for my mother, who patiently taught me how to level the playing field.

Our large backwoods family became renowned as principled hunters who never failed to bring down an animal responsibly and ethically. Before the Cherchez youngsters could hunt, they first had to complete a mandatory read, *Beyond Fair Chase*. The little handbook was packed with the basic tenets of an ethical hunt. My father considered this read the compulsory first step to any hunt.

Memorizing the paperback's content from front to back was just the beginning. No one touched a gun until properly trained and educated. Jules and Luce Cherchez patiently explained that hunting is a privilege, that the best shot taken is an instantly fatal one, and that safety is and will always be principal to the hunt.

———•◆•———

Mom worked hard to find a balance for her only daughter. We read whenever we could find time. Most reads were beloved books, but we also scanned hundreds of magazines, gleaning information atypical of our surroundings. As time passed, we rarely missed our daily reading, sharing the classics, stories of adventure, Frommer's travel guides, and fashion magazines. My mother believed that we two women had to work twice as hard to comport ourselves civilly due to our surroundings.

By the time college presented itself, I was a voracious reader. The night before leaving, Mom and I hid behind the stove for one last private read. We talked late into the night. Not able to let go, we finally drifted off on the cozy corner side couch until the morning light flooded our hideaway.

Chapter 11-
MSU'S WESTERN CHIC

A main street dive of Bozeman, Montana was just one of many places I worked as a bartender. The Rocking R Bar provided supplemental funds for university books and outdoor gear. This western township was a gentle easement into Montana's rural society. The similarities between Bozeman and my own Gaspé hometown felt thickly relatable.

The bar's creaking floors and dim lighting gave the locals' favorite saloon added charm with an overstated Western ambiance. Cowboys, farmers, and college kids frequented the place from opening to closing.

I watched the fetching giant walk into the Rocking R Bar. The king-sized Colossus stood out, not only due to his immense stature, but also his attire. Dressed like a model straight from *Gentleman's Quarterly*, the very fit and dapper man looked a bit out of place in the mucky surroundings.

Lizzie, the barmaid, knew more about the townspeople than the local rag. I was informed that the giant's name was Henry Wildbird. She provided a colorful scoop about both the giant and his twin sister Mattie. After graduating with a master's in business, Henry sought start-up funds to open a casino. Lizzie went on to explain that he wasn't having much luck. "Montana's good ole' boys weren't about to loan him and his twin sister money on account that they're half-breeds."

I warned Lizzie not to use such an inflammatory label. The barmaid passed it off, considering me just another crazed woman from back East. She went about the business of delivering a loaded tray of beer like nothing was ever said.

A couple of hours later, the giant's Windsor knot looked more than a little askew. Tall tales and laughter gushed from Henry Wildbird's table, just like his multiple rounds of beer. Lizzie made sure an order of Pickle Barrel sandwiches found their way to the big fella and his companions, thereby ensuring a very large tip. Just prior to closing time, the giant of a man ducked out quietly, but not before taking a protracted glance my way.

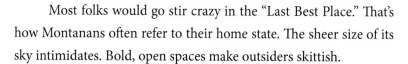

Most folks would go stir crazy in the "Last Best Place." That's how Montanans often refer to their home state. The sheer size of its sky intimidates. Bold, open spaces make outsiders skittish.

As it turned out, Bozeman, Montana was bliss, second only to the Gaspé. The local culture and surrounding Bridger, Gallatin, and Madison ranges are incredibly analogous to the Canadian Shield.

What I did miss was my family. Especially my mother, Luce. The distance between home and college meant the Shield was out of reach for a long three-year stretch. Seeing the Chic-Chocs out the plane's window made my heart skip a beat.

After a little downtime and more than a few good reading sessions in my favorite hideaway, I made plans to get a job with Parks Canada. First, I'd master wildlife protection as an undercover agent for Ministere de Resources Naturelles, regardless of stereotypic skepticism. Once I proved myself in Canada, I planned to invade the hallowed halls of the United States Department of the Interior. Women gaining access to the wildlife section of the DOI was generally thought to be a vain endeavor. Regardless, this vocation was my one and only strategy.

————————•◆•————————

Finished with the latest historical file, Tee pulls a coverlet over herself as she leans back in the chair. Her rebellion against sleep fades. A file labeled "White Earth" falls onto the nearby floor as the second cup of tea finally overcomes. Tee Fairfax yields to an edgy sleep, but not before one last, soft testimony to the deceased. "Sam the Seeker": Now, that's a name not easily forgotten. Tee's Ink Prayer reverie engulfs her sleepy subconscious. She shares a collective existence between life and dream state with her lifeless companion.

The night skies fill with pregnant clouds of sorrow. Massive raindrops spew down with anger, and the cabin's curtains swing wildly against the room's glass doors. In advance of drumming thunder, a flash of light illuminates Mattie's petite frame. Tee awakens with a deafening start, only to find the corpse's dead brown eyes agape with excitement. Mattie gropes at the young journalist's cotton flannel shirt and pulls Tee Fairfax into the depths of Bandy Hawk Lake.

Chapter 12-
BANDY HAWK VISIONS

Extreme cold dominates the mortal soul. Tee floats, frozen in place, amid dark and light veins of water. A penetrating chill asserts itself but is wholly ignored, overridden by trepidation. This callous space is irrational. The war-tested journalist tries to make sense of the nonsensical images, pushing glasses up her nonexistent nose for a better view.

Drafting tainted Wildbird memories, Tee is forced to observe Mattie's arm incongruously dangling off Henry Wildbird's mass as he tows his twin sister to the bottom of Bandy Hawk Lake. Crimson red bleeds into the crystalline blue waters, merging into a protracted trail of stain.

Sharing the twins' harrowing past imparts an overwhelming revelation. Where is hope? Tee tracks the giant boy through the lake's abyss amid futile calculations, considering her own last breath. When Tee closes in on the otherworldly pair, Mattie shapeshifts into a bear - the same bear the journalist narrowly avoided on the trail to the cabin.

Henry suddenly reverses course. Entangled, he drags his inert victim to the narrowly lit shaft of light, presently inhabited by Tee's spectral presence. The bear winks and then throws hulking arms around the young journalist's shoulders, dragging her essence through the horrid experience of near-death. The sensation is unfathomable.

Pleas for salvation go unanswered until Henry Junior forcibly shakes the woman from her hallucinations of terror. His giant arms swallow the sobbing Tee Fairfax into a calming embrace.

It takes time to adjust from this ghostly nightmare. Henry's wife comforts the young woman with another warm blanket in an attempt to relieve her quaking tears.

"And sometimes things are behind."

Chapter 13-
PURE GUT

An eerie sensation suffuses the trail leading to the old medicine woman's cabin. The sun sleeps deeply on this earlier-than-usual gathering, lost within the moon's fullness. The ether is charged with transformation.

The dizygotic twins arrive at their destination soundlessly, each deep in meditative preparation. Their need to speak was left behind long ago. An easy genetic stillness descends upon the two. They feel each other, understand one another, and converse wordlessly. Repeatedly, this proves both a blessing and a curse.

The pair see Hinmah's summons as inevitable. Henry and Mattie are prepared. The tribal shaman is far wiser and much sharper than either, paired or not. Even in unity, they fall short of Hinmah's wit and incisiveness. Experience and knowledge always surmount rawness.

As the two climb the cabin stairs in solidarity, they share a quick glance. Why should they fear the outcome? They have two votes to her one. Both agreed in advance to honor Hinmah with due homage, as behooves a tribal elder. That aside, Grandmother must be reasonable.

The twins decided early on that blunt honesty is their only course of action. The medicine woman must admit that they can no longer meet the String's demands. Specialized reinforcement in areas of information technology, transitional special effects, accounting, military tactics… hell, even sales, requires greater attention. The String is big business now.

Wet birch simmers in the fireplace and permeates the air. Grandmother's cabin is a place filled with an incantation, and the medicine woman is dressed in ceremonial clothing meant to invoke ancestral powers. This premeditated act is intended to remind the young people of her sovereignty.

Mattie and Henry enter with respect and move to the place fronted by waters where the tribal leader regularly holds court. The young giant kisses the old woman's soft but wrinkled cheek, and as Henry kneels, he applies a blanket to warm her, a move she immediately recognizes as an attempt to diminish her power. Mattie follows with a second kiss and then tucks the blanket in to signal unity as well as deference.

The old woman smiles at the twins' cleverness. It's evident they've come prepared. She leans back with a pride-filled consent and begins,

"I asked you here to share this precious time. We have never actually spoken about what happened at Bandy Hawk. It's too painful."

Piously, the medicine woman declares, "Life's benchmark has always been excessive for Tree and Isabelle's offspring." The old lady exhales deeply. "I'm here to beg your forgiveness."

The soundless room dares not disturb as the twins exchange a discreet, yet surprised glance. A small tear appears on the old woman's face.

"We have been in a perpetual state of combat for more than a half decade, a battle of ideas, a war of principles. All this has supervened without your consent."

Henry stands and turns to the lake, unable to respond. Mattie has always done their talking when concerned with matters of the heart, but even she is shocked into silence. Everyone takes a moment to breathe before Henry jumps in.

"I know you consider the String the act of a madwoman, but it has restored my dignity. Without it, I would have done something stupid, in rage."

Henry looks at Mattie, extends his massive paw, and adds, "Grandmother, your craziness saved our lives. If you went to the sacred place today, we two would continue to build the String."

Hinmah takes his hand in comfort. Mattie only shakes her head in agreement and smiles at the giant in celebration of his pronounced declaration.

Hinmah rocks in her chair for a moment without a word. After a time, she characteristically moves onward.

"What does it take to be a part of change, something grander than the norm, a real maker of a difference? Pure gut! It fills me with consternation, but ambitions of this nature are complex and dangerous."

The old woman presses on.

"Your grandfather and I have concluded that the String's circle must be widened. This risky next step is crucial. It's also perilously daring. It only takes one wrong choice, one mistake, and all we have worked for is lost. Knowing this doesn't alter the fact that we need outside help."

Another round of silence fills the cabin, followed by a ground-swell of elation as both Mattie and Henry feel immediate relief. Henry's rare demonstration of exultation sends him into a burst of blasphemous rambling.

"Holy shit, Hinmah." He catches himself. "Oh, pardon, Grandmother, I mean to say how glad I am." Buoyant laughter fills the room.

———◆———

Diminished by one, the original five members of the String felt frayed when "Apple" Tamer Gray left to pursue higher education. Hinmah and Delsin forced their adopted grandson to walk a different path. The two elders knew of Apple's infatuation with Mattie, but that was not their motivation.

Hinmah hinted at this purposeful measure more than once, but the twins could never find the reason to send him so far away. Today, it's decided that the String will get a much-needed boost. The twins are shocked to hear that this enriched plan includes the return of their adopted brother, "Apple" Tamer Gray.

The Ink Prayer's medicine woman will handle this delicate homecoming. She aims to contact the Department of the Interior deputy director personally. Grandmother's espoused son has held this prized position at the DOI for two years now. Today, it has been decided that Apple return home. His knowledge and influence demand the deputy director's return.

———◆———

The medicine woman and her accomplices build and calculate a list of possible candidates meant to bolster the String's inner circle. It's a treacherous move, and each choice is grave.

As time presses the team forward, doctored tea steams atop the counter. Various topography maps that include Bandy Hawk and its tabletop plateau sit alongside two laptop computers. The relics of lunch sit at the edge of the work surface as an aria floats softly over the conversation. Colored pencils, a giant ruler, and graph paper sit on the counter as Hinmah and her grandchildren survey the list of long-thought-through indispensables.

Mattie's assigned the procurement of the best information technology specialist available. She has a CIA contact that has provided her several names, but the man who best fits is an ex-CIA technician named Winslow Sharp.

Charged with tracking down a tunnel expert, Henry has already narrowed his options. Dagmar Eiksund, a Norwegian engineer, has just retired. At present, he acts as a consultant on some of the biggest excavations in the world. There had been some noise that he wasn't well after losing his wife of forty years.

Henry will fly to San Francisco, where Eiksund is grooming a team of experts attempting to reinforce the underground system known as the BART, or Bay Area Rapid Transit. Henry must determine if this fine gentleman is up to the task.

Enlisting talent of this caliber will be a precarious challenge. The twins have two weeks to garner these professionals between and around other important business regarding the String.

Before this morning's meeting convenes, a plan is made to acquire internal help within several states' bureaucracies. This list includes someone inside the governor's office; the Department of Natural Resources; legislature; Revenue; and Fish, Wildlife and Parks. Mattie insists that the frustration of underpaid state employees can practically promise key players throughout as many departments as dictated.

The governor's office will be the most difficult, owing to the holder of the throne, but the internal staff is frustrated by the governor's vulgar, unscrupulous mandates.

Hinmah suggests, "Crebo Lund is nothing if not tyrannical. More than a few want his head. It's a place to start."

The medicine woman moves to the fireplace for soot. With gnarled fingers that act like a paintbrush, she smudges ashen wings on her grandchildren for added protection and fortification.

Chapter 14-
DAGMAR'S BLISS

Bandy Hawk Plateau is a cave dwellers fantasy. That is, if you know about the caverns, with their myriad passages, chambers, and pools, all concealed deep beneath the surface. Few do.

Henry Wildbird discovers the caves accidentally, out of necessity. Dagmar Eiksund, a second-generation Norwegian civil engineer, exalts them as the eighth natural wonder of the world and has made them into something of an engineer's playground, building a multitude of camouflaged entrances, tunnels, and egresses.

Henry first meets Dagmar at the Hilton-Union Square in downtown San Francisco. The engineer assumes both men have business in San Francisco. Dagmar is to give a presentation to civil engineers hard at work modernizing BART, specifically the Berkeley Hills segment. This tunnel runs three-point-two miles underneath the city and is the fourth-longest vehicular tunnel in the United States.

Dagmar's real expertise is adverse environmental engineering. Early in his career, he returned to the family firm in Norway as a favor to his aging father to build the Eiksund Tunnel. The younger Eiksund engineered and supervised the planning and construction of the project. It was completed, on time and on budget, four years later.

Poised as the deepest subsea tunnel at 942 feet below sea level, it runs a remarkable 4,832 miles long. Since then, Dagmar's firmly established reputation moves him from mere civil engineer to the deity of tunneling among the world's elite scientists in the field.

Today, as a sixty-nine-year-old widower, he has applied every type of tunnel construction in the discipline. Box jacking, boring, shaft, underwater, enlargement, cut and cover: you name it, and Dagmar Eiksund has lived it.

Now a private consultant, he travels from project to project, "giving something back," as the modest engineer is often heard to say.

The loss of his beloved wife Elsa, combined with his bout with cancer, render him less capable in the field, a problem he has not yet learned to manage. It means Dagmar can teach but not live the dig. For an active man like Eiksund, these setbacks affect the flavor of his life. He is determined to go out in a hard hat, Carhartts, and a well-worn pair of steel toed Asolos.

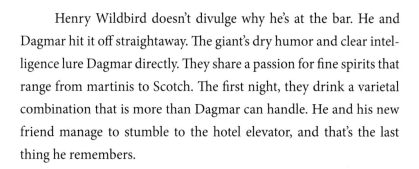

Henry Wildbird doesn't divulge why he's at the bar. He and Dagmar hit it off straightaway. The giant's dry humor and clear intelligence lure Dagmar directly. They share a passion for fine spirits that range from martinis to Scotch. The first night, they drink a varietal combination that is more than Dagmar can handle. He and his new friend manage to stumble to the hotel elevator, and that's the last thing he remembers.

It's rare when a Scandinavian suffers from a lack of self-control, so the following morning, Eiksund feels discomfited when next he sees Henry. That doesn't last long. The giant puts Dagmar at ease instantly.

Both men struggle through their hangover with a Bloody Mary and succor of bacon, eggs, hash browns, and toast. Not once does Henry make Dagmar Eiksund feel as if he's past his prime.

That day, the slight-of-build Norwegian invites his new friend to the Bunker Hill project. Dagmar shares his wealth of knowledge as the giant ducks through the worksite.

Engrossed, Henry pays close attention to even the most detailed of explanations. It's evident the young man has a great capacity to learn. His questions are well-rounded and concise. Dagmar asks the giant if he has previous instruction in the field, but Henry merely shakes his head as the tour continues.

That evening, the two enjoy another delicious meal of San Francisco's finest fish while they scan the Pacific Ocean in search of its easternmost edge. Tonight, the two newfound friends temper their drinking.

Henry asks Dagmar if he has ever traveled to Montana. Dagmar realizes he knows almost nothing about the man beside him.

"No, I've always wanted to, but never had the time," replies the engineer as his skin tingles with the sense of great promise.

Something about this young man makes the hoary engineer feel needed, for perhaps the last time.

"I'm going to ask a very odd question."

The engineer sits forward, much closer in the giant's space. Henry Wildbird doesn't flinch.

"I assumed you had business in San Francisco. Am I that business, Henry? Do you have a job for me?"

The giant wipes the last vestiges of wine from his lips with a starched white linen napkin and says, "No, sir, I have a mission for you."

This declaration hangs heavy over the table as Dagmar deliberates his next move.

"During the past six, nearly seven decades, I've learned to trust my instincts. It's obvious that you're a man of integrity. You don't strike me as a person who idolizes money or power. I'd wager my future that whatever plans you have will be for the greater good," says the elderly gentleman as he peacefully leans into a sip of fine cognac.

Stillness falls over both men as they watch the colors of dusk flee on the back of an outgoing tide. Dagmar's newfound solace morphs into something more vibrant. He can only liken it to going home.

As darkness sets in, the Norwegian realizes his prayer to be useful has been answered. He contemplates the act of "doing good" and then asks, "When do we leave?"

"I arranged a flight for both of us early tomorrow morning. Forgive me for taking the liberty, but our work is pressing. I have two first-class tickets to a small town called Missoula. From there, we'll travel by truck down the Clearwater along the Black Foot River to Bandy Hawk," says Henry matter-of-factly.

"What exactly are we doing in Montana?" asks the legendary engineer.

"The very thing you're most celebrated for," replies the giant.

The distinguished Dagmar Eiksund's weathered hand finds a place atop Henry's massive paw. With a tear of joy in the engineer eyes, he adds, "Thank you."

Chapter 15-

WINSLOW SHARP

The five-foot-three-inch man works hard to appear average. Melding with the locals is considered an asset in his line of work.

As a rule, Winslow is obsessive about his weight and appearance. Handsomely appointed with an unusual shade of auburn brown eyes and western European features, Winslow Sharp is attractive. Even his nails and cuticles are meticulously clean. In these parts, he would be regarded as a standout metrosexual.

Today, Winslow exhibits greasy mouse-brown hair with a patchwork mustache, wrinkled flannel shirt, and jeans that display a worn, circular hole in the rear pocket imprinted by a can of chew.

This slightly thicker version of Winslow Sharp (assisted by a small couch pillow) makes his way back from the local electronics store into an early-model Jeep Wrangler.

A single empty gas tank dangles off the rear of the filthy rig, and the windshield is streaked with dry mud. Winslow focuses on the wider but only slightly cleaner section of the smeared glass. The well-worn wiper blades encumber the vista.

Such personal incongruities require tremendous personal patience, but Sharp revels in the role of scrounger and will do anything to best himself. His line of work requires that he's constantly aware of his surroundings.

Winslow absorbs every detail before making even the simplest move. Exploiting the facade of mountain-man survivalist, he looks the part as he rummages for a camouflaged, weather-resistant CCTV surveillance camera. The type he seeks is not easily found nor often discarded.

Mr. Average isn't worried - not with his knack for acquisitions. Most, if not all, of the paraphernalia Winslow needs to build and maintain his mind-bending technology attracts a lot of attention.

Fanatics have made it far harder to acquire sensitive parts and supplies without exposure, as if just locating the proper gear to do the job isn't trouble enough. No matter. Winslow Sharp has a reputation to uphold.

During his stint with the CIA, his colleagues respectfully referred to him as the Sterile Scrounge. Fact is, the ex-CIA agent has developed access to even the most restricted paraphernalia, in whatever quantity.

Winslow's real value is in the field of surveillance. Couple that with his ability to design and reproduce anything needed to get the job done, and he's invaluable.

Many of Sharp's business contacts share a rather dubious background, but this only enhances his reputation as the best in the business. Connections on both sides of the law make him a highly sought-after surveillance and procurement specialist.

Somewhere along the line, Winslow Sharp recognized that government work can be ethically sketchy. Personally, he agonizes over his contributions to the overall demise of the populace's right to privacy.

The argument for and against surveillance is a thorny subject at best, but more to the point, Sharp doesn't agree with the CIA's use of his many technological innovations.

He decided to walk away or, more precisely, vanish after his stint with DARPA, or the Department of Advanced Research Projects Agency, where Winslow worked on armed unmanned aerial vehicles and hybrid insect bugs, real insects surgically mounted with electronic circuitry guided by GPS to specific targets.

It cost Winslow a couple of cold beers and bar snacks to understand how the CIA's high-level vanishing masters back out of an old life slowly. They're a shrewd lot, eager to share the tricks of their trade. He was told to take his time and created an extensive list of disinformation to minimize his social connections.

From that point, he had to find a credible reason to leave the agency. He told his immediate supervisor that private sector work surpassed government pay. In part, this line of reasoning was true, but Sharp didn't care about the money. Still, his own startup had proved very lucrative. It took months to create the deception to make a clean break from DARPA. Finally, the Sterile Scrounge vanished, hidden amongst the masses.

This ex-CIA procurement technician rarely trusts anyone, so when the stunning Native American woman approaches him at the Las Vegas Surveillance Convention, Winslow is immediately suspicious. State-of-the-art technology is on display annually at this convention, so everybody in the business attends, including a well-disguised Winslow Sharp.

It's rare to see both sides of the law under one dome, a trick only Las Vegas entrepreneurs can pull off, supported by a large chunk of change and a backroom political agreement. Capitalism at its best.

People immersed in the surveillance trade are wary of strangers. Mattie introduces herself, hands Winslow a business card, and asks him to contact her at the state of Montana Department of Fish, Wildlife and Parks. Talk about brilliant. There is no greater ploy than candor. The question is, how did she recognize a disguised Winslow Sharp?

Curiosity eventually takes its toll. Winslow uses a throwaway cell phone to place the call. Sharp completes a week-long investigation into his mysterious contact before he reaches out to the enigmatic Mattie Wildbird, Chief Legal Counsel for the state of Montana's Fish, Wildlife and Parks Department.

The two agree to meet for breakfast in a small town called Whitefish, Montana, just twenty-six minutes from Glacier Park. Winslow had never been to Glacier Park but had read about its sheer magnificence. More to the point, one could get lost quickly inside the expansive wilderness. The Rocky Mountains' staggering heights and lavish forests provide plenty of space to hide.

Winslow makes fastidious plans for this straightforward encounter but leaves nothing to chance. Multiple escape routes and a fake passport give the very thorough Mr. Sharp an advantage. It's best to be prepared. Multifarious getaway scenarios are a prerequisite.

You can always trust the locals to know where to get a delicious meal. A late brunch at the Buffalo Café on Third Street hits the spot. The food is hot and hearty, and the company mouth-watering.

The bantam-sized, transparent Mattie Wildbird asks her spooked breakfast partner to consider splitting a four-egg omelet with plenty of green chilies and vegetables.

"Portions here are always more than I can handle," confesses the genial FWP attorney.

After listening to Mattie's proposal to build a unique wildlife ecosystem under the government's nose, he wonders about this notion named "The String." Can it somehow help expunge his own past transgressions? After all, a guy can't go for a walk without wondering whether the fly that just buzzed by is a common housefly (*Musca Domestica*) or a cyborg listening device in the employment of the CIA.

Winslow Sharp, a typically cynical sort, falls in love directly. It isn't just the woman's eye-catching appearance but more her earnest conception of how the world should operate. For the first time in many years, Winslow thinks his skills might have a well-intended purpose.

A fresh start means more to Winslow Sharp than anything imaginable. To hide his euphoria, he signals the waitress for more coffee. After all, he's a master of his craft, sober in all things. There's no sense in tipping his hand.

Mattie quietly explains the concept behind the String. Then the ex-CIA agent asks a pertinent question.

"How do you know I won't give you up?"

Without hesitation, she replies, "I know your old boss." Bells and whistles explode inside the ex-CIA specialist's head. Mattie senses Winslow's panic.

"Your cover is intact! Your ex-boss is an old friend who recognizes my specific needs and sympathizes with the cause. Cunning expertise is rare, and few people have your talents. He knew you couldn't resist the temptation of the raw technology my organization requires. It isn't out of the ordinary for me to locate you at the Las Vegas function, but I understand how hard you've worked to disappear from your old life.

"I leave it to you. It's entirely your decision but recognize that this is a commitment that goes beyond the norm and, more importantly, the law. I want to be up front about that segment of this bargain. Come and join us. This thing will end one of two ways. If all goes well, you'll be an ecological champion."

With that, the self-assured woman picks up the tab for brunch.

"What if things go south?" probes Sharp.

Mattie challenges Winslow with a whimsical smirk.

"Well, let's just say your disappearing skills will be a great asset."

Jovially, she adds, "You have two days to decide. If I don't hear from you by then, I'll be forced to look for someone else. Hopefully, you'll join us. I don't often settle for the next best thing."

Sharp watches Mattie walk away without looking over her shoulder with even a slight display of apprehension. It takes a bold determination to see this modern-day coup to its end. Mattie Wildbird is beyond passionate.

Winslow thinks about the proposal as he walks to the local pub. For the first time in years, he doesn't double back on himself. It's not often he gets an offer to work with an official benefactor of integrity. In fact, he's amazed that there might still be someone interested in a genuinely righteous cause. It's an atypical event.

The ex-CIA agent downs a shot of whiskey. He realizes he doesn't feel a bit guarded or skeptical about the scheme. Winslow picks up his backpack and heads for the train station. He finds himself whistling. What the hell.

"Imagine," he says to no one in particular, "a bona-fide honorable cause."

Chapter 16-
SWEET BROWN BETTY

Peering through glazed windows in search of warmth, Brown Betty shivers with the dawn. Everything in Montana waits on the morning sun except her damnable employer.

Betty started work at the gigantic delivery company on the Louisville tarmac. As a logistics specialist, she was charged with directional package flows over enormous sorts on elongated belts. For some time, millions of packages found their way to the appropriate aircraft in an orchestrated dance. Sweet Brown Betty meticulously adjusted box flows while creating new shortcuts for greater efficiency along hundred-mile beltways.

Betty's computer talent dumbfounds most, but so does her temperament: thus, the sarcastic moniker. She has little patience for pompous managers who don't give a damn about the workforce.

Previous employers readily acknowledge Betty's lack of tolerance for such foolishness. She's never sure what's worse: the company's day ladies (middle management) or putting up with the night supervisors. Inevitably, credit for all her innovative designs ends up bolstering some white guy's resume.

Brown Betty's creative capacity has gone unappreciated for some time. Last Thursday, the night manager (a.k.a. Mr. Arrogant) pushed Sweet Brown Betty over the edge. Beyond angry, the slightly over-gross computer phenom applied for one of the company's short-haul driver's jobs in the first place available; damned with where she landed.

Naturally, Betty left a little something behind for her friend the night supervisor. Emails from coworkers verified that Mr. Arrogant was fired two nights later. The portentous boob could not resist boasting about the innovative ideas he had for the entire beltway transit system just before he triggered Betty's final software application. Packages flew off overcrowded belts, ended up on the wrong side of the 100-mile long sort, or were found crushed because belt speeds reached seventy miles per hour. Mass package mutilation was widespread and extensive.

As conveyed, Sweet Brown Betty isn't exactly known for an even temperament. Her general attitude reflects the caramelized comfort of the Southern pudding whose namesake she shares - Apple Brown Betty. The sweet, buttery dish is covered with a caramelized crust just as Betty's disposition is.

Extorting pain from whoever annoys her isn't unusual. Nor is it atypical for her to pay a personal price. Reactionary and excessive behavior is rarely complimentary.

The upside of Betty's notorious sentiments is her scrupulous concern for others. Her vibrant sense of humor draws even the meek to her side. She uses her plump profile like an artist's canvas, bedecked with a variety of flamboyant colors accompanied by a welcoming smile.

Let's face it: a mulatto woman in Montana is somewhat of a curiosity. There aren't a lot of sisters to trade crowns (church hats) in celebration of Christ at each Sunday service.

It's evident that Sweet Brown Betty is a bit of a spectacle just about anywhere she lives. As for Montana, Betty doesn't exactly blend in, but she considers this place and its animal inhabitants an addictive splendor.

The edgy over-girth woman often talks to herself. This morning's dialogue is about the cold.

"Girl, you need to toughen up! I swear, if I didn't know you better, I'd think you were a city princess who can't break a nail without carrying on. It ain't that cold, so just stop thinking about it."

As a child, Betty was given up for adoption. She spent time in no less than eight foster homes. Her prospects looked bleak until she volunteered at the local animal shelter to avoid going home after school.

The animal shelter's manager took Betty under his wing like any stray in need of a break. He encouraged Betty to stay in school and gave her jobs at the shelter that fortified her confidence while giving her refuge from the violent lifestyle in her foster care environment.

That's how Betty discovered an aptitude for computers. Before long, these skills helped to finance a new animal shelter. She personally created software used by veterinarians to locate lost animals. This cutting-edge talent gave the young girl a pecuniary chance towards emancipation from the flawed and treacherous foster care system. Betty went on to acquire a scholarship to DeVry.

Chapter 17-
EXPRESS VAN BLUES

Having taken its sweet time, a glorious sunrise explodes into crystalline coldness. Betty's two-wheel-drive van brawls to hug the highway between Helena and Winston.

Covered in abstract veins of cold smoke, the valley runs for miles. Highway 287 takes the delivery van straight into a penetrating morning sun. Betty can barely make out what's going on a half mile further ahead.

Four, maybe five pickups are parked on the side of the two-lane paved highway. Exhaust smoke from tailpipes, light reflecting windshields, and men dressed in winter branch #7 camouflage make it difficult to reckon.

They seem to be ogling something on the ridge just below the Elkhorn Range. Betty detects a commotion through the stream of ice flakes dusted up off the fallow wheat fields.

Once abreast of the activity, the express van is pelted by a variety of projectiles. Full-blown hunter insanity turns truck hoods into shooting platforms. Luckily, Betty avoids the shootout, but line of sight takes her to a place of carnage.

Condensation rises off the carcass of a fallen bull elk as the remainder of his herd circles in panic. The fatal realization of the herd's impending slaughter hits Sweet Brown Betty all at once. Her infamous temperament kicks in as she executes a perfect 180-degree spin on the icy pavement before accelerating with purpose.

Guns, boots, hats, binoculars — all take flight as hunters become targets, the van becomes a weapon, and Sweet Brown Betty turns savior with an extended middle finger acting as a testament. The van careens off the highway, spewing gravel at dazed hunters, adding insult to injury.

Other, less demonstrative drivers have notified the sheriff's department. Officer Stoltz approaches the situation with caution. He witnesses the chaos and immediately calls for backup. Sweet Brown Betty's speed doesn't help her cause. She flies by the sheriff, running better than ninety miles per hour on roads that demand greater prudence.

It takes time to contain the crime scene. Whirling lights make it clear that everyone involved better think twice about running. The sheriff's second response comes by helicopter. This flying patrol reinforces the notion that slipping away isn't an option.

In the end, the only real victim is the herd's bull elk. The cows and calves make it safely to cover, just like the hunters who leap atop their pickup hoods.

Everyone is inside Helena's jailhouse on Breckenridge Street before morning's end. There is little doubt that Betty's future as an unemployed black woman in the middle of a red state holds few employment options. Scheduled for the following Monday, a court hearing will determine her immediate future.

— ◆ —

"That ink dries fast. Here's a paper towel."

The handsome redhead about six feet tall reaches across the counter and offers Betty a segment of Kirkland's best from the nearby towel rack. She scrutinizes the sheriff cautiously as he fingerprints the new inmate. He is methodical, and his kind smile betrays his solemnity.

"Between you and me, I was impressed by that one-eighty you pulled out there, particularly given the icy road conditions. It was tight and reasonably controlled."

The sheriff looks over his shoulder to see if anyone else is nearby and then chuckles.

"Those good old boys must have leaped ten feet into the air."

Sweet Brown Betty stares, not saying anything, but carefully follows the sheriff's instructions to the letter.

"You'll need a good lawyer," details the attractive rosy-headed man in uniform. "I think I know someone who has the type of skills that can get this thing behind you," says Sheriff Drake Stoltz.

Betty stiffens and then decides to take the risk.

"Why would you want to help me?"

The genial officer ignores the question as he escorts his newest prisoner to lockdown.

"I'm going put you down this hallway, away from the rest."

The newly booked tenant struggles in cuffs and ankle chains. These trappings aren't conducive to taking a stroll. Stoltz takes Betty's left arm to stabilize the inmate.

He explains the situation.

"Those others may think you're responsible for their plight. Fact is, their unruly behavior placed them in the stew. Between you and me, I hold bad hunters in a harsh light. As far as I'm concerned, the laws, well, they just aren't stiff enough. Anyhow, this portion of the jail is unoccupied, so your stay should be pretty uneventful."

The sheriff opens the cell door, and a reticent Sweet Brown Betty walks into a tiny, very claustrophobic, and confining space. Her size makes it even more difficult to tolerate. Stoltz asks Betty to turn towards him. He towers above her on the opposite side of the jailed door.

"Put your hands through the bars, please."

Betty follows his command, chancing a quick glance into his eyes. The sheriff gently unlocks Betty's leg chains first and then handcuffs adding,

"Yeah, I know a gal who is pretty good at this legal stuff. She's busy as all get-out but has a thing for wildlife. I'll give her a call if you want. She might show an interest."

The cell door locks with a loud clack, but not before the sheriff tips his hat and laughs one more time at Sweet Brown Betty's audacity.

She settles into the corner of the cell. As he saunters down the hall, Betty can hear the sheriff say, "Mattie will get a kick out of you."

Brown Betty has a lot of time to think about her predicament. She starts by contemplating her attraction to a tall, white sheriff that, at present, is kind enough to look after her.

Chapter 18-
DAMNATION COUP

Adjutant General Markay receives an oddly unidentifiable text on his cell. GPS coordinates present a tip about an illicit, pending raid. The general immediately contacts his bureau connection. The FBI works to track the informant's identity, but the process takes time. That's the one thing Markay lacks. He makes the decision to intercede.

The general's Garrison Colonel, Brad Clarkson, develops an operational strategy within the hour. The squadron is in place by early afternoon. The regiment's planned mission feels foolproof to a confident Clarkson, who declares that these skirmishes will end as abruptly as they began.

Later that same evening, the night skies are illuminated with lambent stars. Rigid air satiates the dormant field with electricity and expectation. Not much separates the hunter from its prey except for, perhaps, a sixth sense. The fully camouflaged garrison colonel can't make sense of things.

He whispers to his second, "There's no way these insurgents can detect our presence. Applied, proven tactical counterintelligence is fully implemented. We came early, followed the rules of concealment. How could they possibly detect a trap? Dammit, they've been standing there for over half an hour! Hell, their horses haven't flinched."

Scowling, the colonel continues his rant.

"I can't believe I have to stand out here all night to track down a bunch of eco-terrorists."

The lieutenant hands the night vision goggles to the fulminating colonel.

"Sir, this doesn't make sense. No one is that disciplined!"

At ground level, the officer thinks he detects a strange shimmer, almost a radiance, as he crouches low to the ground for a distinct perspective.

The binocular's object lenses sheath everything in a green hue. The colonel makes the necessary adjustments to fit his angular face.

As if on cue, the principal raider's nearly indiscernible hand gesture gets an immediate reaction from the colonel. This blatant misdirection sends command and guardsmen into frenzied action, but the eco-terrorists stand their ground.

An explosion from behind the squadron provides the rider atop the chasm time to vanish, but the well-trained National Guard tactical unit reorganizes, waiting for the inevitable attack.

It's too late. The coup is complete. The colonel's strategic operation didn't include a near-silent attack from his flank. Tampered chase vehicles are completely undriveable.

The colonel barks at the lieutenant via handheld radio. "Get that chopper up now!"

Moments later, the captain and his metal bird lift off from a backup position where the concealed helicopter waits for just such an opportunity. Surveillance is a priority now.

The air chase, with a rather weakened ground component, widens the pursuit just as the sun rises to the east of the bloodless battleground. The flight's captain and its crew have one objective: expose the riders' identities. The riders have two — go undetected and escape.

Like their namesake, the Ink Prayer riders flow over the mountainous terrain. This admirable chase is dangerously exciting and immensely significant. Much is at stake.

The incursion is perfectly choreographed, part of a greater plan. Each rider has a predetermined role and awaits the order to employ evasive maneuvers.

Simple hand signals are a lifeline in the daring composition of this escape. There it is: the lead drops three fingers. Some of the riders modify their strides, swinging to the left of the pack. This variation alters the chase, as does the terrain.

The sleight-of-hand deception distracts the helicopter's pilot just long enough to allow the remaining strap hangers to slide underneath a craggy outcropping and into a shallow riverbed. Once they reappear, only four are left. As previously instructed, the captain pursues the largest group.

Wet and glistening in the early morning sun, the remaining Ink Prayer riders move towards the plateau at lightning speed as each animal deftly eludes the perils of haste.

The helicopter clamors thickly off their right shoulders in hopes of catching a telltale image of anyone daring to ride for this outlaw faction.

The plateau's crest demands the lead provide an additional signal. This gives the pilot a split second to decide whom to chase. He orders the private first class running the video camera to focus on the lead.

Three riders veer to the right and find cover under a stand of trees, leaving the last exposed and unaccompanied. The helicopter presses the remaining rider forward as both horse and machine rush across the golden tabletop of Bandy Hawk Plateau.

The plateau's inevitable edge makes a clandestine promise as the masked horseman reigns in the ride with intensity. The dust settles on this single soul, who baits the pilot with a breathtaking smile and then reins the horse backward in a slow, unflinching prance that evolves into a gyratory dance full of a promised finale.

Total exhilaration, unreserved passion, full-blown insanity takes the strap hangar's proud paint to the end of the plateau. The pilot can do nothing but watch as the animal leaps horizontally over the edge into perilous flight. The impending impact will indisputably kill both animal and rider.

The pursuers themselves are now in a death brace against the helicopter windshield. No one can believe what they just witnessed as their flying machine hurls past the scene of the unmitigated leap. The cameraman slams against the windshield as the pilot hits the brakes to avoid a second helicopter carrying a news team.

The National Guard captain throws his metal bird into vicious recoil. The aircraft's turn and slip indicator vaults to the far right. The pilot's war-like screech rises above the strained helicopter's din as he jerks the craft into position.

The private's grasp fails as gravitational force overwhelms. The video camera plunges to the floor. He strains to collect the small metal box as it lurches back and forth across the cabin floor, erratic proof that this pursuit has been one hell of a hullabaloo.

By the time the copter has made the 180-degree turn, nothing is left. Not a single trace of horse or rider on the rocks below. No blood, no broken bones, not even a feather from the outlandish mask the horseman wore. The banshee vanished.

Mattie's pursuers search the plateau's floor as the amused escapee watches from within the rocky vestibule five feet below the cliff's edge. Poised, even after the leap, Virtuoso the trick paint horse ducks inside the cavern's sheltered opening.

Chapter 19-
STATESMANSHIP

Crebo Lund despises statesmanship. As governor, his punishing tactical responses are infamous, even beyond the state's borders.

Like the rest of the country, Montana is politically paralyzed, divided between conservative rural populations and liberal urbanites. Lund is grateful for the chaos. There's no better place to hide a dark agenda than within pandemonium.

The governor's father had grave doubts about his son but died before Crebo obtained any real power. One of Lund's great regrets is the missed opportunity to shove his gubernatorial victory down the old man's throat.

Besides, he's just getting started. Lund makes no bones about his political ambitions. More than once, he has declared, "One day, I plan on ruling the ruling class."

———◆———

National Guard Adjutant General Regal Markay and his garrison colonel Brad Clarkson are forced to wait in the governor's forward office. Markay has played hardball with the best, so this type of petty tactical maneuvering rolls off his back.

The adjutant general is a trim, sixty-one-year-old veteran who has seen plenty of active duty in his day. His official military dress makes his five-foot-five frame look taller. His square jaw and muscular physique augment his professional image.

When the general speaks, he does so with his entire face. His animated eyes and finely defined features are more than demonstrative. Markay's stature defines military excellence, even six decades into his life.

Clarkson, a tad bit more fidgety, quietly dreads the unfortunate circumstances that bring him and his commander here. It's impossible to explain how the riders escaped. The colonel's humiliation is nearly palpable as he checks a nearby mirror to make certain his appearance is immaculate.

Lieutenant Governor Greyson Chance strides out from an interior office that adjoins the governors. He respectfully salutes both officers, even though his post as lieutenant governor doesn't warrant such behavior.

Chance's attire reflects his present role. The dark-blue, three-piece pinstriped suit complements his graying temples. He takes his position as a political leader earnestly.

Ostensibly, these three men hold each other in high esteem characteristic of proven military records. Eventually, the threesome makes their way back to the governor's office for what Lund has labeled crisis intervention.

In a show of power, the governor separates himself behind a massive oak desk.

"Well, gentlemen, come in, come in. Please have a chair."

The adjutant general is forced to reach across the lengthy desk to shake the governor's hand, as does his second, Colonel Clarkson.

After this awkward exchange, Lund uses the intercom to invite an information technician in with a video-equipped flat-screen monitor.

The governor waits for the technician to leave before he starts.

"Gentlemen, I want to thank you for the visual record of our latest attempt to capture these pesky camp robbers."

Clarkson's face reddens as the governor diminishes the eco-terrorists to something like mischievous field mice.

"There wasn't much to see," continues Lund, "so I had my man loop the videotape for a deeper inspection of these petty hoodlums."

The shrinking garrison colonel can no longer contain himself.

"They're hardly run-of-the-mill street crud, Governor. In fact, they're an expertly prepared and very organized group."

Adjutant General Markay slips his hand atop Clarkson's sleeve to restrain the colonel.

A cheerful governor responds. "Well, hell, Brad, you sound like a fan. What I want to know is how this band of raiders continues to evade you and your elite squadron of highly trained tacticians. What is this, the third time you've lost these… organized raiders?"

Greyson Chance glares at Lund. The governor is entirely absorbed by the power to humiliate. He points at the flat screen.

"Look at your squad. Most of them are afoot. These two characters drove one of the only operating Jeeps remaining into a damn pre-dug trench; it's like a scene from the Keystone Cops out there."

The looped video continues in the background, and still, Regal Markay rests unaffected. Crebo Lund stands directly between his audience and the flat screen.

"Apparently, Greyson hasn't yet conveyed the importance of an upcoming visit. The state of Montana gets little good press on a national level. I've managed to do some extensive networking with this nation's Secretary of State. Let me make it clear: By the time Tully Neff arrives, these hoodlums, or whatever you want to call them, better be under wraps. I hope I've made myself clear."

With this pronouncement, the governor moves in front of the screen. Crebo laughs as two chase helicopters barely evade one another. The National Guard helicopter pilot screeches in the background.

"Whoa, that was close," laughs Lund.

The camera's visual record swings wildly back and forth across the cabin floor, followed by static. Then the embarrassment begins again.

Regal Markay gets up and signals to a visibly shaken Clarkson to follow. The governor, seemingly engrossed in the tape, pretends not to notice his guests are on the way out. The lieutenant governor follows the guardsmen out.

"General Markay, please let me apologize for the governor," declares the lieutenant governor.

Markay turns to Chance.

"How the hell can you stand that conceited megalomaniac?"

A sincere Greyson Chance responds.

"Someone has to keep this office upright, Sir. As a public servant, I can't afford to do anything less."

"This thing isn't over. It's been my experience that the governor's office will need the Guard sooner than later. I have to say, at this point, I've lost interest. It's pretty evident your boss has little respect for the uniform or its representatives," declares a solemn Regal Markay.

With that, the general offers one last salute before he and his garrison colonel withdraw.

Chapter 20-
MARLEY WOMACK

What sends a dedicated employee like Marley Womack over the edge? She survived the loss of her first husband to cancer and her only son to a car accident. Somehow, throughout each challenge, she maintained a gracious dignity.

Today, a hard-earned balance permeates Marley's world. People are drawn to her serenity and depend on the calm they feel in her presence.

For more than twenty-five years, Mrs. Womack has happily worked at Trust Land Management, or TLMD, with the Department of Natural Resources.

TLMD is charged with administering the state's timber, surface, and mineral resources that subsidize Montana's future. Funds earned from these renewable resources are used to underwrite apportioned expenses incurred by the state's school systems. The work is more than credible.

Marley sets a prototypical employee standard by example and passes on a sense of stability to younger workers during severe fire seasons, not to mention the fiscal year's end. She always reminds the less experienced that they managed in the past and will survive the future.

Few things upset this well-seasoned accountant. At sixty-one, Marley Womack easily finds compassion for the lonely, sick, and uneducated. She doesn't pretend to be the perfect human being. Marley accepts the flawed and damaged traits of the middle and lower classes. It is, however, an understatement to say she cannot abide arrogance, greed, or most of the supercilious upper class.

Naturally, life's adversities test the accountant on a fiscally recurrent basis. As Trust Land Management comptroller, she's thrust into the midst of the very behavior she despises.

Mrs. Womack's job demands she sponsors monthly public land management board meetings. The problem is that the board consists of Montana's top five elected officials: the governor, attorney general, commissioner of securities and insurance, secretary of state, and superintendent of public schools. Marley recognizes the exception but feels that as a rule, high self-opinions accompany this level of state government, so much so it creates its own continuous squall.

Regardless, everyone, including Womack, is paid to make sense of items that range from the sale of land banking parcels to grazing leases. The business of trust lands places a weighty responsibility on the shoulders of each board member, but none more significantly than the governor's.

Marley has watched Crebo Lund intimidate members of the board for years. The only exception is Attorney General Scott Tabor, simply because he belongs to the opposing political party and has political ambitions of his own. These political perspectives bolster Scott's opinion of Crebo Lund. He doesn't give a damn what the governor wants. Still, Lund controls the land board four to one and mocks Tabor at every turn.

Despite the absurdity, Marley Womack and Land Board Secretary Lily Parks work hard to maintain a modicum of peace. These women sit directly across from the U-shaped table occupied by the haughty politicians.

Both DNRC representatives are professionally dressed and competent and apply various learned techniques to advance the agenda with as little infighting as possible.

Lily records and transcribes the day's business. Marley's job is to present the program and provide a status report on TLMD fiscal matters, something she can do in her sleep.

Neither Lily nor Marley enjoy this segment of the job but understand the significance of the work. They muddle through as best they can. The pay is insufficient and doesn't justify the stupidity they're forced to witness, but Marley and Lily find reason enough in their purpose.

Bad blood between Governor Lund and Attorney General Tabor spills over on a consistent basis. As a rule, disdain permeates the entire room and fully engulfs those who dare enter the fray.

Lily whispers to Marley regularly. She tries to lighten things up and jokes,

"We'll need a lot of peanuts to get through this circus."

Thank goodness for Lily's dark humor. Otherwise, Marley might finally lose control of her temper. She has been tempted during many incidents to inform these blowhards how petty they really sound.

Today's last agenda item, 1013-2, deliberates the sale of land banking parcels in Madison and Gallatin counties. It's no surprise that Tabor opposes the vote to purchase these properties, particularly as it's Lund's idea. Secretary of State Lindeman acts as the governor's front to sponsor the proposal.

What does come as a shock is Tabor's verbal accusation that Lund would directly profit from the sale. With this pronouncement, the room goes dead quiet. Crebo Lund loves a fight, and Marley can tell he's more than happy to perpetuate Tabor's frustration.

"Well now, Scott, when the attorney general of this great state makes a claim like that, it requires substantiation."

Embarrassed, Tabor has let his displeasure take him too far. Marley shifts slightly in her chair. Exasperated by the politics, egos, and power, she just wants to see things done fairly.

Why on earth would the attorney general tip his hand? "Does Triad Realty ring any bells, Crebo?" asks the frustrated Tabor. Just then, the governor's chief of staff interrupts the land board meeting. Timing is everything. The governor's luck holds out. Greyson Chance interrupts the meeting. A massive fire is raging through Custer National Forest. It's dangerously close to the town of Red Lodge.

The meeting concludes quickly as the governor calls for a vote. The sale completed, Lund heads out for a fire briefing, but not before he winks at the snickering attorney general. Everyone gathers their belongings and departs quickly. Crebo Lund's scorn is something most people work to avoid.

The attorney general is the last to leave. He calls Marley over for a private conversation.

"I'm sorry. I hadn't planned to disclose this reported information during the Land Board meeting."

Tabor stands sheepishly before Marley. She doesn't physically react as Lily watches the two chat.

"Do you have evidence, Scott?" asks Marley.

Abruptly, with discomfort, the attorney general leaves after confirmation of a business partnership - "Triad Realty".

The two women are left to collect the meeting's pencils, spare agendas, empty cups, and leftover doughnuts. They do so in silence until it's clear everyone is out of earshot.

Lily can't stand it. She bursts into laughter.

"What the hell just happened? It was like a bomb dropped. I'm buying the vino tonight, girlfriend."

"Okay, but with one caveat… no talk about the job," declares the weary comptroller.

An hour later, Marley drops Lily off and then heads straight home to do some in-depth research.

"So, it's true… Triad Realty."

It takes Marley twenty minutes to inspect the secretary of state's business certification database before she discovers trouble. She could care less about politics unless it concerns the String.

Triad Realty's registered agent acts as a front for a unique partnership. Well, maybe "unique" is an understatement, given the circumstances. After a thorough search of the UCC records, Marley recognizes an inexplicable, bizarre alliance.

Chapter 21-

WHITTLED BUT WILD

Whittled down by seventy-three eventful years, the six-foot-three septuagenarian moseys more than walks. Anne Creekbaum finds herself inside the old Parrot Confectionery. Like her, this little establishment has seen a fair share of history. Creekbaum instantly feels at home.

The former chocolatier proudly supports a soda jerk alongside its line of great handmade chocolates and a lunch menu that boasts an original homemade chili recipe that dates back to 1910.

Gracefully poised against a cozy back booth sits an enigmatic young woman. Anne Creekbaum, Professor Emeritus, quickly studies the woman's coal-black eyes and approaches with caution.

"Gracie Holdsclaw said someone here wants to talk to me. Would that be you? Because if you are that person, here I am."

A cup of hot coffee sits opposite the Fish, Wildlife and Parks chief attorney in anticipation of a new arrival. Mattie stands by way of introduction, points to the seat across from her, and simply adds, "Yes. Would you like something to eat?"

"That depends," responds the brusque professor, "on what you want."

Gruffness is a tried and true instrument used by the aging as a means of deflection. It doesn't work on Mattie. Moreover, it's evident that this mysterious lady is comfortable in her own skin. She does nothing to hide her prosthetic limb as the lanky Creekbaum folds into the tiny booth.

The young woman takes a sip of coffee, sets the cup down, and slowly pours a supplementary cup for her guest, asking, "How'd you get your start in film?"

What Creekbaum recognizes but doesn't mention is that her coffee is fixed just like she loves it. The two women measure one another a moment longer until the inducement to affirm her history lures the professor into conversation.

"Early on, I lied about my age to get a job on the set of Warner Brothers Studios. I worked on a swing gang. It wasn't much; we cleaned stages and moved props on movie sets."

Creekbaum takes a moment and decides against subtleties. "That's when I fell in love with Olivia de Havilland. She was on the set of *Santa Fe Trail* with Errol Flynn. Ronald Reagan was in that film, too. You might remember him."

It doesn't appear that either topic bothers Mattie Wildbird, so Anne presses on.

"In my opinion, de Havilland was the finest actress of her time. She wasn't just a beautiful face. Olivia understood the business and encouraged me to build a career of my own, but not as an actor. She felt that side of the trade was too rough."

Mattie leans in closer as Anne reflects.

"Women in the industry were unheard of, particularly gangly types like me."

The professor's self-deprecation makes Mattie grin.

"Anyhow, de Havilland introduced me to the director of *Santa Fe Trail*. Like most folks, Michael Curtiz loved Olivia and would do just about anything she asked.

"The truth is that's how the first camera I'd ever operated fell into my hands. De Havilland pulled at Curtiz's heartstrings to give me my one and only chance. I worked seven days a week to perfect my skills with anyone who would let me shoot film. I guess I got pretty good after a while."

Mattie garners every word of this extraordinary personal history as Creekbaum ruminates between swallows of cooling coffee.

Saddened now by the memory, the professor laments, "As time passed, I lost track of Olivia. Heck, she dated the likes of Jimmy Stewart and John Huston. I didn't stand a chance. Still, I worked with some of the best Hollywood had to offer."

Mattie doesn't interrupt but can't help admiring her seasoned and experienced guest.

"After that, things got dodgy in Hollywood. I was labeled a communist sympathizer, along with a lot of other discerning people," said the immersed storyteller.

"That fat bastard McCarthy did a number on a bunch of us. What a fear-mongering extremist. Anyhow, after too many months without work, I took my camera and headed out. Hell, this must be boring you near to death."

Mattie uses her patented smile to encourage the professor.

"Please go on. It's critical to our future."

Creekbaum gives Mattie a peculiar sideways glance before she continues.

"The movie industry revolves rapidly, so I decided the only way to stay on top of the trade was to teach. The perfect job opened at Montana State University. I jumped at the chance because it permitted me the opportunity to feed my two great passions. Who could ask for better film material than the durable characters of Montana and the rugged mountain ranges that surround Bozeman? It seemed to be a sacred sign."

While Anne finishes her coffee, Mattie takes a moment to interject.

"The university is proud of your accomplishments."

A more modest Creekbaum responds with a simple, "Thank you. The exultations of eminent university academics along with praise from my students are icing on my cake.

"You see, as I already mentioned, film technology made massive advancements throughout my residency. Picture shows and nature have afforded me my very own celebrity status. As a semi-retired professor, I can do as I please, with access to everything that makes me content," beams the silver-haired woman.

"How's it you came to know Gracie Holdsclaw?" inquires a relaxed Mattie Wildbird.

"I'm not sure how my private life is a concern of yours," admonishes the professor. "Besides, my guess is you already know about Gracie and me."

"Montanans aren't exactly avant-garde about such things," says an empathetic Mattie. "Did you know that many Native American tribes revere gays as two-spirit people? We believe that you possess a transcendent aptitude and heightened genius. From my personal perspective, your relationship and love for Gracie is something to be admired."

Anne's moist eyes shine with pride. She signals the waitress.

"Would you please bring two bowls of that old-fashioned chili? I'm buying," declares Creekbaum.

Chapter 22-
INDIAN RACES

What the more-aged woman thought would be a short conversation turns into a pleasant afternoon. Anne found an unusual comfort with Mattie.

"You know, Gracie's oldest boy Pete is an active team owner and Indian mugger on the Native American horse circuit. That's how I met my lover in the first place. Everyone in Bozeman kept talking about this wild-ass sport called 'Indian racing.'

"After a while, I was besieged with curiosity, so I decided to take a drive to the Crow Nation with my camera. It turned out to be the perfect subject for a documentary.

"There's so much to like about the sport. Indian racing is utterly full of tussles. That kind of action is film's best friend. Pete tells me this form of racing stems from counting coup. Personal honor and courage are the primary features reflected in the sport.

"Anyway, Gracie and her family were kind enough to guide me through the sport's chronology. They shared their knowledge, food, and, on occasion, their homes.

"Pete lives for these races. As he tells it, these competitions are the closest thing to living life just like his ancestors did."

Mattie feels Anne's passion, so she interjects.

"I'm a rider, but not for any team. I have a specially trained paint named Virtuoso with whom I accomplish similar feats. He's an amazing animal, and I hope to introduce you to him sometime."

The professor ponders this comment.

"Have you and Pete done much riding together?"

"As a matter of fact, we have. But please, finish telling me about your documentary," deflects Mattie.

The professor flashes Mattie another inquisitive look and then goes on.

"Everyone who participates in these races acts as a representative for his or her tribe. Gracie claims it gives their young people a steely-eyed purpose.

"Come to think of it, I've never heard one of those young people complain about the long hours, toilsome work, or danger involved. It's been my privilege to meet many of the riders. Numerous clans are mightily represented.

"In the end, I won an Academy Award for the documentary. Montana PBS funded and then promoted the picture at the Park City film festival. This gave Gracie, Pete, and me a taste of what it feels like to enjoy movie star status. Oh my, we celebrated for a week. That old Western ski town knows how to put out the red carpet.

"Since then, the sport has gone viral, vernacular and all. Pete is fluent in the jargon, and that's a good thing, because he's getting too old to be a mugger. The best part of this whole story is that Gracie and I ended up together. She's my last hurrah."

Chapter 23-
INVITE WITH AN ICE CREAM SIDE

Mattie signals for the waitress and asks her to bring a banana split with two spoons. Once the server is out of sight, Creekbaum continues. The next Creekbaum reveal is delivered with a smirk.

"Turns out Gracie's oldest is involved in a lot of wild-ass things. He and at least five other teams ride for something called the Ink Prayer."

Without a wince, Mattie places her napkin back on her lap and waits for Anne to continue.

"Of course, they didn't approach me for a good year. Maybe they thought an old communist like me couldn't be trusted," winks the professor.

"One day, unexpectedly, Pete invites me to take a ride with the family along the Bob Marshall Wilderness's Chinese Wall. Naturally, I jumped at the chance. Who wouldn't want to witness that country-side firsthand?

"Our trek started in the company of a stunning sunrise. We three gained access to the Wall laterally along the Benchmark side of the Rockies. I'm sure you know the place."

A giant banana split is delivered. Mattie mines a chunk of strawberry from the ice cream and shows it to Anne.

"I've eaten my share of these at exactly the spot you mention. The wild ones taste much better."

It's as if these two women have shared a lifelong friendship. Their conversation flows effortlessly, and Creekbaum's general attitude reminds Mattie a great deal of Hinmah.

"You know, Gracie loves the West Fork of the Sun. We followed that river for miles before actually setting foot inside the Bob Marshall Wilderness," adds the professor.

"The three of us eventually found ourselves at a bridge atop the river. We made a sharp left into a vast open meadow filled with countless wildflowers."

Mattie's eyes widen.

"Doesn't that whole valley stun? I mean, it's incredible, the width and breadth of that place. Its geological composition seems surreal, but oddly enough, it's just the opposite."

"I know what you mean," qualifies Creekbaum.

"A regal transformation consumes Gracie and Pete once engulfed in that teeming meadow. It was if they wear the scenery. I suppose it makes sense. The Sun River is a part of Holdsclaw's DNA. It just verifies that a sizable portion of society is detached from the land and water, completely disoriented in a back-wood setting. Most of us will never experience our environment like them.

"Anyway, around twelve miles in, we made our way across the West Fork of the Sun River, at a place called Indian Creek Trail. The water runs cold and fast at that crossing. It's a good three feet deep.

The horses handled it with little trouble, but I'm not that comfortable in the saddle; the river's span got the whole of my attention."

"I think I know your destination," reports Mattie. "Indian Creek leads to White River Pass."

"Right," confirms Anne as she sets the maraschino cherry to one side. The two women finish the ice cream as Anne continues.

"Curiously, Gracie led us off the main trail and down a saddle to the north. I remember we set up camp early. I teased Pete a bit, thinking he was taking it easy on the old women.

"Preoccupied, he just smiled. Pete's a handsome man, but I can't figure out what he's thinking. Gracie tells me he had a drinking problem as a youngster. She recognized Pete was going down a dangerous path. Gracie felt that a worthy pastime was the only hope for her son. That's when they came across Indian racing.

"Anyway, I remember that night at the base of the Rocky Mountain Front as pure magic. Stars carpeted the dark skies in numbers too vast to count. Wrapped in thick wool blankets to ward off the cold, we two old women huddled together as Pete imparted many traditional stories passed down by his grandfather and his grandfather's father. That young man's voice is spiritually laden, full of ethos. Sadly, I sense that Pete is torn between his tribe's rich history and an immense struggle to create a realistic future. Making sense of life seems to weigh heavy on his generation.

"Gracie thinks the tribe's young are convinced their heritage holds them back. The truth is no one can ignore their authentic self. If he thinks it's hard to face what he is, I'm here to tell him it's worse to hide from his true self. Gay people know a little something about living a suppressed existence. I was forced to live that way, so I know what I'm talking about.

"Anyway, when Pete put a voice to his ancestral legacy, I realized the magnitude of his many gifts. That land is sacred to him. You wouldn't happen to be an Ink Prayer native, would you, Ms. Wildbird?"

Mattie wipes the indulgent remains of the ice cream from her lips.

"As a matter of fact, I am. Maybe I can shed light on what Pete faces. The slow extinction of his people's history is just the beginning. The one unbroken mandate most native people still share is a deep commitment to protect the land and our animal family. What if I told you this was the reason for our meeting?"

A less-than-surprised Anne Creekbaum replies, "That's why I'm here?"

Both women chuckle at the blatancy of this remark. The professor doesn't hesitate to speak from her heart.

"Gracie and Pete have never asked anything of me. It's an honor that they might trust me enough to share this, their loftiest ambition. I don't know what you all are up to, but I have confidence in the Holdsclaw clan. I could never deny them anything. They're all the family I have. Gracie tells me you direct a cartel of like-minded folks that can use my services."

Mattie uses her fabricated limb like a drumstick against her tight stomach.

"I'm afraid I've overdone it again. Chili and ice cream are my two personal favorites. Please, let me thank you for sharing your rich personal history. It just so happens that every Thursday night, a group of enlightened people meets to discuss the sustainability of wildlife in this very erratic ecosystem. It sounds quite meek, but I can assure you, it's fraught with the unexpected," asserts the very poised Mattie Wildbird.

Without mincing words,

"By that, you mean, illegal?" whispers Professor Creekbaum.

Standing fully upright, Mattie's tiny frame appears unaffected by Creekbaum's brash statement. In no rush, she buttons her light jacket.

"Join us, and then make a decision. The way I see it, you can make both Gracie and Olivia proud one last time."

Chapter 24-
CREEK BAUM'S INDUCTION

When members of the Holdsclaw clan enter each other's home, they tender a gratuitous blessing. This tradition is lost on most of society but is still held sacred among Gracie's tribe. Eagle plumage soars with feathered consecration.

A wave of excitement diminishes any thought of age as Professor Anne Creekbaum patiently embraces this ceremony as a prelude to the next stage of her life.

A convivial Mattie Wildbird stands in the doorway with open arms. The professor pauses behind Gracie as her lover hugs Mattie and another, even tinier woman, whom everyone calls Hinmah.

Beside this elder stateswoman stands a giant of a man who doesn't speak but welcomes Anne with an affable smile. Hinmah introduces Delsin Wildbird as her husband. One of his charcoal black eyes reveals a dull sheen, and the right side of his forehead bears a scar from some past encounter.

Dignity permeates Delsin Wildbird. He and his wife hold the status of tribal forerunners with ease. Mattie explains to her new guest that this elderly couple is principal to the whole of the Ink Prayer tribe. It's obvious that Delsin and Hinmah accept this fundamental responsibility with a practiced distinction.

The room accommodates another colossus who mirrors the first, but with less age. Henry Wildbird is deemed twin to Mattie Wildbird and grandson to Hinmah and Delsin. Anne's a big-boned woman with large extremities. Even so, Henry's palm easily conceals the whole of Creekbaum's hand.

The professor wonders at the remarkable difference between this rare set of twins. Mattie and Henry's substantial divergence is more than conclusive of their duet classification.

Creekbaum is the star of tonight's String agenda. One by one, the members of the intrepid Ink Prayer band introduce themselves to the newcomer. Beer eases her inclusion as Anne slogs through the direct exposure, trying to remember everyone's name.

Mattie begins, "Well, Anne, I guess I should walk you through this banal group of colleagues."

"Nice," bleeps Winslow Sharp.

"Ah! A volunteer," banters Mattie.

Winslow turns red and tips his fake cap at Creekbaum.

"This shy guy is head of all things dark, to include the Internet, onion domains, and futuristic shadowing. Whatever we need, he acquires, and without detection. Most often, you'll find him in command of the surveillance and reconnaissance over more than five hundred miles, up and down, the length of what you'll learn is called the String. Winslow builds, repairs, and overhauls any and everything," reports the party hostess.

Mattie moves to the left and continues.

"Next is the industrious Marley Womack. She works for the Department of Natural Resources, or DNRC's Trust Land

Management Division (TLMD) by day and the Department of Transformation at night."

Typically, discreet, Womack joins the banter.

"After that introduction, I think I'm going to need a new cape."

Hinmah snickers in the background because she recognizes Marley's overt behavior means she has consumed more than one glass of white wine.

Now every member of the party joins in with witty rejoinders. The hostess makes a half-hearted attempt to regain control of the meeting.

"Marley Womack has the most difficult job here. She keeps us honest."

Uncontained laughter spills over as the group can't help but agree with Mattie's description.

"She works full-time for the state as a comptroller tending books, assessing land values, and tracking land board acquisitions. She functions as our eyes and ears inside the TLMD. Marley's role is identical inside the String.

"Seated to her left is Dagmar Eiksund, engineer and overseer. This elder statesman spends most of his time crawling around in the mud at Bandy Hawk. Take a good look at him now, because you'll probably never see him clean again," smiles Mattie.

Flirting with Creekbaum, the still handsome but graying blond from Norway moves towards the towering professor and kisses her hand.

"Rest assured, sweet lady, nothing could be further from the truth."

Henry looks at Sharp.

"Damn, Winslow, maybe we should take lessons from lover boy here."

Delsin gives Dagmar a high five to celebrate their refined and more practiced rank.

"Anne, if you haven't figured it out by now, Dagmar is a tunnel expert who has managed some spectacular engineering feats. In fact, he's world renowned," finishes Mattie.

The room fills with jeers as the senior man takes a bow.

Chapter 25-
PETE'S PROCLAMATION

Hinmah enjoys these gatherings. She and Delsin thoroughly relish the witty denigration. They're delighted with this tongue-in-cheek hilarity. It's family. The insanity of Tree and Isabelle's murders overwhelmed everyone, but none more so than Tree's parents. After this, their greatest loss, they could not imagine a returned contentment.

The twins' ongoing repartee about Pete's header at the last Indian race brings Mattie back around to introductions. "Speaking of the race, Anne, directly across from you is a gentleman by the name of James Tarkio. He's the director of Fish, Wildlife and Parks."

A visibly content man wiggles a few fingers in Anne's direction. Jim's first-hand holds a mug of cold beer, and the second is full of party appetizers.

"Culturally embedded, Tarkio is permitted to ride with Pete and his team of raiders. He's also our eyes and ears, defusing danger with advanced information of pursuit," adds Mattie.

The polished political appointee's precisely trimmed chestnut hair and mustache are the only things to suggest his professional status. Otherwise, he wears comfortable, well-worn jeans and a T-shirt that reads "Join the cause before there is no cause to join."

Tarkio gulps down a slug of beer before protesting, "Why, Mattie, I think you've hurt my feelings. What exactly do you mean, 'permitted'?"

With a slam of his coup stick, Pete jumps in. "What our illustrious hostess aims to explain is that we let you ride because she makes us."

The entire gang cracks up in delight.

Slender, with wiry strength, Pete moves to the center of the room. His eyes now focus on Anne.

"All humor aside, Professor, counting coup is the reason we ride."

Pete looks sternly at Hinmah and then moves to the center of the room to plead his case.

"We have completed many raids without assistance, as proven by this staff."

The feather connected at its top notch is dyed red. He makes a show of the stick to Creekbaum.

"This indicates that the owner has endured injury during a coup. We riders are warriors inside this environmental battle and as such have regained a sense of honor. It's not only a ritual but our sacred duty. The professor's ruse insults the purity of this sacred act. The coup is sacrosanct. Science is insolent, and Creekbaum's application is bald-faced," declares a brazen Pete Holdsclaw.

The room goes quiet. Creekbaum takes in the unexpected blow, shocked by the declaration. Hinmah slowly makes her way to Pete.

"This isn't the first time two sides of a copper penny coin have found their way into this room. Today's culture is based on science and reason, while our spiritual heritage relies on belief and faith."

The old woman works the room.

"Anne Creekbaum is an intelligent creator whose invention is founded in science. My tribal relative, Pete Holdsclaw, finds his roots in a traditional ethos. Each has its power; neither is wrong. I wonder, can they not both find a principled alliance?"

Pete Holdsclaw respectfully bows to the Ink Prayer's tribal medicine woman as he lays his coup stick at Hinmah's feet. The elder's husband bends to gather the coup stick with reverence as Hinmah continues.

"While Delsin and I are extremely absorbed in this dispute, I think we should dedicate some time to our new guest, Professor Creekbaum, if you please. I'm anxious to hear about your particular skill set and how it might be employed to assist the String."

Deliberately avoiding his mother's scrutiny, a furious Pete Holdsclaw storms out of the meeting, seething with Hinmah's declaration.

Pete's heated display of emotion more than surprises Creekbaum. Anne takes a long gulp from a tallboy as Gracie bolsters the newcomer with a quick knee squeeze.

The lanky professor stands up to Pete Holdsclaw's snub. "I've spent an afternoon with Mattie. She didn't exactly explain your purpose, but Gracie here has approached me about using my invention to protect the Ink Prayer riders during raids. At first, asking me to participate in such illicit activity irked me."

The room falls quiet. Trying to lighten the mood, Anne looks directly at Gracie Holdsclaw.

"To be honest, I'm still miffed. Why did it take you so long to ask me to join in the nefarious activities?"

Momentarily mollified, first by Pete's behavior and now by Anne's, Gracie leaps in.

"Well, you old communist, you've way too big an honest streak for the likes of Pete and me."

It's at this point Hinmah acknowledges that the lanky professor will fit right in.

Chapter 26-
TECHNO ACCELERANT

A level of optimism reignites the gatherers as Gracie Holdsclaw busies herself with a small metal box. Inside is a micro LED Rivulet projector with Targus laser pointer. Holdsclaw carefully arranges the system as an invigorated Anne Creekbaum stands tall and purposeful.

"Misdirection, distraction, and diversion are all well-qualified tactics applied in this group's line of sedition. What my invention adds is invisibility."

Now the long-limbed woman has the team's all-inclusive attention.

"I understand that these raids are increasingly dangerous due to the National Guard's technically advanced tactical maneuvers. As a practiced protester and counterinsurgent, I might have a way to help.

"In the late thirties, I worked alongside the head artist for several major Hollywood film studios. A Broadway designer, Tommy Cracraft, mesmerized Hollywood studio executives with astonishing backdrops and set designs. His work augmented some spectacular movies. The set I admired most was for the film *National Velvet*."

The soft-spoken and somewhat dreamy-eyed Marley Womack whispers, "I loved that film."

Creekbaum smiles at Marley and then continues. "Cracraft's backdrops were remarkably lifelike. Artists like Tommy saved movie moguls millions because they could film on a studio set. Since then, the cost of quality filmmaking has skyrocketed.

"Now, for more than a decade, I've worked towards the expansion of film media. The objective is to build more pictures for less and without the financial support from major film studios. This new strategy means to reconcile the financial side of moviemaking while retaining a characteristic value. So, using the latest technological advances, I've built an apparatus to assist smaller filmmakers. I call this new instrument a portable hologram rivulet. It gives small-budget films the means to film on-site but appear as though they're on location."

Creekbaum may have well been spewing out Mandarin Chinese given the looks on the faces around her, but she pushes forward.

"This mechanism projects a direct live backdrop with complete peripatetic capabilities."

The excited professor grasps the laser pointer and then moves to the east side of Mattie's living room.

"Are you ready, Gracie?"

Gracie beams with pride and hits the switch on the micro-LED invention. Grace aims the Targus at the people closest to her. Mattie, Henry and Hinmah utterly disappear. What remains is a hologram of Mattie's household and its belongings.

The professor goes on.

"I've managed to keep my invention under wraps for now. It's not common knowledge, so in that vein, I think it's perfect for this covert application. Imagine what we could accomplish with a hologram rivulet in combination with Winslow's - may I call you Winslow?"

"Absolutely," responds the not-easily-mystified ex-CIA agent.

"With Winslow's surveillance system," finishes Anne.

Everyone at the gathering is wholly astonished. From what appears to be the newly vacant space in Mattie's living room, Creekbaum adds, "I understand Bandy Hawk mountain is at the core of each egress. I'd bet money that Mr. Eiksund has already incorporated a multitude of tunnels with influx and exodus routes. We can use the rivulet's hologram to overlay images that will mask these portals. The goal is to bamboozle the pursuit."

Stunned, Eiksund asks, "You say this gadget is immediate and streaming, but please confirm that it's portable?"

"Indeed," answers Anne as Gracie disengages the device. "I can place a pinned version of the rivulet on a single event, just like Cracraft did with his various backdrops. If I have pre-determined coordinates, we can make anything vanish. In its place, an accurate bionetwork display appears."

Gracie demonstrates the machine's capabilities again. The distinguished trio evaporates. She clicks a second time, and Henry, Mattie and Hinmah reappear.

"The only restriction is advanced conduit placement. Because these routes are pre-established, that shouldn't be a problem," declares Professor Creekbaum.

The entire group is sufficiently astonished and impressed.

Hinmah asks, "What about sound? How do you reproduce the bird's song, the creek's warble?"

Creekbaum loves a challenge and, if possible, stands taller than her six-foot frame projects.

"Ah... good question," answers an invisible Anne as Gracie further demonstrates the machine's audio liability. The professor is invisible but adds, "I'm the first to admit that a sound engineer is a vital component. Over the years, I've acquired bites, tracks, and loops that will work, but the real test is Pete's ability to quiet the animals as the pursuit passes. One off-cue snort, whinny, nicker, or neigh could change the entire outcome."

A final click of the Targus and Anne stands front and center of the crowd.

The old medicine woman turns to Tarkio.

"Do you have any idea how you might keep them silent?"

"No, but I believe the trickster spirit in Pete Holdsclaw will find a way," declares an amazed Tarkio.

"Jim, I trust you and Professor Creekbaum will work together to find a solution."

Hinmah slowly turns to each member of the Ink Prayer's inner circle.

"All of you must find a way to make this work in order to fulfill our obligation."

Chapter 27-
TARKIO'S TRYOUT

Murmurs infuse the gathering as Jim Tarkio signals to Mattie for the opportunity to speak.

Mattie moves to the center of the room and announces, "Tarkio has the perfect challenge to test out the professor's gizmo."

Jim wipes the sauce from a chicken wing off his chin and then begins.

"As director of Fish, Wildlife and Parks, I have the distinct disgrace of working shoulder-to-shoulder with our illustrious governor."

Boos and jeers fill the living room.

"I received a call from Lund's office yesterday. It appears the governor has invited a special guest for the opening of bow season. Tully Neff, United States Secretary of State, is on his way to spend a weekend in Montana."

Henry jumps in.

"Are you certain about this?"

"Unless the Secretary's schedule changes at the last minute," declares Tarkio, "he'll be here. I know Tully Neff. He's a rather rotund fellow. I can't see him tromping through the forest with a bow or on foot. You can bet every hunting law in the book will be broken."

Eiksund, forever cautious, jumps in.

"Let's remember, this gentleman undoubtedly carries as much political weight as he does girth."

A far less prudent but very cagey Henry declares, "It's exactly what we need to draw the national exposure to fortify the String."

The room breaks out into an overexcited conversation. Finally, Hinmah moves beside Mattie.

"You're all aware that there is a vast difference between gambling and precise risk. First, we must work as a cohesive group, and that means finding a way to help Pete Holdsclaw reinterpret his heritage."

Gracie Holdsclaw intercedes, "That challenge is mine."

The medicine woman smiles with pride at her old friend. "You and Tarkio have made a good team. Pete is a gifted man, and I'm confident of your ability to sway him, Grace."

The old woman turns to Dagmar Eiksund.

"I believe Henry is right. We must take this gamble. The larger the impression we make, the greater the likelihood the String will remain intact and survive over time."

With this declaration, the elder stateswoman halts in front of the professor and grips Anne's hands. Hinmah adds a kiss to each palm in a sign of deference.

"You come to Black Bear and Coyote when needed most. You're real people now. Thank you for the benefit of your knowledge."

Graciously departing, Delsin and Hinmah bless all at the gathering as they take their leave.

Anne looks at Gracie with humility and then asks quietly, "Who or what are Brown Bear and Coyote?"

"Animal totems," whispers Gracie. "Pete's totem means he's a man of paradox. Coyote is the tribe's trickster but is also known as a contrarian. Mattie's black bear totem means she's our people's great helper and companion. She affords power to all who seek its source."

Once the elders leave, the meeting goes into overdrive. Henry hollers across the room at Eiksund.

"We'll need PERT calculations by six tomorrow evening."

"I'm on it," responds the engineer. "Am I to include the hologram?"

Professor Creekbaum bows in confirmation.

"Make certain your ideas are concrete and plentiful, ladies and gentlemen," warns Eiksund.

The group breaks into smaller units as everyone separates into lesser clusters. The professor is left to wonder what just happened. She and Gracie busy themselves gathering the remaining equipment.

Earnestly, Anne declares, "I had no idea Pete felt this way, or I would never have extended my services."

"Why do you think I kept his reactionary behavior from you?"

The secretive Gracie Holdsclaw leans close to her lover as they gawk out the living room window. Jim Tarkio has found his way to Pete Holdsclaw's truck door.

"When Pete's father took off, a kind of darkness made its way into my son's heart. I thank the everywhere spirit for the horse races and Jim Tarkio. Over time, Jim has managed to sneak in through some tiny crack of Pete's sorrow. Don't get me wrong, Pete still misses his no-account father, but somehow, Jim manages to reach past those feelings of dejection. Tarkio will apply supple means to convince the coyote trickster to modify his convictions."

Mattie recognizes Anne's reticence from across the room as the two women worry themselves over Pete's conflicted behavior. She makes her way towards them.

"Congratulations, Professor Creekbaum, you're officially a member of the Ink Prayer inner circle. Welcome to the String."

Now, all three women watch Tarkio work his magic before Mattie adds in a matter-of-fact tone, "Henry indicates week's end will see us field-test your apparatus. You have a lot of work to do, ladies.

"Oh, and Gracie, your idea to use the Internet as a supplemental vehicle to support the cause is a brilliant idea. My guess is that you can create a media crusade sympathetic to the cause. Constructive film coverage that promotes our work is just one more powerful tool we can implement. Please speak to Winslow about applying past and future camera footage along the String to develop the YouTube takes. The systematic destruction of unlawful hunting camps should make for great entertainment."

"Thank you for the opportunity. The downside is that it can bite us in a court of law, but just imagine the upside," declares Gracie.

Chapter 28-
TULLY'S FOLLY

Brown-nosing suck-ups are commonplace in today's political arena. Few are better at this than Crebo Lund. The governor's plans to schmooze Neff are vital to his autocratic ambitions.

Months ago, Lund had been asked to speak at a political convention on behalf of mining interests. It was during this Kansas City conference that he and Neff shared a rare bottle of the finest bourbon. The two self-absorbed men hit it off straightaway, and soon plans were hatched for a shared Montana hunt. Scheduling was a problem; Tully's political responsibilities didn't jibe with Montana's hunting season. The nation's Secretary of State is heavily committed, but his calendar is momentarily clear in mid-September.

Power is a drug that weakens most people's sensibilities. Lund and Tully consider themselves above the law, and after a brief discussion about the restrictive bow hunting season, they decided to create their own rules. The two declare that prerogative belongs to the privileged.

The power-hungry governor boasts, "My hunting camps are as opulent as can be found in the rugged Rocky Mountains. I'll spare no cost to ensure your comfort. Trust me, you'll feel quite at home. My crew will pack in only the finest of everything, including spirits."

The Secretary of State's arrival isn't made public. Scottish and very fair-skinned, Neff arrives comfortably dressed in Duluth Trading Company's best camouflage pants. Tully's balding red head is covered in an expedition-style cap to protect him from the sun's rays. He's garbed in an extra-large, lightweight, bush poplin hunting shirt with accompanying safari bush vest.

Once at camp, the politicians settle in with a few locally crafted brews and cigars flown in from Cuba. After the first day's hunt, the governor plans to break out his reserve of rare bourbons. Between the food and spirits, it's one hell of an indulgent feast. Lund means to capitalize on his investment by solidifying his relationship with the powerful Secretary of State. He'll spare no effort to advance his political ambitions.

Neff takes full advantage of the hunting camp. He thinks himself a powerful man, and as such, demands special treatment. His private flight to Montana was charged against his federal government expense account. Of course, the trip is declared strictly business. The two men have much in common. The privileged and powerful always feel that equality is nothing more than a form of repression.

Early the next morning, in complete darkness, a news helicopter flutters east towards the impending sunrise. As a backdrop, the enormous sky is softly lit by a large harvest moon slumping thickly to the west.

Inside the aircraft, a thin-boned woman works hard to keep her composure. The copter's belly shifts radically in the reedy air. Anxiously, she struggles with scarf, coat, and microphone. In her late twenties, the reporter strenuously grasps the metal handle with strap beside the "yank and bank" door on the right side of the craft. She shares the copter's large aperture with her cameraman.

"This is Macy Percy, reporting live for KXLH. It's nearly daybreak on the third day of bow season in Western Montana. It may be difficult to hear me above the aircraft's din.

"About an hour ago, we picked up a Mont-tip notification on the sheriff's radio band about illegal hunting activity near White Earth. We're scrambling to get there, but it looks as if we'll have company."

The whirl of rotor blades rips through the crisp, early morning air, bouncing off the ghost-lit valley floor.

"It's still faintly dark, but with the help of the harvest moon, I can make out several National Guard helicopters headed due east," continues Perry.

"Just beneath us, multiple Jeeps and Humvees advance along Highway 287, running east-northeast. We're closing in on the location now. All this activity can't possibly be aimed at one bad hunter. This whole area is crazy frantic."

Perry speaks into the helicopter headset.

"Jeff, set this thing down, so we can get a better idea of what's happening."

As the copter begins its descent, the reporter asks, "Is that who I think it is? The camera is rolling, right? Zoom in on the big guy staggering down the road. Is he nude? Forgive me, folks; I'm a bit stunned by everything going on.

"It appears a naked United States Secretary of State Tully Neff, now blanketed, has been loaded into a National Guard helicopter and is being spirited away from this hunting camp. The governor is with him; you can see Crebo Lund slipping into the copter right behind Neff."

The news crew touches down and bounds into action.

"Jeff, record everything," screams the newscaster as she ducks under the rotary blades and runs towards a disheveled campsite.

Percy launches into a litany of hunting indiscretions. "Ladies and gentlemen, there are several vehicles suspended from surrounding trees. Others simply sit on blocks, tireless. The few rigs left intact look to have been siphoned dry." She smells the residue from an abandoned garden hose.

"Simply incredible. This place is orderly chaos. All these guns are broken down into multiple pieces. Look, they're all lined up in a neat row below the carcasses of several slain animals."

The cameraman goes in for a closeup. The reporter shouts over the chaos.

"Animal carcass everywhere. It appears these firearms were expended on the many kills."

To the right is a rocky ledge full of cell phones, minus batteries, along with a parade of empty beer and bourbon bottles. The camera pans in and then follows Percy to the hunters' tents, suspended in the trees five feet above their metal frames. The messy confines are exposed and easily examined. Perry begins.

"Let's just say these accommodations are less than tidy."

Percy explores a broad set of Duluth jeans.

"Look at these pants; the leggings are sewn shut. No wonder the governor and his companion left without proper attire.

"Folks, there doesn't appear to be a single bow or arrow in sight. So much for hunting regulations."

Just then the camera is jostled. Lunging, a hulking guardsman grabs Percy's microphone.

"Hold on! Hold on!"

The stout and overly physical National Guardsman spews at the news reporter.

"I'm in command of this incident." He places a large hand over the camera lens and then barks, "Turn it off, now!"

The camera goes dark, and a lot of background noise is transmitted.

"We're being forced to leave. Wait a minute, wait a minute! As a reporter, I have a right to—"

The audio feed is cut. Macy Perry and her crew are physically ushered back to their helicopter.

"Bastards, don't you give a damn about the First Amendment?"

Furious, the reporter screams at the guardsman, "What the hell happened to freedom of the press?"

Macy attempts to straighten her clothing and presses her free hand against her red locks as she yells, "Guys, stay focused. Catch up to the other helicopters. What the hell?" shrieks Percy.

Now airborne, the news team films the National Guard engaged in a ground skirmish. A single horse and rider float across the dimly lit expanse like a tumbleweed dodging captivity. Several other riders make a mad dash to join the first, jumping over fallen tree stumps, dry creek beds, and boulder fields. From overhead, Percy witnesses the tightening formation as it flees its pursuers.

Dawn stretches out at the horsemen sweeping in and out of shadowed forests with speeds far too dangerous for the hour. The sure-footed animals seem to magically avoid each obstruction. The treacherous footing and diminished light add to this dicey adventure as the riders spill onto the open plain at breakneck speeds. In a race against a jealous sunrise, the riders press hard toward a vast woodland. Too late, they're bathed in an eerie and revealing light, betrayed by the rising sun.

For a split second, Percy's cameraman gets a glimpse of the group just before they disappear under the forested canopy. The local reporter from Montana immediately recognizes she and her news team just netted a segment on the evening's national newscast.

———◆———

Fractionally restrained by the helicopter's seatbelt and stunned with the remnants of inebriation, a sunburned Tully Neff shivers with the realization of what just happened. A guardsman wraps the obese Secretary of State with another blanket to spare everyone further humiliation.

Wrathful, the governor, himself half-clothed, seethes with indignity. He made it clear that if this absurd band of renegades muddied Tully Neff's reputation in any way, there would be severe repercussions. It never crossed the governor's mind that Henry Wildbird would dare go this far. An infuriated Crebo Lund works hard to control his breathing. For now, Neff is a priority. Getting the Secretary of State back to Washington, D.C. without further exposure is the governor's first concern.

Lund wipes his face with a wet hunter's orange shirt and throws it angrily over his upper torso. He signals the unfortunate guardsman whose assignment is to assist the hungover politicians.

The young private leans in to hear what the enraged man wants and then backs away from both the excessive spittle and Lund's horrific breath. He pushes the intercom button attached to his headset. An immediate course change to the north takes Tully Neff away from the escort and out of the fray.

An hour and forty-five minutes later, they land at a private landing strip on Crystal Lake deep within the Kootenai Forest. Waiting, Greyson Chance provides a change of clothing for the bulbous bureaucrat. A Learjet stands fueled and ready for takeoff. Five minutes later, the Secretary is in Canadian airspace, on his way home, without further humiliation but forever infamously counted among Ink Prayer coup.

Chapter 29-
CREBO'S CABIN

"I don't think I need to remind you what's at stake, Chief," says an animated Lund.

Crebo's cabin, nestled on an island in the middle of a pristine mountain lake, secluded between the Seeley Swan and the Bob Marshall Wilderness, feels more like a lodge. Just buying the land to build such a dwelling screams money.

The governor's private hideaway doesn't see a lot of visitors. Separate shorelines, cold, clear water, and privately protected access preclude the typical Montanan admission. The only witness to the midnight meeting between Lund and Henry Wildbird is Greyson Chance. After all, these three partners have much to discuss.

The latest of the terrible triad's acquired holdings isn't pristine, but it is red hot. The property in question is the single drainage that sits on an old, unnoticed mining claim. For years, it has acted as a public gateway to the back side of Moonlight Ski Basin. This small strip of land contains access to the resort's best and most challenging runs.

Greyson's real estate knowledge has, once again, proved most advantageous. He discovered the mining claim, and, after a lengthy investigation, his research paid off. Together, this unholy threesome has managed to acquire more than thirty properties with minimal outlay and maximum yield. Tactics that enhance these assets' total value are often considered blackmail. Over the past several years, this trinity of thieves made huge financial gains through in-house official tipoffs, complicated land swaps, right-of-property easements, and mining patents.

That's when Wildbird's Tall River Casino comes into play. It's a seamless tool used to filter dirty revenue. One must work hard to uncover the partnership. The company's financial assets appear, at first glance, to be nonexistent, even to experienced forensic auditors. Henry Wildbird makes certain all sullied funds are well-hidden. Chance and Lund's access to these monies is obtained via Bitcoin accounts. The governor's contribution is simple: Anytime Triad's holdings are scrutinized, he runs interference.

Tonight's deliberations address two pressing topics: in-holdings and Henry Wildbird's diversionary tactics. The governor pours himself another glass of bourbon and settles into a chair beside a massive stone fireplace. Lund doesn't offer his two guests a chair or a drink.

He starts in, "Those coups have been a great distraction."

Lund's eye-piercing stare stabs at Henry and is full of brazen hatred.

"You probably consider the latest raid a superlative achievement. After all, those riders thoroughly embarrassed a seated Secretary of the United States," sneers the aggressive Crebo Lund.

Emboldened now by his second bourbon, Lund continues his verbal assault.

"Still trying to even things up, Henry? We aren't even cut from the same cloth. You can't compete."

The giant shows no reaction, so the governor doubles down.

"Greyson, why don't you tell your boyfriend Henry here what happened during our last land board meeting? Perhaps you can convince him that our little business venture is starting to fray around the edges."

Greyson, leaning against the credenza, straightens and walks to the bar. He pours himself and Henry a cup of coffee.

"It seems Attorney General Tabor has stumbled upon Triad Realty's free agent. It's only a matter of time before he connects everyone in this room to the Moonlight Basin purchase."

With pure disdain, the governor eyes Henry as he waits for a reaction.

"But you already knew that, didn't you, chief? Hell, you probably leaked it to the AG yourself."

The fireplace light distorts Henry Wildbird's size as he moves to collect his coffee from Greyson Chance. Intermittent flickers of dark and light cast an enormous shadow on the cabin walls, exaggerating an already massive Henry's size.

"Neither Chance nor I perpetrated any legal infraction in the acquisition of Moonlight Basin, nor any other properties acquired through Triad Realty," states Henry.

"Profits from each sale have been properly cleaned through Tall River Casino and then placed in a Bitcoin account, just as agreed. I'm not obligated to protect anyone's reputation. You're both big boys. I'm sure you considered the political risks connected to our business affiliations. If the AG feels the governor benefited from some form of insider knowledge, I cannot be held responsible. I believe you gentlemen are liable for your own standing."

Seething now, the governor rips into Henry.

"Don't you worry about me, boy. I can take care of myself. As for those raids of yours, well, let's just say the governor's office can't possibly turn a blind eye. Nationwide news coverage puts an end to any safeguard I can provide. The Federal Bureau of Investigation has stepped in because you and your raiders attacked a seated federal official. They'll be here soon, I imagine, along with anyone else the president decides to direct our way. It takes a real dumbass not to recognize that such an embarrassment would draw a lot more attention than we need."

Henry finishes his coffee without the slightest reaction. Greyson attempts to change the tenor of the meeting.

"The Moonlight thoroughfare purchased at a fair market price is a boon. Wildbird made a clear declaration that the public could no longer use his private land without fair compensation. If the Moonlight Corporation continues to allow people to cross the property, it will result in legal action. We paid thirty thousand for that strip of land. Moonlight has offered to buy it for five-point-five million. The resort owners have already screamed blackmail without much repercussion. While incensed, they have little choice."

Chance's attempt to distract Henry fails. The giant man eyes both men.

"The raids have been and still are the perfect distraction, but things are getting a little too rough. If anything happens to those riders, Governor, I'll hold you accountable."

Henry purposely sits the empty coffee cup down beside Lund.

"You don't want to find out what happens should that happen."

The giant's abhorrent glare penetrates the governor's false courage. Crebo squirms while holding his breath. It isn't until Henry leaves the room that the marginally inebriated governor breaks into a wry smile. With renewed courage, he takes a poke at the absent Henry Wildbird.

"I think the chief just threatened me, don't you, Chance?"

Greyson shoots Lund a stern look and follows Wildbird out. He hopes to placate Henry with a promise to protect the Ink Prayer riders.

"That's right, Chance! You best go repair your little bromance with the chief," hollers Lund.

Alone now, finishing his bourbon, the governor moves to a leather couch. He smiles as he pours a fourth. Hate is the stoutest emotion and, consequently, the most powerful. He reserves this sentiment for a special few. The Wildbirds are presently at the top of his list.

The governor rarely ponders his emotional state. Kentucky's finest bourbons do that to people. The lovely elixir allows him a little self-scrutiny. The bottom line is his addiction to power; it's the one thing he admires more than bourbon.

A haze falls over the governor as he slips into the past. Years have passed since the chief's parents stumbled onto one of Lund's bourbon-laden hunting parties. At the time, Lund was a younger version of his magnificent self. He had not yet acquired the taste for choice bourbons and failed to drink them neat. His hunting buddies had even less experience with this potent elixir, especially that dupe Greyson Chance.

"It was never anyone's intent to shoot down that long-winded public servant. The unwelcome idiot lectured me in front of my posse. Accident or not, I couldn't leave the game warden's murder to witnesses. Henry Wildbird, that witless giant of a boy, got lucky.

I don't exactly know how he and his she-devil sister managed to escape that ill-fated moment. Crebo's sure the mash had something to do with it."

The velvety legs and rich, brown sugar undertones of the bourbon bring vivid memories of Bandy Hawk Lake to the forefront of Lund's muddled mind. He whispers to no one in particular.

"How did that one-armed little bitch manage to survive her wounds? She's spent the last decade fouling my plans." Shifting uncomfortably, the drunken governor murmurs, "I'd love another shot at her."

Crebo Lund drifts off into a drunken stupor.

Chapter 30-
AT ODD ENDS

Standing at her tallest, Mattie Wildbird is barely noticeable opposite the bulletproof glass. Lotner hits the buzzer that allows the serene attorney into the interior office.

"You should have said something, Mattie. How long you been standing out there?" demands the middle-aged woman over the top of her readers.

Mattie waves the woman off and passes straight through to Drake's office. Flustered, the clerk's glasses now dangle by a thin chain as she drops everything to warn the sheriff by intercom. By then, it's too late; Mattie Wildbird is very quick on her feet.

With the intercom blaring in the background, a wry grin takes form on the young sheriff's face. Mattie finds a new way to make his jail clerk ill at ease with each visit. No one materializes so covertly as a member of the Wildbird clan. When Mattie enters, Drake laughs quietly.

"You spook the hell out of Lotner."

Mattie's eyes sparkle with pleasure as she confesses her need to surprise Lotner has turned into a weird form of amusement. Laughing inaudibly, the two look down the hall as the lawyer lands in the chair to the left of the sheriff's bookcase.

"Everybody is talking about this kid. Is it true? Did she run those old boys atop their truck hoods?" asks the minuscule attorney.

Drake loves Mattie's visits. His entire world comes alive.

"I didn't see the whole thing, but what I did witness was pretty damn impressive. First, she isn't a kid, and second, you probably haven't seen that many black people in these parts."

Drake walks around his desk to pass the attorney a file for perusal.

"That gal pulled off one of the prettiest one-eighties I've ever seen. But you need to know, this Betty woman has what you might call 'anger issues.'"

"So what? I'm an Irish Native American attorney with an unruly attitude and half a left arm," remarks Mattie.

Drake's smile deepens with appreciation.

"What do you think? Can we help her out?"

"You like her," smiles Mattie, hoisting herself from the chair. She heads down the corridor towards Sweet Brown Betty's cell.

Drake's lengthy inseam easily offsets the small woman's lesser stride, but he lags a couple of steps behind. Otherwise, Mattie might notice his blush.

The jailhouse cell feels a lot smaller than six-by-eight and reeks of industrial cleaning solvent. Earlier, a female guard informed Sweet Brown Betty that she was "lucky." The old jail (now the newly remodeled Myrna Loy Theater), not more than a half-block from the new one, was so overrun that inmates shared a space no bigger than four by six.

With her back against the cold cinderblock wall, Betty's thoughts return to the sheriff. After all, she has more than enough time to consider her plight. Betty cogitates over her newfound friend, Sheriff Drake. Fair-minded, he believes in justice. That's something they have in common. Tall and handsome, just the way she likes her men. He also seems kind, and to Betty, this is a weighty attribute. When she requests that someone look in on her animals, Drake volunteers, confessing that he loves animals more than people. That's another mutual viewpoint she appreciates. Betty smiles as she considers the sheriff's attractive traits for a while longer before returning to the problem at hand.

Somehow, a petite woman in her late twenties materializes no more than a foot away from the preoccupied inmate without detection. Startled, Betty feels a presence before seeing one.

Just over five feet, the smidge of a woman looks vulnerable in this place of internment. The sheriff stands back. Neither woman speaks for what feels like an eternity. Finally, the minuscule lawyer (who in Betty's estimates couldn't weigh more than a buck "0" five) introduces herself as Mattie Wildbird.

Incredulous, Betty doesn't trust her own eyes.

"You ain't that terror of an attorney Sheriff Stoltz told me about?"

Mattie ignores Betty's comment as she scans the arrest documents. She waits for Stoltz to unlock the cell and enters. Sweet Brown Betty is flabbergasted. Mattie climbs into the bunk and sits off the inmate's right shoulder. Stoltz is struck by the distinctive picture these two women make sitting beside one another: complete opposites.

Sweet Brown Betty watches Mattie shuffle quickly through the file with her artificial limb. It doesn't seem to inhibit the pocket-sized woman as she rapidly gleans the information needed to summarize her thoughts. In time, Mattie shifts so she can look directly at Betty.

"I think I have the gist of it. It sounds like you came across a bad case of elk fever. It's not an uncommon phenomenon in these parts. Judge Melos won't be impressed with your response, but my guess is he won't blame you, either."

Mattie is on the move now, pacing, deep in thought. Sweet Brown Betty, still in shock, throws a "*What the hell?*" gesture at Stoltz. He grins.

"Let me tell you how this'll turn out," announces the very official-sounding lawyer. "My guess is you'll lose your job because the corporation you work for won't want the publicity. The judge will look down on that, and he isn't going to let you leave without bond unless you have someone to vouch for you. Do you?" questions Mattie.

Flummoxed, Betty just shakes her head no. Mattie moves to stand at attention.

"No one got hurt," continues the miniature lawyer. "You scared the crap out of those hunters, but they had that coming. Your employer will want the van repaired, but I'll see to it the problem falls to the defendants charged in this incident. Drake here will pick up something other than your delivery uniform for court this afternoon. Get cleaned up, be prompt, and keep it brief when you speak to the judge. See you in court."

That's it; the interview is at an end. Betty isn't sure what exactly transpired. Mattie leaves as abruptly as she appeared. Drake Stoltz gives Betty a moment to catch up.

"She's the lead counsel for the Fish, Wildlife and Parks Division. Mattie Wildbird only takes cases that mean something to her. I'd say you should be out of here this time tomorrow."

Brown Betty can't remember precisely when she consented to representation. Obviously, Drake considers Mattie Wildbird the best person for the job.

"Thank you, I think," replies a still-bewildered Sweet Brown Betty.

———————◦◆◦———————

The courtroom is linked to the county jail by an enclosed runway off its northeast side. The fresh air makes every inmate realize just how badly they want out of their tiny cells. At this point, Betty will agree to anything.

Judge Melos dispatches judgement on a prior case in a deep baritone voice just as a handcuffed Sweet Brown Betty is ushered into the second pew.

"Mr. Lahaderne, this court finds you guilty of eight counts of fraud. The sentence for fraud is two years' imprisonment for each count. You're lucky I don't throw more time at you, given your proclivity towards breaking the law and bending the truth more ways than imaginable."

The gavel drops hard atop the bench, and the jury is dismissed. The bailiff signals Betty forward to a seat directly in front of the bench. Mattie Wildbird storms in just as the previous defense lawyer exits. Mattie makes herself at home behind one of two huge tables with three chairs fronting Judge Melos' bench. The clerk reads aloud several charges. The judge looks straight past Betty.

"Mattie, it's good to see you. Looks like you've found another cause."

"Good afternoon, Your Honor. I can make this easy. Mostly a black and white situation: My client was traveling west on Highway 12 when she passed a group of hunters pulled off the road to her right. Her vehicle was pelted with a variety of ballistics used by the accused. There was substantial damage done to the vehicle. Thankfully, my client was not hurt. It appears she came across a severe case of elk fever."

A blond and very underweight prosecutor takes this moment to stand and object.

"Judge, this is a simplified version of the circumstances. Ms. Wildbird fails to describe the retaliatory antics displayed by her client."

Judge Melos interrupts.

"Sit down, Jake; I can read the file. Okay, I have a couple of questions. My guess is you're no longer employed. Is that correct, Ms. Kumba?"

Sweet Brown Betty answers with a succinct, "Yes, sir!"

The judge quickly returns to Mattie.

"What's the plan?"

Mattie Wildbird provides the details.

"I'd like you to release this young woman into my custody. There's an opening in the FWP mailroom. Ms. Kumba is more than qualified," asserts the tiny attorney with confidence.

"She has no previous record and isn't a flight risk. I suggest a minimal fine and a get-out-of-jail card."

Once again, the prosecutor shifts his limited girth upright.

"Judge, I appreciate a good sense of humor as much as anyone, but the truth is Ms. Kumba could have killed those men."

"Well, she didn't, did she, Jake? Damn it all; those idiots were shooting across the highway. I'm not sure I wouldn't have done the same damn thing."

With that, Judge Melos attaches a thousand-dollar fine to thirty days in jail, suspended for time already spent. "Ms. Kumba, you'll work in the FWP mailroom for no less than three months."

Melos's wooden gavel drops as firmly as his judicial decision. That's it. Sweet Brown Betty walks out the courtroom, a free woman. She has just one question: What exactly does she owe Mattie Wildbird?

Chapter 31-
APPLE'S RETURN

Hinmah calls Apple home from Washington, D.C. in a way that always transcends his sensibilities: She arrives in his dreams.

Early next morning, he finds himself at the White House consulting with people he had never aspired to encounter. Hinmah's poignant visit proves correct by the conclusion of this session.

Apple's new boss, Reilly Geo Mac, Secretary of the United States Department of Interior, accompanies Apple to the meeting. The two men enter the Oval Office. Andrew Delahunt, President of these United States, or POTUS, and a mortified Secretary of State Tully Neff watch the morning news.

"Apple" Tamer Gray sits apart, hoping his share of whatever unfolds won't include last night's national news coverage. Uncomfortable in his surroundings, he senses what is about to transpire.

"These people are little more than the latest brand of eco-terrorists," rages Tully.

The president lets the humiliated Secretary of State rant on as he signals Mac that he wants to scan the FBI file in Apple's possession. The contents of the green GSA manila file folder are far more enlightening than anything Tully contributes:

US Department of Interior, U.S. Fish & Wildlife Service- Employee #41000-Samantha Cherchez

- Sam Cherchez is French Canadian with a dual US citizenship. (The Seeker's parents and several siblings live inside the Canadian Shield.)

- The Cherchez family lives near a Canadian attraction called National del la Gaspésie (Gaspésie National Park) at the base of the Chic-Choc Mountains, an extension of the Appalachians.

- Quebec has the world's largest freshwater reserves, with only 0.1% of the world's population. The Cherchez family is deeply rooted in conservation efforts to protect these waters.

- Luce Cherchez (mother), a freelance journalist, concentrates on environmental issues.

- Sam Cherchez is the youngest of eight children who grew up on a remote, 120-acre, backcountry homestead that has been in the family for generations.

- The Cherchez children are highly successful in their chosen professions. The Cherchez brothers are excellent resources in a variety of fields: two Canadian Olympic athletes, a Canadian Royal Mountie, two renowned government wildlife biologists, a well-known comedian, and a Royal Canadian Air Force pilot.

- Cherchez (a.k.a. Sam the Seeker) is a highly ranked member of the elite undercover branch of the US Department of the Interior Fish & Wildlife Service.

- Employee #41000 leads the department's agents in overall closures and arrests. As principal investigator, Cherchez has built a talented and diverse team that investigates a vast array of criminal behaviors, from manhunts to judicial corruption. Cherchez's dynamic law enforcement team has closed 763 cases to date with a 99.2 percent conviction rate. Cherchez is said to be driven, direct, and intense when in pursuit of a suspect. The entire undercover team completes these duties utilizing tenacious principles and anonymity.

As POTUS scans the contents of the GSA file, Secretary Tully fulminates. Finally, when the president can stand it no longer, he silences the dishonored politician.

"By morning's end, I want your letter of resignation on my desk."

Tully Neff's reddened face takes on a deeper shade of crimson as he looks to others in the room for support. Finding none, he storms out of the oval office.

Andrew Delahunt looks to the DOI Secretary. "I like your plan, Mac. It sounds like you may have found the right man to deal with things out West."

Just then, a regal woman in her late twenties dressed in a professional yet attractive business suit is escorted into the Oval Office. Reilly Geo Mac introduces the elegant Sam the Seeker to the president of the United States. A wisp of a smile settles in as Andrew Delahunt shakes the delicate hand of the covert operator. Mac offers Samantha Cherchez the obligatory refreshment, but she waves it off.

"I understand you gentlemen need my assistance?"

Delahunt begins.

"You have an excellent track record, Ms. Cherchez. I'm very impressed that your team has managed to keep your fabled in-house skills anonymous while ferreting out an incredible amount of felonious activities. Please let me introduce you to the Interior's Deputy Secretary and Chief Legal Counsel, 'Apple' Tamer Gray. I imagine the two of you will know each other well before this mess is properly contained."

Gray looks across the room in stunned realization; Sam the Seeker won't be going back to Montana alone.

———————◆———————

The sleek Gulfstream G650 flies at Mach 0.8.25, so the flight to Great Falls, Montana doesn't take long. Apple Tamer Gray's new co-worker looks serenely out the window of the private jet. She doesn't say much, not that he cares. His plate is full enough, given the circumstances. He needs to focus on his unexpected immediate future.

Passing beneath the thin-skinned jet is a land of open spaces filled with patchwork farms, grasslands, craggy mountains, and fast-running waters. Apple finds it difficult to do anything but watch the naked countryside unfold. It has been far too long since he left the city.

The president's request that he act as liaison and interpreter for Cherchez is, of course, undeniable. It doesn't bode well for anyone's future to refute POTUS. Just because Apple speaks Ink Prayer fluently doesn't mean he shares any real connection to a native people who shunned him in his youth. Nothing has changed. He is still Apple, the half-breed. Apple's unusual nickname is tribal slang. It stands for red on the outside, white on the inside. Hinmah taught him to sport it as a badge against bigotry.

The loss of both parents when very young forced Apple to grow up rather quickly. Early on, the Wildbird family made the boy family. Together, he and two other children came to recognize that their mixed blood made them different. To this day, harsh discrimination marks the worldly perspective of all three. The tribe's children taunted Henry, Mattie, and Apple mercilessly. The Wildbird children often came home bloodied. Henry's size made him a valuable warrior, as did Mattie's speed. Apple's brilliant tactical mind compensated for his lankiness. The three relied on one another to survive the tribe's cruelty.

Hinmah didn't tolerate troubled excuses for fighting. She felt being cultureless was a problem cured by creating one's own. All three people are genetically linked to the Ink Prayer tribe. Whether Apple likes it or not, he's bound by this fact and a dark, violent act that affects each one and will do so the remainder of their days.

Grandmother believed knowledge to be the only means of survival for her family and tribe. Instruction found a crucial forum under the medicine woman's roof. All three of her orphans were expected to reap its benefits. No one escaped that house without proper schooling. In the end, Hinmah produced two attorneys and an economics professor with a graduate degree in forensic accounting.

Decades after his adoption, the promise of sharing time with his espoused family feels surreal. He is both reticent and euphoric. Age does funny things to a heart and its memories. He doesn't know what to expect. Whatever happens next is long overdue. Apple left behind a meaningful relationship, half-finished, or at least that's his interpretation. He failed to express his feelings, lacked the courage to follow his heart and gut, and that's something he regrets. Hinmah has her reasons for calling Apple home, but he has his own for making the trip: most significantly, to face Mattie Wildbird, the one woman he will always love.

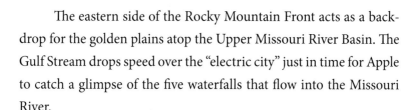

The eastern side of the Rocky Mountain Front acts as a backdrop for the golden plains atop the Upper Missouri River Basin. The Gulf Stream drops speed over the "electric city" just in time for Apple to catch a glimpse of the five waterfalls that flow into the Missouri River.

Apple peers out from the plane's signature oval windows, searching for America's shortest river, "the Roe." This place holds meaningful memories: his mother's funeral, his grandmother's Ink Prayer dance, his first love's kiss, and their last goodbye.

Cherchez watches a poignant smile wash over the attractive man's face as he peers down upon the vast expanse. It's hard to hide the kind of emotion "Apple" Tamer Gray presently feels. He looks much younger than his twenty-nine years as the window's changing light plays off his face. Samantha Cherchez sits motionless, as witness, not wanting to invade this tick in time.

The jet's Rolls-Royce engines cut short Apple's reverie as the ninety-three-foot wings shim into a graceful rolling stop on the tarmac of the Great Falls International Airport.

The GSA flight attendant lowers the steps to an awaiting entourage, including Governor Crebo Lund, Lieutenant Governor Grayson Chance, and Regal Markay, Adjutant General of the Montana National Guard Joint Forces.

Apple gives thanks to the attendant and follows Samantha Cherchez down the plane's steps before turning to greet the confreres.

Governor Lund takes a firm hold of Apple's hand, trying to compensate for the difference in the two men's stature.

Lund thinks himself strikingly handsome. His arrogant stance confirms an outsider's first suspicion that the governor indeed likes himself. Sporting a fair complexion with Romanesque facial features, Crebo Lund adjusts his tie over a starched white shirt. His suspenders are attached to expensive pin-striped black slacks, accompanied by sockless tasseled penny loafers—all in an attempted *I'm extraordinary* look.

Apple, with his six-foot-one stature, black wavy hair, and dark black eyes, gives onlookers a sense of peace. Self-confident, he looks people squarely in the eye, just as Hinmah taught him. His mere presence establishes a level of involuntary poise.

Samantha Cherchez stands completely overlooked in the background, aiding the standard good-old-boy assumption that Apple is in command. She can't resist the humor of unrealized chauvinism, even in its regularity.

The governor welcomes both members of the D.C. team with enthusiasm, right up until he's informed that Cherchez is, in fact, the president's answer to his problems. Incredulously, Lund looks at the well-heeled woman standing before him and laughs. Slightly above average height at a lean one hundred thirty pounds, Cherchez looks as if a strong wind might blow her off her Christian Louie Viton pumps.

Lieutenant Governor Greyson Chance, a soft-spoken second-generation Scot, leans into the fray just in time to soothe any potentially ruffled feathers. He welcomes Ms. Cherchez and guides the entourage back to the terminal.

The small gathering waits to collect the D.C. team's personal baggage, as a sniggering Governor Lund cannot resist taking a superfluous poke at Cherchez.

"I see you travel light, Mr. Gray."

Apple grabs one wide-mouth beige leather duffle that looks to have seen some mileage. There are no less than seven bags, of every shape and size, remaining on the carousel. The porter steps up to load Samantha's luggage as Apple excuses himself, heading towards the men's room. He never reaches his destination.

Chapter 32-
LOVER'S REUNION

It's a rare thing to confront time. Mattie runs headlong from Sweet Brown Betty's hearing to do just that. She knows this moment is inevitable but can't explain why her heart feels as if a ricocheting bullet is trapped inside her chest. Regardless, today, she aims to realize her future.

Mattie Wildbird makes up for her late departure from the courthouse. The Gulfstream flies in overhead and touches down just as Mattie pulls into the clearly marked, drop-off-only curb painted a bright yellow. The tiny attorney leaps from the Jeep and enters the airport terminal as inconspicuously as possible.

Apple tracks the wisp of a woman immediately. Mattie's furtive entrances alarms most, but Apple finds it part of her mystifying beauty. He doesn't make a show of his departure as he extricates himself from the entourage to shadow his past. The two escape out the east exit without detection.

The Jeep Wrangler's exposed interior provides Tamer the perfect opportunity to demonstrate his agile vigor. Apple throws his wide-mouth duffle into the back seat and takes his best shot, landing just short with his trail leg. He rolls his eyes, looking up from Mattie's lap.

Laughter rushes at him. The city-slicker attempts to right himself as Mattie throws the Wrangler into gear, hurling the two back into their guileless past.

The Jeep darts from the airport to the frontage road as if in flight. A torrent of light, color, and sound floods Apple in whimsical waves. Montana's largesse emboldens imagination as the legless air infuses his sense of liberty.

Mattie moves over dirt roads and blind hills with intemperance. Heat rises off wheat fields; the plains are dotted with fallen barbed-wire fencing, jagged rocks, and passing barnyards.

Massive irrigation pivots stand guard on mounted wheels, spraying bullets of moisture over fields of green. The overindulgent driver swings wide from the paved frontage road to a single track, bouncing from pothole to pothole, some dry, some wet. This mad dash slams to a halt just long enough for Apple to get his bearings.

The Jeep explodes into reverse, then settles behind an enormous boulder. Mattie leaps to the ground without a word, pulling off her shirt, bra, pants, and shoes. Distracted by Mattie's beauty and attempting to multitask, Apple falls out of the Wrangler, exhibiting the same poise he used to get in. Upright once again, he strips off the remainder of his three-piece suit while watching Mattie glide over fields like a native bird.

The race is on against galvanized trusses to win or suffer a steady saturation from the gallant soldiers of irrigation. Apple can taste the clear, chilly water ahead. He catches a glimpse of Mattie just as she makes an exposed leap into the green-blue depths of their favorite childhood pond. Her beauty stuns. He forgets his nakedness and joins her without a sound, a trick from childhood, a feat lost on city dwellers.

Apple craves Mattie's touch like that of a wanton paramour. They return to a place in time, a state of unrestrained need, conditioned anticipation, a reckless yearning as Apple sinks abruptly under his first love's spell. Mattie rushes at him; they kiss, caress, and find themselves linked in a passionate embrace, sinking to the water's floor. With erotic prowess, she pulls Apple inward as if a practiced courtesan. The two make love in a place of turquoise light and indulgent lust, lost in a shared primordial darkness. Both lovers hold fast at the edge of a collective acuity. From a common center, they pursue an innocent ecstasy. Mattie's desire withstands Apple's strength. She breaks from his embrace and swims to shore, beckoning him to join her in nature's bed of soft flora. He watches as she stretches out like some wild creature native to the lakeshore; once again, he finds himself gently provoked, yet fully aroused.

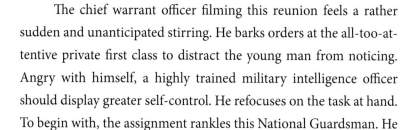

The chief warrant officer filming this reunion feels a rather sudden and unanticipated stirring. He barks orders at the all-too-attentive private first class to distract the young man from noticing. Angry with himself, a highly trained military intelligence officer should display greater self-control. He refocuses on the task at hand. To begin with, the assignment rankles this National Guardsman. He detests the governor's command to film such private matters.

"I'm damn sure neither of us signed up as voyeurs. We've followed the order to keep track of this guy, but taping his personal activity is just damned sick."

The private is still filming the events as they unfold and doesn't verbalize his thoughts. The chief determines that a record of this private affair is contemptible.

"Can that camera roll without you or me as a witness?"

The private tears himself from his duties.

"Yes, sir, but I can't promise how the video will turn out."

"Well, hell, son, I don't plan on winning an Oscar. These folks work for the government just like you and me. All I can say is that Governor Crebo Lund is a prick. Pack it up, Private."

Chapter 33-

A CHANCE ENCOUNTER

Historically, a mix of wind, rain, and sleet makes every Labor Day weekend in the Queen City a challenge. This one is no different. The governor's Yukon pulls up to the FWP headquarters. Clad in rain gear, Lieutenant Governor Greyson Chance exits the vehicle and hops over a cement curbing filled by downpour.

Shaking the excess water from the brim of his felt hat, Chance smooths back glistening bronze hair. He takes a minute to brace himself, then strides down the hallway to stand at the door of the chief legal counsel's office.

Serenely lit by the window's tepid sunlight, Mattie Wildbird is dressed modestly in her weekend apparel, blue jeans with a light-blue cotton shirt, layered by an oversized dark-blue corduroy jacket. The hard-working attorney sits behind the very desk her mother occupied years ago. Isabelle's flaming-red hair, long legs, and emerald-green eyes are at odds with Mattie's high cheekbones, dark black eyes, and diminutive frame.

Mattie has three fields of concentration. The first is the law. The second is to see the String completed. Only then will the chief legal attorney give her full attention to the third, matters of the heart.

The last two decades of Mattie's life have revolved around the String. At first, this family goal was merely a dream, then a religion, and now reality. Every step towards its achievement is in honor of her parents' principled ambitions. Building the String is dangerous work. Once finalized, the String will provide wildlife a far better opportunity to survive. Only then can all the contributors honestly and openly make claim to their scrupulous attempts to conserve wildlife.

The federal government's official position towards most conservationists is a twisted aim to vilify. In other words, they could give a damn about purpose or cause. Labeling the Ink Prayer riders "eco-terrorists" amounts to a public campaign to criminalize the work of building the wildlife corridor.

As for the misdirecting raids, they shine a light on perpetrators who break hunting laws without regard to mandate, environment, or ecology. Animals are poached. Examples of trashed environments and destroyed habitats are copious. The raids must continue to act as a blind for the String.

Mattie's toughest task is to control Henry's focused pursuit of retribution. She and her brother deal with the brutal murder of their parents in distinct ways. How far they stray from the law requires keen discipline. Mattie views each penny earned illegitimately justified when redirected to the corridor's construction. The use of state excises, dues, and assessments to acquire land falls within the Ink Prayer's just philosophical margins. Acquisitions using a series of cleverly designed tactics pinch finances from varying forms of state income. These pass-on funds go towards crucial shards of real estate. Each of these properties is accurately recorded with the owner's name: the great state of Montana.

Henry Wildbird, a forensic accountant, is held to justification with a form of checks and balances. The String's internal auditor, Marley Womack, devises and applies these measures. Hinmah intentionally assigns changing and redundant auditory practices to ensure no one falls prey to greed. Henry's financial prowess isn't the problem. It's his deep-seated need for retaliation. Can Mattie and her grandmother control Henry's vengefulness even with Marley Womack's ever-vigilant eye on the casino's second set of books? It's more than a cause for concern. Triad Realty makes that evident.

Mattie's fretting is visible when Chance breaks her reverie by clearing his voice. His keen eyes take her in whole.

"What's going on?" asks the silky-voiced lieutenant governor.

The interruption doesn't startle Mattie. She just reroutes her thoughts.

"I'm putting the finishing touches on a pro-bono case that involves bad hunters and an express delivery driver."

"How is it going?" asks a genuinely curious Greyson Chance.

"My client got a slap on the wrist and some public service. The hunters lost their licenses for a year," responds the FWP's chief legal officer.

"Oh, I read about that in the paper. Those guys got off way too easy; it's a pretty weak response to the menace of elk fever," replies Chance.

"Well, we can thank an FWP's feeble commission and a legislative body more interested in hunting fees than the well-being of the public and wildlife. In the end, the only one to pay an actual price was the trophy bull that used to run his herd along the base of the Elkhorn's," reports Mattie.

The room goes quiet again until Chance reports,

"The governor and I hoped to see you at the airport yesterday."

"Oh, I was there. What can I do for you, Chance?" asks the miniscule attorney.

He quickly halts the conversation to answer his cell phone.

"She's here; let me ask. The governor would like to know if you have a moment to meet someone."

Mattie merely nods. She expects this visit.

Chapter 34-
THE SISTER SETUP

Chance wanders down the hallway and waits for the governor and his companion to arrive through the downpour. Seconds later, all three of Mattie's visitors are at her office door.

The chief legal counsel has disappeared. A furious governor turns bright red as he looks to Chance, who in turn calmly offers the femininely dressed Samantha Cherchez a chair.

With tray in hand, Mattie sets hot tea, coffee, sugar, and milk on her desk, waiting for an introduction. Chance stands in front of Mattie on the far side of the room, where he has just offered the mysterious Ms. Cherchez a chair.

Mattie calmly walks behind her desk and offers both gentlemen a seat facing her. She exchanges a weighty look with Cherchez and politely offers her guests a morning cup of coffee. The room settles into an uncomfortable silence as the two women pretend to focus on their hot drinks while gauging one another. Sam can't help but recognize the magnitude of Mattie's natural beauty, framed by daylight through the window's exposure. Similarly, Mattie takes in the sophisticated clothing and bearing of this, her newest predator.

The governor, with all the fanfare of a circus ringmaster, makes the introductions. He is obviously pleased with himself as he watches the two women's initial confrontation.

"Ms. Cherchez, this is the chief legal counsel for Fish, Wildlife and Parks, Ms. Mattie Wildbird. Mattie, this is DOI Agent Samantha Cherchez."

Samantha is direct.

"How did you lose that arm?"

Once again, silence envelops the room. Officially thrown, the gauntlet dropped.

A very tranquil Mattie replies, "My guess is you already know the answer to that, Ms. Cherchez. The governor was kind enough to inform me that the president has assigned you to address our current difficulties. I would imagine you've done significant research in advance."

Sipping her coffee, Sam the Seeker steadily measures Mattie.

"I'm sure you did as well, so tell me, what did your research reveal, Ms. Wildbird?" asks Sam.

"My resources indicate that you and your highly skilled team of agents share the highest DOI statistical arrests and convictions on record. In short, your team rarely fails to apprehend a suspect."

With such a detailed narrative, Sam the Seeker glances at the governor, smiles, and turns a deadpan gaze back to Mattie. "Well, if indeed I am undercover, how is it that you know so much about me?"

Crebo Lund smiles with delight. The lieutenant governor stiffens and then intervenes.

"Ladies, we're on the same team here. Ms. Wildbird is a loyal and trusted member of our operation, and all of us have to work hard to bring this situation under control."

The governor snickers again with obvious amusement. "Christ, Chance, everyone here recognizes our number-one suspect is Mattie's brother."

Chance looks at Lund with displeasure. Once again, a profound silence envelops the group. Mattie is first to break the stillness, looking directly at Sam the Seeker.

"Obviously, I recuse myself. This investigation is far too important for such profound distractions. By the way, Governor, I have something here for you."

Mattie stands with poise to cover the distance between her and Lund. She slips a legal-sized envelope into Lund's hand with her fake appendage before returning to a chair adjacent to Sam's.

Meanwhile, the Seeker places her coffee cup on Mattie's desk and then rises to prowl like a wild cat around the exterior of the office, taking in anything that could offer clues about Mattie Wildbird.

Shelves covered and brimming with books about wildlife migration provide additional impetus for the Seeker's investigation. She skims the first few exposed pages of a book open on the counter, the Trust Land Management and Enabling Act. Beside it is a copy of *The Theory of Island Biogeography*. Both books have been visibly referenced with sticky notes interspersed throughout. She makes a mental note to have Beggs grab a copy of these reads.

"Ms. Wildbird, I want to thank you for your dedicated assistance in wildlife protection. You have proven yourself a time-honored and principled public servant. I'm sure the governor shares my gratitude for your service, and I look forward to working with you.

I understand that you've already reunited with my associate, Mr. Tamer Gray. We'll be in touch."

Sam turns back and looks Mattie squarely in the eye before benignly walking out of the office, followed by Greyson Chance, who thanks Mattie for the coffee before he leaves.

The governor, who seems very pleased with himself, can't resist a parting jab.

"I think you two will become great friends."

His intentions are all too evident. Both women are the targets of Lund's farcical wit, but the governor plays a weak hand.

Mattie watches Sam the Seeker gracefully saunter from the office. The attorney returns to her reverie, this time considering the added twist that is Sam the Seeker.

From the hallway, she hears the Governor yell at Chance. "That little bitch just subpoenaed me and Tully Neff, for Christ's sake."

Greyson quickly ushers the governor from the building. Mattie picks up the phone with a wide grin and tells Henry about the governor and his friend the ex-Secretary of State's upcoming court date.

Chapter 35-
PYRITE SMART HOUSE

The view from the smart house overlooks the north valley, just minutes away from the State's capitol complex. The town itself, steeped in vividly rugged history, began early. In 1864, the well-traveled valley revealed its riches when four down-on-their-luck miners stumbled onto a rich gold vein meandering down what came to be called the Last Chance Gulch.

———————◆———————

Forced into the great expanse of the western United States, Beggs Cooper copes with its ruralness. Montana isn't what he considers a bucket list-worthy priority for anyone except wild-child types like Sam. The IT specialist prays this assignment will be more pleasant than last year's Wyoming foray. After that, any reasonably minded city slicker would have resigned.

Beggs feels the state of Wyoming should shut its doors during winter. At least the present mission is in early fall, with long, warm days turning cool at night. Sam jokes that Montana is a reliable place to get a sunburn and frostbite in the same twenty-four hours. Beggs hopes this is a jest. Her sense of humor makes these far-afield assignments bearable. Add to this his love for the cursed woman.

The Helena Airport is new, well-appointed, and only ten minutes from the smart house. The farthest exit south of town takes the taxi to a sector known as the Bull Run Addition. Cooper's driver explains that it isn't unusual to see elk or deer make their way back up into the southern hills after a midnight stroll around the Capitol. Helena, Montana, like many small towns, writhes with urban sprawl. Wildlife forced to seek water and long grass around far-reaching neighborhoods lined with gullies must contend with people. These animals have found ways to live under, besides, beneath, and around their human counterparts.

The cabbie pulls into a secluded lot at the far end of a cul-de-sac fronted by a three-car garage. Cooper thanks the cabbie, grabs his bag, and pays his fare before entering the security code on the gate. He stops abruptly, stunned by the view. Additional lodging sits atop an outbuilding, providing Sam a private retreat. Based on this vista, Beggs can only imagine what it looks like from Sam's new accommodations.

The entire complex is secured and protected by video surveillance. Apparently, the owner loves wildlife and is determined to share the two-acre property with deer, elk, fox, and even a favorite skunk that keeps the hornet population down.

Guests are immediately drawn to the spectacular panorama off the north deck as the valley sprawls onward, fronted by a favorite local landmark. The Sleeping Giant lies supine in snow-covered splendor. This mountainous marker is attached to a wilderness area comprising 11,000 acres of very steep and rugged landscape.

Direct access to the very private compound overlooking the entire Helena Valley is restricted. Cooper gains entrance to the house through large double French doors on the north side of the property.

The house itself is tastefully appointed and has every modern convenience. Not a single animal suspended in its death throes adorns the living space, nor are there signs of antler art light fixtures. The Wyoming expedition left Beggs with nightmares of lifeless animals leaping from frozen mounts straight into his sleeping subconscious.

Instead, Cooper finds granite countertops, Viking appliances, hardwood floors adorned with crimson rugs, and a fireplace with an enormous oak mantle embellished by a painting depicting a light stand of birch trees. The furniture is a combination of leather couches and overstuffed cloth loveseats. Pleasantly surprised, Cooper drops his bag, removes his shoes, and then falls into the luxury of his new quarters.

Just as the IT specialist gets comfy, the intercom announces the arrival of a semi-truck loaded with computers. Several large men pushing dollies loaded with state-of-the-art central processing units follow Cooper to the basement entrance of a large daylight apartment. This space will act as a command center for the newest Sam the Seeker investigation.

The frenzy to pull the center together is immediate. Cooper's transient operation is in full assembly mode before he even gets a chance to grab a second cup of coffee. Beggs is an integral part of Sam the Seeker's highly accomplished squad. This mission charges the covert team with the detection, identification, and capture of multiband eco-terrorists responsible for raids on hunters' encampments.

The IT specialist has an uneasy sense about the assignment. His perception of the evidence gathered thus far leads him to believe a deeper set of circumstances underpin the raids. The Seeker's team members don't concern themselves with guilt or innocence. Sam demands that her unit focus on detention. Nothing else is of concern. Beyond that, Cooper has never been a major fan of the pompous Tully Neff. Beggs could care less that these environmentalists humiliated the U.S. Secretary of State, particularly if he and the governor were involved in such heavy-handed activities. The entire affair smacks of conceit.

One thing is for certain. Sam the Seeker doesn't give a damn what or who happens to be her criminal target. Still, it's undeniable, given the power and prestige surrounding this case, much is at stake.

Chapter 36-
MIGHTY RELIC

An abundance of pine needles coupled with huge granite rocks lines a trail that leads to the cabin surrounded by lake and sky. A steep climb presents nothing but blue heaven until the ridge gives way to dark-green lake waters. Sam stops, not wanting to miss any of the surrounding splendors.

Children's laughter breaks through a hushed reverie. The undercover agent follows its echo to the porched cabin with a screened doorway. Approaching serenely, Sam the Seeker stands enthralled, listening to the medicine woman's account of a beloved tribal allegory about a white hunting party. Sam smiles at the happenstance; it was just yesterday when Beggs's research referenced the same story.

Hinmah's allegory has serious underpinnings. The arrogant British nobleman is wealthy beyond comprehension. Sir George Gore arrives in America committed to an ambitious hunting excursion. The narcissistic villain from a privileged heritage surrounds himself with the creature comforts of his inherited wealth.

Hinmah, as a storyteller, adds her own brand of humor to soften this miserable tale of destruction. Her reference to Sir George is filled with disdain as she mocks the "nobleman" with various facial contortions. The pride and power in her voice makes it clear that the tribe's forebears would not tolerate this reprehensible waste. The Ink Prayer people ran the fool out of the country preventing the slaughter of hundreds of more animals for mere bragging rights.

Hinmah's expression inspires frenzied laughter as the youngsters demonstrate a keen interest in the tale. Without turning, the diminutive elder whose back faces the doorway speaks to Sam.

"You may join us if you wish. I didn't expect you this soon, but please come in."

Hinmah hugs the anxious child curled in her lap and then dismisses all seven youngsters with a tease.

"Go play in the traffic." The older children deliver another round of glee and then head out through the screen door, with the youngest child in tow.

Sam finds herself alone with the minuscule woman sporting a set of foreboding, dark-gray eyes and bobbed, silver-white hair, a style that adds at least an inch to her diminutive frame. Graceful, confident, and comfortable, Hinmah directs Sam to a rocking chair fronting the large, plate-glass window overlooking the lake.

"I pray never to take this view for granted. Please, get comfortable," says Hinmah.

Leaning over a nearby table, she pours two cups of tea and a dab of something from a creamer. The medicine woman makes an offering to Sam. Hinmah occupies the chair beside Sam's, folding her tiny legs alongside the armrest of the swaying rocker.

Sweet awe takes hold of Cherchez. Between the view and sips from the steamy mug, the DOI agent falls into instant bliss.

Her hostess smiles. "I like to add a little something to make the tea palatable."

Sam clears her throat in appreciation. Another long silence settles in as both women fall victim to the tranquility that seems to extend forever within the vastness of crystalline waters.

"You said you hadn't anticipated my visit so soon," remarks Sam. "How is it you expected me at all?"

Hinmah looks puzzled. "Smoke signals." With a deep grin, the old woman quickly clarifies. "It's a small town."

"I'm here because the cloud leads me to you," responds a smirking Cherchez.

"Ah, brilliant, I assume your computer search was fruitful?" laughs Hinmah.

With a serious tone, Cherchez shift gears and hits hard. "Tell me how an educated woman like yourself sells spiritualism."

The undercover agent delivers this question with incredulity.

Without the slightest show of humiliation, Hinmah responds.

"It's true that our young people feel that our tribal beliefs and rituals hold them back. I hear the neophytes' complaints. To be frank, you're much like the young people of my tribe, judging their history as, and I quote, 'mere bullshit.' I understand their reticence and yours. But customs are important to all people. For example, a Christian celebrates Christmas. My people live the circle. There is an ancient pan-tribal belief. It avows,

> *'Man follows earth. Earth follows heaven.*
>
> *And sometimes things are ahead,*
>
> *and sometimes they are behind.'*

"While I don't know you, I can guess you share similar sacraments defined by your culture," smiles the unflappable old relic.

Sam's host is way too comfortable; it's best to have one's prey off balance. She throws the tribal leader a hardball.

"Can we talk about the loss of your son and daughter-in-law?"

Hinmah's response is slow. It comes from a long-ago place, deep within and coated with grief.

"Based on your research, you probably know much about my family details, like the fact that my husband has no hearing. The day my son and daughter-in-law died was one of the few times I'd ever heard a sound from him. It was guttural, anguished, and animal-like.

"The distressing news came in a very unusual way. Our only grandson, Henry, wet and covered with blood, carried his twin sister to this very cabin. She was close to death, with her left arm severely damaged by the bullet of a semi-automatic rifle. Henry was in shock and reacted instinctively, out of pure survival."

A stillness falls over the two women until Hinmah adds, "How does anyone overcome such devastation? Of course, no one ever really does. My son's children became our responsibility, no, our privilege."

The old woman takes a long pull from her teacup.

"It wasn't until Apple Tamer Gray appeared that our family of misfits grew whole," says the little woman as she drifts back to the comfort of the view and is once again swallowed by it.

Instinctively, Sam knows that's all Hinmah intends to divulge. Moments later, the old woman snaps out of her deep reflection.

"It's kind that you responded to my invitation."

Cherchez sets the empty mug on the coffee table and rises from the comfort of her rocker.

"When did you invite me?" asks the Seeker.

"We have much in common, Ms. Cherchez. It has been my privilege to spend time with you," says Hinmah with a cunning smile.

Standing, she faces the splendor of the lake.

"So, you know, my instincts suggest that what happened at Bandy Lake is the real reason I'm here."

She turns and looks straight into the old woman's eyes for some manner of emotion, but she sees none. The screen door slams resolutely with the Seeker's departure.

Hinmah scrutinizes the young woman and decides that Samantha Cherchez is a worthy opponent.

Chapter 37-
THE CRITICAL TURN

"What's safe to reveal?" asks a composed Mattie Wildbird.

Family and friends, all dedicated members of the String, gather around her fireplace. The team's work is seditious. The need for privacy forces them from their digs at the local pub.

From an outsider's perspective, the gathering at Mattie's place passes for a book club or a study group. Inside, the discussion is pointed and incisive. Equals here, everyone shares ideas about how best to expose the primary target. All suggestions are germane; no one idea is too preposterous.

This group, not unlike a military tactical unit, has come to depend on one another. Their tremendous commitment and dedication make them veterans of an exclusive war. Outsiders may see them as criminals, but this gang considers itself a rare breed that takes pride in their very distinct liability.

"Let's give 'em Creekbaum," proposes Tarkio. "She drinks more beer than any of us."

The room explodes in laughter as the leggy elder pounds down the rest of her tallboy and then belches unabashedly.

Another round of hilarity bounces off the ceilings.

"Okay... Okay, let's get down to work," demands Mattie. "Winslow, why don't you tell us a little about this Betty Kumba character?"

The ex-CIA's presentation is tidy.

"This young lady has skills. She played us. I believe the elk fever episode was real but a fluke."

Creekbaum breaks in. "More like providence. It takes a lot of ire before I'd purposefully drive in front of six or seven hunters with elk fever."

"Well, that's the one consistent trait this particular person displays. 'Passion' best defines Ms. Kumba," responds Winslow. "There is a larger problem. Our background check provided a dubious lead. After a few aptly placed inquires, I tripped across Ms. Kumba's financial status. Drake, I'm sorry to say your new friend hasn't exactly been forthright. It turns out she's working for the enemy and is seriously flush. We're talking exceedingly rich," asserts Winslow.

Mattie watches Sheriff Stoltz's eyes widen.

"Don't feel bad; Betty's a credible opponent," adds the String's tactical leader. "Here's the thing. There was no pretense in Ms. Kumba's poignant reaction towards the fool huntsmen that slaughtered that bull elk. When she ran those crazed stalkers atop their truck hoods, she meant business. I believe this reaction reflects her true self."

"Well," adds Sharp, "the financial red flag made me look a little deeper. The sheriff was kind enough to provide Ms. Kumba's fingerprints. I forwarded them to my CIA contact, who in turn tapped his IRS associate to confirm our suspicions. It turns out Betty Kumba, a.k.a. Betty Amara, is a social media prodigy who made a substantial profit from the sale of her high-tech software. Her creative algorithm restores lost domestic pets with their owners. At the mildly worn age of seventeen, Betty Amara became a multi-millionaire.

"Today and for the past decade, she has played a role as an undercover agent with an IT background for the Department of the Interior's most efficient wildlife protection team. Kumba, or Amara, is one of the government's best and brightest."

With this last detail, everyone in the room goes silent. A deafening beat passes before Creekbaum breaks the stillness. "It might be the beer talking, but if I'm going down, I want that particular privilege earned."

"So, Winslow," asks Mattie, "Tell me: Is this woman that good?"

"My source says she and her covert team are precisely that," responds Winslow.

A new round of emotional chatter erupts.

"Listen, everyone, she's no doubt incredibly talented, but a turn might be easier than you think."

Mattie looks to Winslow to explain in greater detail.

"Apparently, Betty's active and tight-knit group is very principled," adds the String's techno-geek.

"In fact, it appears Betty is at the heart of this principled behavior. She and her colleague, Beggs Cooper, work in tandem. Cooper operates behind the scenes, while Betty is generally embedded. The real threat lies with the team leader, a Ms. Samantha Cherchez, otherwise known as 'Sam the Seeker.'"

The deliberate Drake Stoltz interjects,

"So, what if we use this Betty Kumba… I mean, *Amara*… in reverse. What if we come clean incrementally? You know what I'm saying, don't you, Mattie? Immediately after her highway skirmish, she realized she didn't have anyone to care for the two dogs, horse, and mule left unattended. Hell, it turns out the horse is an old Mustang headed to the glue factory. If she hadn't adopted that animal… well. The woman obviously loves these critters. She drove them all the way across this country. That says something," determines Drake.

Tarkio interjects.

"I've run into people like Ms. Amara at the FWP commission meetings. I sense that animals mean more to them than their own self-preservation. For example, there's a woman in town that attends nearly every meeting relating to deer populations. The city handles the problem in the cheapest manner possible. Trapped inside a collapsible meshwork, the netted deer are deadbolted the following morning. It's inhumane. There are better ways to handle the problem. The commission's fallback plan is always to do it inexpensively, whether it's right or wrong."

Appalled, everyone in the meeting mumbles their disdain.

Tarkio goes on with his story.

"This deer advocate despises the use of deadbolts. You can actually see injury in her eyes when she besieges the Commission to show compassion. Eventually, deer entrapments are mysteriously saturated with coyote urine. Not a single deer is captured when city police check the traps. I have no tangible evidence, but my guess is that woman takes matters into her own hands. Her view is that culling is an ornate word for killing. In many ways, this Betty Amara behaves similarly. It's a fair supposition that she'll find honor in our cause."

"Seems reasonable," declares Gracie Holdsclaw.

"So, folks, what do you think?" asks Mattie.

"Should we make a soulful solicitation? And if so, how best can we approach Betty Amara?"

Marley quietly sips at a glass of white wine, wipes her lips with a napkin, and then makes a case for the obvious.

"Ms. Kumba, or Amara, is a part of a family not dissimilar to our own. She has much to risk. We must appeal to her personal sense of integrity."

"Marley's right," affirms Creekbaum.

"She has to be able to honor her prior commitments while slowly digesting the purpose of the String. I believe the authenticity of our work will appeal to this woman's sense of decency."

The room erupts in multiple conversations.

"Whoa," says Tarkio, "you all understand that she's part of an undercover DOI task force sent to arrest 'us' criminals?"

Murmurs of concern and disagreement bubble throughout the room. Mattie patiently listens. Ten minutes later, it's decided.

"Okay, we have a plan," says Winslow.

"I'll plant the metadata into Betty's FWP mailroom computer. All Ms. Amara will have to do is cross-pollinate domains and use a little common sense. For someone with her skill set, discovery will be immediate. If she goes to Mattie with the evidence, we can progress incrementally."

Everyone in the room agrees and then calls it a night. The idea is now fully entrenched in the group's game plan. No one will sleep tonight.

The ever-clandestine Sharp stays behind to address Mattie.

"It's risky, what we're about to do. I hope you and Henry have an escape plan."

Mattie walks towards the ex-CIA genius, whose affection for Mattie is obvious. She hugs him.

"I wish it were that easy, Winslow. There are only two outcomes for my family. Complete miscarriage or total victory. We're tied to this cause like the earth is to the sky. The day my parents were gunned down settled that."

Chapter 38

MARKAY'S- NO MAN LEFT BEHIND

Regal Markay often invites his staff over, especially in late summer, early fall, but that doesn't soften the probabilities for Chance or Robbins. They know what their commander has in mind.

"The two of you should bring your partners by tonight for a barbeque."

Montana's adjutant general is held in high esteem. His long and decidedly decorated career began over thirty years ago in the Marines. Time spent in service included several years at the Pentagon, networking with corresponding branches of government, all working to keep this great nation safe.

Eventually, a man wants to come home. A Montana native, Regal's homegrown status is just one reason his troops consider themselves lucky to abide his command. Markay cares.

The general hovers, cajoles, and insists on perfection. Meanwhile, he's a fair man who goes the extra mile for anyone who needs support. Regal Markay lives the aphorism "Leave no man behind."

It makes sense that he and his joint chief of staff suit one another; he's so much like Gig Robbins's own father. The two just fit. Regal Markay and Gig Robbins foster a family of friends that just happen to work together.

As Lieutenant Governor, Captain Greyson Chance makes Regal and Gig's work easier, but they pity him for having to deal with Crebo Lund. Greyson often acts as a buffer for his commander. The old man has little time for bull-crap, and that's the sum of Crebo Lund as far as the general is concerned.

The Friday night party is held on the big deck overhanging a wide, lush valley. After a full complement of barbeque, the over-indulged couples relax under the spell of a splendid fall evening.

The gang's laughter echoes down the canyon. Below, Mrs. Markay's gardens boast the noblest of colors. Tonight, even the general's plant life appears to stand at attention.

Time floats past as the evening fades. As is normal, Regal asks Gig and Greyson to stay behind, a practice to which each spouse has become accustomed. Gig's husband will drive Danielle home while the remainder of the party huddles against the hour in a late-evening work session.

Regal's wife excuses herself when the old man lights up a cigar. He allows himself one more drink. A small pit fire offers comfort as the evening cools.

Gig is fully aware that the general is upset after his meeting with the governor. She has spent the last week avoiding him at every turn. When the old man gets a burr under his saddle, there's generally hell to pay. In all fairness, Markay can't understand how these insurgents continue to evade his command. It makes no sense. Tonight's meeting is the adjutant general's version of a come-to-Jesus talk.

The three relax as the twin fawns rise from the tall grass to join the small herd in the north field. A varietal wash of tinted colors satiates the endless sky, lost between darkness and day. Both Gig and Chance know this calmness is a false betrayal for an impending storm.

The old man takes a long draw from the cigar normally forbidden to him. He tilts it left and right, savoring the feel and aroma.

"I'm sure there's some explanation for our inability to capture this lot. Make no mistake; they're indeed modern-day brigands, but that's not an explanation."

Neither Chance nor Gig wants to field the question for one simple reason: There is no excuse. Is the old man about to flush them out? The general waits patiently. Finally, Chance braves the profundities of the historically established military requisite — failure is never acceptable.

"Sir, I think a new course of action is necessitated. We think these riders unsophisticated when, in fact, they employ unconventional technologies combined with a weighty understanding of military tactics. These unique strategic fusions demand that we up our game."

Gig shoots a look at Chance as the old man sits back into his chaise. Regal takes another puff.

"When a garrison colonel with twenty years of experience is humiliated like poor Clarkson, I can't find one reason to disagree."

Regal bounces out of his chair across the deck. He turns back towards the trapped audience to vent with grandiose flair.

"Now we have the damnable feds involved, and I don't mind admitting to you two that's it's an embarrassment. Just what the hell do you suggest?"

Gig shifts uncomfortably in her seat as Chance presses forward.

"We must alter our tactics. First, a command post must be established at Bandy Hawk, twenty-four-seven. One of Clarkson's men reported he may have detected the use of an elusive technology. His description of events indicates that a sophisticated illusion made it appear that all the riders were together and stood a half-mile in the distance across a ravine. Admittedly, things happened quickly, but in hindsight, that man thinks only one rider was on the opposite canyon while the full complement attacked from the rear. It's apparent to both Gig and I that these insurgents are getting help."

Chance let that sit for a moment. The general is hidden behind a puff of smoke. Gig has no idea where Chance was headed but decides it's best to play along.

"Surveillance isn't restricted to the confines of the military, sir. Our best guess is that the riders have more than one set of eyes."

Regal leans forward.

"I was starting to worry about the two of you. We've been getting our hats handed to us, and neither one of you have applied yourself. I thought you two had twisted yourself up in something sordid."

The two military specialists suffer intense apprehension but maintain their composure. Gig thinks, How the hell did this old guy figure things out? Regal looks closely into Chance's eyes like a father protecting his children.

"Tell me you two aren't having an affair. You wouldn't destroy both careers over some silly-ass thing like sex?"

The dense atmosphere parts when Gig and Chance break down into hysterical laughter. The old man would never know just how close he came to learn the real facts surrounding the raids. After he regained his composure, Greyson Chance answers forthrightly.

"No, sir, I can honestly report that Gig wouldn't make that mistake twice, but I think we have finally reckoned a way to grab these slippery characters."

Gig nods but doesn't add to the complicated storyline.

After Regal's cigar burns to a fraction of its original size, the two officers head out.

Stunned by this new plan, Gig asserts, "What the hell, Greyson, I'm not going to be the one who tells Hinmah that we're setting up shop at Bandy Hawk. You better have a good explanation, my friend."

Chapter 39-

SPECIAL AGENT IN CHARGE

The FBI task force assigned to Finch888 arrives a full week after the wholly immersed undercover unit from the Department of the Interior.

Bureau agents fly directly to the Bert Mooney Airport (BTM) in Butte, Montana from the regional office in Salt Lake City, Utah. Landing at BTM is a bit tricky based on locale and weather. A ninety-foot statue of the Blessed Virgin Mary hovers atop the Rocky Mountains just east of the airport, for good reason. The primary runway is only nine thousand feet long and a hundred fifty feet wide, just large enough to handle a 737. Touchdown is delicate business, even in pleasant weather. One needn't go too far past the runway before gaining entrance to the Holy Cross Cemetery. The locals joke that the boneyard is advantageous should a pilot fail to stick the landing.

The Federal Bureau of Investigation has fifty-six field offices with as many as ten satellites, including the vast expanse that is Montana. In days gone by, the infamous J. Edgar Hoover exiled agents who had fallen out of favor to Butte, Montana. Looking out the plane's windows into the huge copper pit below, Joyce Kingston, Special Agent-in-Charge, thinks the old man must have been vindictive as hell.

Once the plane is safely grounded, Assistant Special Agent Peter Base meets the detail. Peter is a native Montanan dressed casually in Wrangler jeans and an Ex Officio shirt with Merrell hikers. He ushers the four-member FBI team back to Helena in a black Suburban with heavily tinted windows.

The taller-than-average Kingston takes the back seat to her second-in-command for the ride over. She uses the drive to get a better sense of the countryside.

For whatever reason, this special agent-in-charge has never ventured into Montana, nor has she worked with this team of agents. Unfamiliarity with her squad and surroundings creates significant challenges. Joyce is in catch-up mode going forward, on more than one front.

The Feds' team is comprised of a Native American information technologist, an ecoterrorist specialist, a cyber trespass maven, and an explosives expert. According to Kingston's copy of the FBI dossier, their target is local and very much at home.

The sixty-minute jaunt to the capital city winds atop Summit Valley, wherein the mid-1800s' miners cut Mother Earth wide open in pursuit of gold, silver, and, finally, copper. Once past these wounded lands, I-15 spills into a free-fall of coiled curves and narrow canyons wedded to the river bottom. Near the old mining town of Basin, tapered bends straighten to follow clear waters into a beautiful valley. There, a large clearing offers cattle and elk one last vestige of nature before humanity again invades with cluttered ranches, abandoned mining equipment, and urban sprawl. Twenty minutes beyond that, the team finds itself in the Queen City of the Rockies.

The FBI unit is submerged deep inside a gulch named Last Chance. The team stows its gear at the hotel and then meets for dinner at a restaurant famous for its bawdy namesake. Quaint, Big Dorothy's Windbag Saloon links history with local fare. Gold strikes built this entire town, fueled on staunch politics and bordellos.

The diverse FBI team takes this opportunity to bond. Peter Base does his best to articulate how Montana's colorful inhabitants and rich culture have a unique, very independent ethos. Montanans, as a rule, wear baseball caps just about everywhere, as Peter's tan line testifies. His sunburned forehead, broad smile, and candid vernacular build an immediate sense of teamwork.

Kingston starts the meeting with a list she quickly composed on the sixty-minute drive between Butte and Helena. It's forceful.

"After a thorough assessment of the intel obtained from local law enforcement and the National Guard's field evaluations, it has been determined that each raid ends in the proximity of a place called Bandy Hawk plateau. I'm providing each of you GPS coordinates electronically."

Kingston hits the "send" button from her laptop, and a cacophony of electronic signals fills the small room.

"Please familiarize yourself with the attached topography and be ready to hit the ground fast. Government officials must be informed that our full attention will be focused on the Bandy Hawk plateau by tomorrow afternoon. The governor, National Guard, and local law enforcement will be expected to coordinate all facets of the investigation through this unit. I'll direct the necessary reconnaissance to explore the plateau from both the air and ground.

"Peter, synchronize all chase efforts with the National Guard. It's vital to determine what portion of Bandy Hawk sits on private land. We'll need permission from landowners to work those sections. The Department of Natural Resources has been fighting fires in these areas for some time. They have in-depth knowledge of the area where we intend to handle this investigation. Remember, our mission is to discover how the raiders manage to escape. It's not our intention to destroy the plateau — rather, locate all known egress from the mesa."

After Kingston completes perspective assignments, Peter Base recommends the green pepper burger. Moments later, the waiter dispenses five masterpieces with sweet potato fries and a round of ale. A satiated Joyce Kingston and her new co-workers stumble back down the bricked gulch to their hotel with a promise to get on top of the mission early the next morning.

Chapter 40-
FIRST MEET

F BI task force members are used to the cold shoulder. There isn't a law enforcement division or military branch in the nation that doesn't take offense to the broad jurisdiction given the Federal Bureau of Investigation. Of course, the FBI feels the same way about the covert activity performed by CIA spooks.

At first meet inside the National Guard Armory, it's evident to Kingston that the governor is a sexist jerk. The SAC roundly distinguishes Lieutenant Governor Chance as sensible but guilty by association.

The National Guard's adjutant general, a third-generation military man, is used to running the show. Kingston's research highlights that the general's joint chief, a woman with an active track record, is known for competence and precision.

Montana's Department of Natural Resources and Conservation contingent proves to be professional, knowledgeable, and willing. The departmental standout is a Ms. Marley Womack, acting trust land management comptroller.

The local police are a colorful lot, and for the most part, reliable. As is the county sheriff; he's a tall, good-looking man who isn't much for words. Drake Stoltz has been sheriff in these parts for some time. The SAC places him in the asset column.

Kingston plans to get in and get out. Her goal is to do her job meticulously despite the numerous factions involved. At twenty-seven, Kingston is a female FBI field test. Her flaming carrot-top hair and green eyes act as a testament to her challenging and aggressive temperament. The rules are different for women with the Bureau. Joyce Kingston means to supersede expectations for herself and every woman who follows in her footsteps.

Chapter 41-
THE MERCANTILE

It's been several days since Cooper set up shop. Tasked with the mission to unearth the financial means behind the raids, Beggs has, thus far, flamed out. This fact can only be described as atypical. His failure to find financial irregularities manifests as more than a confessed defeat. A "full-blown meltdown" better defines things. The signs are clear. Sam the Seeker is genuinely worried about her chief technician and friend. Usually fastidious, this man has not shaved, his clothes are wrinkled, and he's sockless. A healthful Cooper would never subscribe to such pitiable penchants.

An emergency reunion is Sam's only option. She orders him into the safety net, even if it means the discovery of her protractedly placed undercover agent. A Kumba intervention never fails. Sam the Seeker covertly establishes the intercession. A prearranged Pinterest encoded message will amalgamate the summit. Once Betty responds, Sam sends Cooper in search of his sensibilities. Betty is his touchstone. She's the only one who can help him regain balance.

The Cooper-Kumba brain trust reinforces Sam's accomplishments, but more importantly, these people are her family. A shared history provides them pliable allowances. Individual quirks are customary, and their shared routines enhance their compatibility. Beyond that, they love one another like extended kin.

The cozy little coffee shop chock-full of Montana locals offers a less sterile cup than one might get from corporate establishments. The hometown atmosphere and a rendezvous with his favorite counterpart will indubitably snap Beggs Cooper from his depression.

The disheveled, undercover technician slowly shuffles down the narrow streets of the old mining Gulch. After being inside for days, the fresh air has an immediate effect. The forensic specialist takes notice of his surroundings. Cooper admires this small town's old-bone architecture. It makes a definite statement. In fact, it clarifies the village's gender. Helena, Cooper decides, is indisputably female, flaunting her late 1800s architecture the way only a woman can, with poignant display and piercing elegance. Shadows mute the old girl's nineteenth-century plastered wall advertisements, inviting passersby to lean into her historical seductiveness. The locals call this fetching settlement the Queen City of the Rockies. The moniker confirms Beggs's gender impression.

The morning walk invigorates the IT specialist, who repudiates his need for a respite. The denial contradicts the obvious physical evidence. Of course, Sam is right. The coffee and company will do him a world of good. Once at his destination, Beggs pulls at the handle of the General Mercantile old wooden doors. They don't budge. An observant twenty-year-old directly behind him giggles.

"It happens to everyone, and not just the first time. I still pull instead of push, even though the sign above the handle clearly says 'push.' I think it's the Merc's cunning tease to make us buy more coffee."

Cooper brushes the hair back from his kingly face with a laugh.

"Let me try to get this door one more time."

Triumphant, he holds the door ajar as the amiable youngster passes through to a crowd of college-aged cribbage players. The place teems with life and is cluttered with great gadgetry and old-style candies from generations past. As Cooper walks atop the creaking wooden floors, he notices sweets he hasn't seen since childhood. The countertops are full of decorative antiques and quirky postcards. Historic signage fills every available space. Sporadically dispersed ladders lead to unused lofts throughout the coffee shop and an old-fashioned cash register rings a different era. The light dims the farther one enters. Supplemental trivia flows through the crowd espoused by eccentric bookworms, like the sugar that accompanies customers' high-caliber coffees.

Cooper feels better the more he explores. The aroma and promise of deep conversation beckon him. Hidden in a backroom, Betty huddles over her computer. The one overhead light is disengaged, and the blue glow of her laptop makes her brown-sugar skin even more stunning. Cooper glances behind him before darting into the small space that a brim-filled Brown Betty occupies.

"Be cool, be cool. I miss you too, but let's not get sentimental," announces the large woman, busy at her computer. Without looking up, she scolds her old friend. "Get in here, and don't slam that flimsy little door."

Cooper melts into a hot espresso.

"It's so good to see you. I've been looking at nothing but false expressions for what feels like an eternity."

Betty finally glances up from her computer.

"You look like crap! Why are you all wrinkled and scruffy-like?"

Cooper lifts his head from slumped humiliation.

"None of it makes sense. I've administered the most technologically advanced fraud software in the world, and it hasn't provided a single clue. Not a single anomaly, not one damned incongruity. How is that even possible? Explain that."

Betty's white teeth, turned blue by the laptop's glow, expand into a great smile.

"Maybe you're looking too hard."

Cooper peers over the top of his demitasse suspiciously. "What do you know that I don't?"

Betty loves fieldwork. It offers the perfect mix of social contact and high-tech investigation.

"I can tell you something big is on the horizon. I feel it more than know it. This Mattie Wildbird is a distinctive character, a real do-gooder, if you get me."

Cooper's alarms go off.

"Tell me you aren't falling in love with the bad guys, Betty. Can you imagine how Sam will react? Your boss is a heat-seeking missile on the hunt for her target. Make no mistake; she'll seize and detain anyone who has committed an illegal act, regardless of cause. Don't get between her and the mark," cautions a fretful Cooper.

Betty has a deep-seated respect for the Seeker but isn't easily intimidated.

"I don't plan to get in the way. Did Sam tell you that I came across something in the mailroom? It's a touch suspicious. I did a little research. It took me to a buried article on an old microfiche reader in the downtown library. The news article was hidden three pages deep and recorded two murders at a place called Bandy Hawk

Plateau. This gal, Mattie Wildbird, well, it was her parents that got killed. There's something else that's a bit unusual. Her mom worked at FWP in the very same job this Mattie person holds. That's weird, right?"

Cooper tries to keep up and nods.

"As for fiscal abnormalities, my guess is you won't find any," conveys the embedded agent.

Cooper struggles to accept this last suggestion.

"Well, tell me: Just who funds these riders? They need money from some source. The technological support alone costs more than any environmental group I know could afford to underwrite."

Betty collects her gear and loads it into a backpack. "Well, you better take another look at that casino Mattie's brother owns, because I can't find a thing to support our suspicions at FWP. That by itself doesn't mean anything. Mark my word, whatever it is that we're supposed to find will appear soon enough."

"I think you miss the point. Our boss wants us to find 'whatever' first," declares Cooper.

The two continue their tumultuous discussion. Beggs Cooper feels like himself once more. The hour spent with the incomparable Betty makes him feel in total control.

Cooper presses his old friend about the Wildbird clan. "Sam has already interviewed the grandmother and said the old woman is incredibly intelligent. She thinks the elderly spiritualist is involved but can't pin down exactly how.

"Sam is grateful for the tip. The old woman didn't even try to hide her emotions about the loss of her son. It shut down any further discourse they might have shared. Smacks of a tall tale to me," relays Beggs.

"It's a sad story. Mattie Wildbird lost more than her fair share that day. The entire clan did. That little attorney has an exceptional reputation. Everyone I've met admires her. Just the same, something's not right. I can feel it just walking down the office hallway. Maybe you should look for numbers that are good instead of bad," declares Beggs's corpulent friend.

"So, you think whoever is behind the raids is looking to achieve something good. Are these riders just a distraction for whatever else might be happening?" asks Beggs.

It's just like Sweet Brown Betty to suggest such a conundrum. She smiles wordlessly at her friend in confirmation.

"Well, it's a better idea than I've had thus far. I'll get back to you if I discover anything," declares a renewed Beggs Cooper.

Chapter 42-
TALL RIVER CASINO

Apple needs to see if it's true. Has his "little" brother turned tycoon? DOI operational files designate Henry Wildbird a person of interest but have yet to connect him to the raids. The DOI's internal discovery sends real, bone-chilling concern down Apple's spine. He familiarizes himself with all the intel.

By now, Sam the Seeker knows more about Henry than Apple. The Seeker's crew has worked this case for nearly three weeks, and from what Apple has been told, there seems to be more than enough evidence to justify his concerns. It's the last thing he would've suspected of his brother.

Tall River isn't extravagant. It's best defined as *elegant*. The faux rock exterior on the three-story building is dappled by thousands of small, flickering white lights that welcome patrons into a magnificent portico.

The entrance is designed to make visitors feel as if they flow with the river's current. The glass floor exhibits fast-flowing water below reinforced glass tiles. Patrons literally walk on water. An elongated aquarium full of native fish and plants spans the great hall in its entirety. Overhead, murals depicting picturesque azure skies emboss the ceiling. The river directs patrons into a huge, mesmeric grotto filled with profit-making gaming machines, poker and craps tables, varietal slots, and multiple food courts. At its center is a giant oval bar with a cut-glass enclosed waterfall. Art-deco tile floors surround the bar, with welcoming tables, couches, and chairs all saturated in clear blue light.

A giant of a man leans against the bar and can't be mistaken for anyone but Henry Wildbird. As usual, he's entrenched in reading material. *The Wall Street Journal, The Economist,* and *The New York Times* are sprawled in front of the titan. A tablet is cradled in the man's large right palm, leaving his left hand to scroll through a variety of pages in consultation of his latest stock purchase. The bartender steadily reinforces Henry's coffee cup. A cocktail waitress signals the barkeep of an approaching visitor who, in turn, gives the big man a heads up.

Samantha Cherchez advances towards Henry just as Apple enters the arena from the opposite direction. The DOI deputy director quickly redirects himself behind the nearest slot machine. Henry stands tall to greet the woman as politely as his Grandmother requires. Quietly, almost embarrassingly slow, they appraise one another. Samantha speaks first.

"That coffee smells terrific."

Henry's motion is wasted as the bartender arrives instantly with coffee and all its accoutrements. Cherchez leans in for cream, brushing against the giant. Her arm lightly skims his starched, long-sleeved shirt. He doesn't react other than to watch her stir the coffee. Sam ponders what tactic might work on this guy. It's a struggle to retrieve Henry Wildbird's thick FBI dossier from her oversized Mulberry handbag.

The giant of a man peeks at the file and smiles at Sam. He settles back onto the barstool as the Seeker begins her interview.

"I must look familiar to you," opens Sam. "Yesterday, at the airport, you watched as my associate and I met the governor."

"The fact is the first time we saw one another was a few years back. As I recall, you kept the bar at the Rocking R."

Henry detects a slight moment of surprise on Sam's face. It's difficult to tell, but Henry thinks she's impressed he remembers her from their days at MSU.

Listening in the background, an annoyed Apple realizes much was missed. How could he walk by his colossus of a brother and not notice like Cherchez did? The answer is evident: Mattie Wildbird has a powerful effect.

The giant towers above the woman as he turns her barstool towards him to gain full attention. Henry gazes into Sam's eyes. She meets his stare, each trying to make the other blink first. After a long beat, Henry takes a swipe.

"Yep, I recognize you. Aren't you Apple's secretary?"

"Oh, this is amateur hour. I grew up with six brothers who make a taunt like that look like a compliment. You can do better," smiles the Seeker.

Henry is smitten and replies with a lavish smirk.

"You're no doubt a highly trained undercover agent, dressed to kill. The one who always gets her man. I can't say that would be a total disappointment."

"Count on it," adds Sam, with all the innuendo she can muster.

Perfect, Henry's flirting with Sam the Seeker. Apple can't believe his brother isn't a little concerned. She's attractive and confident, prepared to use any weapon to strip Henry of his freedom. This is a serious game of cat and mouse, and Henry's not the cat.

The file sits open atop the bar, a mere prop. Sam knows the contents inside and out. She begins the interview.

"You're a relatively successful businessman. Tell me, is it luck, or is there some special formula?"

The bar staff have retreated but stand at the ready. Henry Wildbird enjoys the game.

"It's probably a little of both. I mean, I'd like to take all the credit, but that wouldn't be logical. It's important to network. Build connections, rub shoulders, even if you don't necessarily enjoy the company."

They both smile at this response. The giant has beaten her to the punch. Instead, she sips the coffee and presses forward to determine what she can learn from her brainy prey.

"What does a Mec like you do for fun around here?"

The Seeker lures the giant to a nearby couch. Apple is so close now that he and his brother could touch one another, but Henry's distracted by Sam's beauty.

"Probably the same thing as any other Mec. We hunt, fish, hike."

He grins a little and signals the barkeep.

"Please freshen the woman's double-double."

"This is fun, but your slang sucks," declares Sam.

The Seeker's steely-eyed quip is a bit more to the point. "You know a few details about me, but rest assured, I know a great deal more about you than is healthy. This includes your business and family. I'll bet you a toonie that I catch you with your gitch exposed."

With that, the gracefully purposeful DOI agent gathers her things to depart. On her way out, she turns to the giant. "I noticed you aren't sporting a Molson muscle like that brother of yours. You had better get him to watch his weight and give up the smokes. One bad habit will slow someone down, but two kills."

Henry Wildbird is in love and laughs freely as he watches the energetic woman work her Vuittons like few others.

Chapter 43-
BROTHERS' BARGAIN

Mattie and Apple's previous reunion didn't involve much conversation. He was contemplating the event with a mixture of sheer pleasure and total confusion. A hot shower is the one place Apple can sort things out. Heat rises, hot water flows, encouraging solitude. A rap on the glass door shatters any further deliberation. Startled, he swipes the steam from the glass to find Henry, in all his size, sitting on the latrine.

"I don't know what offends me more: the fact that you haven't bothered to speak to me since your return or that your first act was doing the wild thing with my twin sister. A towel is hanging on the door. Let's meet downstairs for breakfast in ten minutes. Don't make me wait," demands Henry.

The hot water helps to abate Apple's trepidation; he stays put until his heart rate goes down. With his head beneath the rainfall showerhead, he changes hot water to cold. It rushes over him with disturbing zeal. What did he expect? He's in the bear's den. Of course, Henry knows Apple booked into the hotel, regardless of the false credentials provided by Sam's staff. He turns off the shower, dries quickly, and jumps into a pair of jeans, loafers, and a brown buttoned-down shirt and then darts down the hotel hallway.

Breakfast in a thriving casino is brisk, twenty-four/seven. Gamblers tend to ignore the concept of time. Gaming's addiction exposes compound causations. Squandered time is just a trite casualty.

Henry is already seated in a loft above the crowd, with an excellent view of the restaurant. He listens in earnest about last night's financial transactions as presented by the fatigued night supervisor.

Henry's giant physique isn't the only reason this meeting is intimidating. The unfinished romance between Mattie and Apple always strained their relationship. Beyond that, Apple and Henry haven't seen each other since they were boys.

Apple distinctly remembers the last time he saw his brother. Hinmah's entire family saw him off to law school. Even then, Henry was large for his age, but now… Both men have lived busy lives. Neither has taken time or interest in each other's careers, never mind updating one another about what's happening in their personal lives.

Apple's return as an employee of the United States government increases a potential conflict. The fact that he's deputy director of the Department of the Interior acts to highlight their dilemma. Henry Wildbird's status as the agency's prime suspect broadens these complications.

Apple Tamer Gray waits to be escorted to Henry's roost. Seconds later, he's guided upstairs, arriving just as the night supervisor completes the evening's financial tally. Apple glances at the man as he disappears without a nod.

"Are you hungry?" asks the giant. "Sit down, little brother, and don't look as if you're dreading breakfast with family. It's not polite."

Apple slides into the seat previously occupied by the night supervisor. The waitress provides him a menu. Stalling for time, he pretends to study it. The waitress returns on Henry's cue. Apple orders two eggs, bacon, and a side of whole-wheat toast. She leaves without taking Henry's order.

"Aren't you going to eat? I thought we were having breakfast as a family."

"Damn, it's great to see you. I have so much to tell you. Hinmah is beside herself with your return," reports the giant.

Literally seconds later, the table is swarmed by multiple waitresses, who fill it with a huge spread that includes Apple's eggs, bacon, and toast. The giant is hungry. Fruit, hot cereal, pastries, meats, and juices are on display atop a hot food buffet wheeled in from the kitchen.

While the two men eat, they talk about old times, but not about their immediate problem or Mattie. The dirty dishes disappear as quickly as the food arrived, leaving behind fresh mugs of hot coffee. Satiated, Henry leans back in silence and stares coldly into Apple's eyes.

"You and I are on a tight schedule. I must bring you up to date since you disappeared. After all, I'm going to need a good lawyer," says Henry with a contagious smile.

Both men laugh as Apple sits as tall as possible in his chair.

"What the hell, Henry, you know I'm deputy director of the Department of the Interior. Representing you would be rather a conflict of interest, don't you think?" says a half-serious Apple.

"Don't you think that the government's use of 'Apple' Tamer Gray in any capacity is a conflict of interest?" asks Henry.

Both men let that comment sit. Henry breaks the silence. "Besides, you won't be working for those guys by the end of the month."

"You're taking a great deal for granted, Henry. I worked hard to get this job, and I'm very good at it. We both know what's really going on here. You're a prime suspect in an ongoing investigation. You're a smart guy; eco-terrorists are getting an inordinate amount of attention these days.

"The FBI views environmental and animal rights activists as the most threatening trend facing our nation, third only to radical Islam and home-grown white supremacists. Let me be clear; they see you as a dangerous fanatic," says an impassioned Apple.

Henry smiles broadly.

"Big brother, you've grown into yourself and sound so official. I'm impressed, but you've forgotten our tribe's basic tenant. Never believe the white man's lies. Active coups aren't an act of extremism. They're predicated on tribal religion and, if carried out properly, are an act of honor and courage."

"Oh, so you admit you've carried out these, what are you labeling them, 'coups'?" spews the ardent prosecutor.

The giant stands.

"Bring your attitude with you; you're going to need it. We have much to see."

If Henry is looking to intimidate Apple, he succeeded just by standing. Apple sits still for a moment longer to appraise the situation and hopes Henry is trying to come clean. He slowly stands.

"Henry, we can get through this. I know some very good attorneys."

Henry's smile is followed by laughter.

"It's you or no one, brother. We started this together, and we'll finish that way."

The two men walk down an employee-only hallway. Moments later, Apple finds himself in a skirmish against three guys who come at him from the opposite direction. He doesn't expect it; the next thing he sees is total darkness.

Henry acts as if nothing happened and proceeds down the hall. The three men throw Apple into an oversized laundry duffel and load him into a dumbwaiter. Two more men await the delivery on the lower level of the casino, loading the duffel into an unmarked white van with blackened windows. Henry is aware that the casino is under surveillance, but Hinmah needs a private moment with her long-lost son. The casino tycoon makes it happen.

When Apple regains consciousness, he feels disoriented. Surrounded by jumbo screens and computers that seem out of focus, he tries to make sense of things. His grandmother's familiar scent falls over him. It isn't until Hinmah places a cold washrag on his forehead that he recognizes it isn't a hallucination.

"Oh, it's good to have you in my arms again," says the old medicine woman.

Apple slowly rises to sit beside Hinmah. He shoots Henry a look of disgust.

"Please, Grandmother, tell me you're not involved in these coups?"

The room erupts in laughter.

Hinmah holds the young man's hand as a gentle reminder. "Do you recall when you came to our family? Looking back, it has a strange symmetry. We all lost many things that fall. I lost Tree and Isabelle; you lost your parents, as did Mattie and Henry. To regain our sanity, we promised ourselves to a visionary ambition. Everyone made a pledge to its composition, even you, Apple."

"Hinmah, I was fifteen years old. You made us believe we could survive anything if we had a purpose. You can't be serious. The String was just an idea," declares a deeply distressed Apple Tamer Gray.

Hinmah stands with arms wide open as she circles the cavernous headquarters of the crusade. Henry holds a position beside several members of the String's inner circle and watches his grandmother work her magic on a man who has lost his way.

"I'm afraid it's more than an idea, Apple. The Ink Prayer's dream to complete the String started the moment we agreed that our dead would act as testimony. All of us bare distinctive scars of loss: your abject singleness, Mattie's fake arm, Henry's need to avenge. Our combined heartbreak still needs mending. The Ink Prayer's String does that for each of us and will do even more."

Now, firmly facing her adopted son, the old woman has fully circled the cavern.

"You must pick a side, Apple, not red or white, but hope against desolation."

Chapter 44-
THE BAR-MISS-FITS

The bar is dark. It takes a moment for Apple's pupils to adjust. His head still hurts, and the stench of old smoke hits him hard. He pushes past it because the tension of his family's dynamics is far worse than any physical discomfort.

The door, floor, and bar are all sticky with the remnants of spilled beer and vomit, as the odor of stale cigarettes is heightened by the trapped heat. Great, no air conditioning.

Poker machines line the east wall and emit an incessant noise. An elderly man leans against a metallic barstool, perched in front of the mechanical poker games. He feeds quarters into the coin receptacle. His nicotine-stained fingers are arthritic, which presents a challenge. He's forced to tilt his cigarette out the side of his mouth to free up his hands. He uses both to drop the change into the slot and does so with a mumbled expletive.

Three guys and a gal whom Apple recognizes as Jen Twenty-Stands play poker in a cheaply adorned back room. A decade ago, Jen was the most beautiful woman on the reservation. Time and gravity haven't been kind. Apple turns away in hopes she doesn't recognize him. He isn't in the mood to be social.

Everyone is here. White Wolf, Big Back, Fire Crow, Yellow Robe, Ridge Walker: these boys, now men, used to beat the hell out of Apple as a kid. He considers all this and decides there isn't much to lose. One brawl has already been lost today. What the hell? Besides, Apple Tamer Gray isn't a scrawny kid anymore. All he wants is a shot and beer.

After further consideration, he doubts that he even counts to these people, Apple the half-breed. Thankfully, no one seems to recognize him. Either they're too drunk, too stoned, or too old to give a damn.

The smell seems to abate after a tallboy and chaser. Apple's agitation subsides the more he drinks. He watches an elderly couple totter to the dance floor. Lost in a juke box beat, they lean and sway to an old Willie Nelson tune. Apple tips his beer at them, but they're too engrossed in the moment to notice.

Gray's been in the bar for a good twenty minutes. No one bothers him. Calm now, he looks around. Things are fine until he realizes Sam the Seeker has tracked him down. Shock fostered by trepidation courses through Apple as he pounds down the remainder of his tallboy. There is nowhere to hide. Samantha Cherchez stands in the doorway, showcasing her elegantly clean lines and unbridled confidence. It's safe to say she's a bit of a standout.

Theoretically, Apple was assigned to Sam the Seeker's DOI investigation as tribal interpreter. The fact is he disappeared the moment they both landed at the Great Falls International Airport. She's got to be disappointed with him on that basis alone. At present, she has caused a commotion just by walking into this place. Sam ignores everyone as she marches to the bar and orders drinks.

"It looks like he's having a boilermaker. Get him another, and I'll join him. Shit, it's hot in here."

Looking at an ash-white Apple, she asks, "What? You think because I wear Christian Dior I don't know how to swear?"

Every person in the bar focuses on the two outsiders. Eagerly, these viewers wait for the impending fireworks. The Seeker perches on a barstool inches away from Apple. It dawns on her that they haven't shared more than ten minutes of conversation since they met. Something has always stood between them: first the president and then this surreal assignment.

Sam considers the forced homecoming for a man who never actually belonged in this place. One can sympathize with the DOI deputy director. Yep… Sam the Seeker knows all there is to know about the shy introvert sitting beside her. It's no coincidence that Apple Tamer Gray pulled this assignment. She's surprised he's not shielding his privates for a little security at this point. Without another word, she takes a pull of the tallboy and thinks back. He's been played, kidnapped, and used for sex. Okay, Mattie's invitation can't have been too bad. Sam is sure Apple probably enjoyed that part. Nonetheless, the whole situation is one hell of a mind game. Given the circumstances, she decides to take a gentle tack. Sam grabs a quick look around.

"Lovely place. Come here often?"

Her companion grins and then tugs at his mustache, an unconscious habit the deputy director executes when amused. He pounds down the shot Sam purchased and then hits the beer for relief. Hell, it isn't this woman's fault that he's in such a bind.

"I should apologize for disappearing on you at the airport."

Looking straight into the bar mirror, she lifts her drink to Apple.

"Don't worry about it," she says, pounding down the boilermaker.

The slow burn floods the Seeker's throat. It makes the impending conversation easier. She signals for another round.

"It's obvious you've been set up. The deputy director of the Department of the Interior rarely goes on a field trip."

She takes another draw from her beer. They watch each other in the mirror, both trying to figure out how to approach the situation.

"I mean, I get the part about duty to the president. That's a no-brainer, but you're in over your head with the whole family thing."

Apple has had just enough stress and alcohol to stab back with an animated quip.

"Exactly what do you want from me, Ms. Cherchez? Let's face it, you probably know more about me than I do myself: my tragic childhood, the loss of my alcoholic parents, my adopted family, and the Ink Prayer people who never accepted me or my siblings."

Angry about everything, Apple asks, "Which part entertains you the most?"

He hammers down another shot and looks around to see who's watching this circus. Curiously, no one seems interested. Apple thinks about that for a minute.

Unintentionally, he verbalizes his impression.

"The old woman has a spell on this place. Nothing is out of her reach."

Sam laughs loudly.

"Come on, you're an educated man. You don't believe in that bullshit, do you? I met your grandmother. She's a remarkable lady, but I don't buy that mystical crap. Your grandmother is a pragmatist who employs substantial resources in ways that benefit her most. For example, to distract her enemies."

Sam glares at Apple as she presses against what she considers psychic crap.

"She's not some phony spiritualist. Well, okay, she's a medicine woman, but don't bullshit me about her methods. That's the only thing I've figured out about Hinmah so far."

A nearly inaudible grunt comes from the old gal who eagerly enjoyed the Willie Nelson song with her toothless partner earlier. Neither Sam nor Apple are sure they heard it, so they both sit in silence, drinking cold beer.

"You think I don't question these strange occurrences? Hell, I know it doesn't make sense. Neither does the visit she paid me the night before you and I met at the White House," says an agitated Apple.

"What the hell are you talking about?" asks an incredulous Seeker.

Sam's austere look penetrates any nonsensical superstition Apple might infer, so he downs the last of his beer.

"Let's get out of here; I can't think!"

Apple, now highly aware of his surroundings, eyes the establishment's occupants. Once again, he's forced to pass the dimly lit poker room and detects a not-too-subtle wink from Jen Twenty-Stands.

The Seeker collects her things and strides from the bar with as much self-possession as when she entered. A shaken Apple Tamer

Gray crawls into the rented Jeep Cherokee. Sam pulls out of the saloon's parking lot, and notices the poker players, outside, wildly amused by all they witnessed. Exasperated, a suspicious Seeker watches Jen Twenty-Stands blow her a kiss in the rear-view mirror. Evidently Apple's spectral suspicions are legitimate.

Chapter 45-
DOUBTABLE ACUITY

Slightly shaken, the two investigators feel like victims of a surreal haunt. The bar's peculiar occupants heighten this discomfort. Sam falls into a muzzled stupor, attempting to make sense of the Hinmah-influenced event.

Five miles down the road, a pull off presents itself and seems like a logical place to reconnoiter. The Seeker veers off the two-lane gravel road, hits the brakes, and slips from the driver's-side door. The agile woman bounds atop a giant outcropping overlooking the Missouri River.

"This place is astonishing."

She signals to Apple, who remains uncommunicative in the passenger's seat of the Cherokee. Akin to some wild creature basking on the flat surface of the large stone, the Seeker calls out to her colleague.

"Why don't you come sit a minute? Take in a little sunshine? I want to talk about what I think we know."

Apple joins Sam, thankful for a peaceful moment and fresh air.

She begins, "Let's be honest: You're in an untenable position. I rarely feel remorse for anyone during an investigation, but none of this appears to be your fault. Apple, my friend, this is a precarious situation. You need an ally, and the only way I can play that role is if the truth surfaces pretty darn quickly."

Apple throws a rock into the river and watches the rings ripple outward without a word.

"Okay, let's start with the easy stuff. My first intent is to find the underlying cause of things, and I'd like to do that without harming your family. What if I tell you what I already know, and you jump in with whatever information you feel safe sharing?" generously submits Sam.

The soreness behind Apple's eyes eases just a bit. He looks at the river, then back at the assertive predator. He makes an attempt to cut his losses.

"Do I have a choice?"

Sam shifts contentedly and adds a rock to the shallows. "I'm not sure what I would do if I were in a similar predicament."

The handsome man takes a large gulp of fresh air and sits tall.

"I have to trust someone."

An hour later, they've defined a list of possibilities. To start with is the glaring fact that it makes no sense that Henry Wildbird is on the take.

"Hell, Henry has always made money easily. There's more to the story. Otherwise, he wouldn't have made himself such a large target," declares Apple.

"No pun intended," smiles Apple's new confidant.

Chapter 46-
PLIABLE TRUCE

Grandmother's cabin seems an odd place to think through this jumbled experience. But that's where Apple's instincts take him.

Just a day prior, Apple Tamer Gray flew cross-country, hoping to clarify his familial standing and, more importantly, his relationship with the first and possibly only legitimate love of his life. Everything after Mattie Wildbird has always felt counterfeit.

Apple's years of study and work behind a desk has had adverse effects. The two-hour hike to Hinmah's cabin takes him far longer than it should for a man his age.

Grandmother waits at the crest of the trail where lake and sky are indistinguishable. The dark fall skies mirror Apple's predicament, but the old woman's embrace is a longed-for antidote. How Hinmah knew of Apple's arrival is a mystery he's learned not to question. As for Hinmah, she has always felt a profound benevolence toward this humble and introverted boy, now a grown man. The old medicine woman hopes his return is a declaration, a prayer answered. They lean into their mutual affection and instantly fall back into the common refuge of adoration. The promise of water and a snack helps Apple complete the last leg of his long hike.

Once inside, the serene cabin transports the DOI deputy back to his youth. Apple scans the pictures displayed on nearly every wall and atop the credenza. The photos evoke an intimate sensibility as he and his grandmother laugh over the cherished remembrances contained within the tidy wooden frames. Apple wonders at the simplicity of these portraits. These timeless snapshots harshly betray his immediate reality.

The two discuss much: Apple's life in D.C.'s Foggy Bottom, his work, even the women he has bedded and then coldly rejected. The family matriarch wants to know of Apple's accomplishments and missed opportunities before moving on to their shared predicament. This tender reconciliation bolsters them both but provides little shelter from the inevitable.

Hinmah's tranquility fortifies Apple. When questioned about the String, the tribal leader doesn't hide behind vagueness or bristle with defiance. What comes from this reunion is an innate openness.

"You must know I left behind my first love," divulges Apple boldly, his eyes direct and probing.

The old woman doesn't budge and returns his stare.

"I'm afraid fate seized each of our futures long ago. Life has been less than generous to you and the twins. In hindsight, I should have considered the loss of your parents further. Please forgive me. So deep was my grief, I couldn't feel yours. Everyone has paid dearly, you every bit as much as the rest."

A respectful silence fills the room.

"My sweet man, please know that I demanded more of you because I wanted more for you. Apple, your grandfather and I didn't send you away to disrupt a shared bond. On this, I give you my word.

It's true, I felt you and Mattie were too young, but that's not why we enrolled Apple Tamer Gray so far afield.

"By now, it's evident that you possess exceptional talent. How else could you have accomplished so much at the Department of the Interior? Your title as deputy director fully demonstrates my assertion. This talent, along with your promise to the String, was our only motivation. George Washington University's full-ride scholarship fell in line with the String's overall strategy.

"This family's compact, made so long ago, has nearly reached fruition. What happens going forward depends on you." Hinmah sighs.

"I leave both the String and your relationship to you and Mattie. Neither Delsin nor I will interfere. You'll always be our son, regardless of choice."

With this pronouncement, Apple recognizes his own deep-rooted insecurity — all these years apart from family, wasted. He had no one to blame but himself. Orphaned by alcoholics and denounced by two cultures, he never understood the gift of acceptance, even when blessed so naturally. Apple sits in deliverance.

"Grandmother, I owe you an apology. You have never been anything but generous, and yet I felt this family lacked devotion. My self-doubt has made me less than a man."

The old woman sheds a single tear.

"We've both made our fair share of mistakes. I question myself daily, especially regarding the String. Please understand that I believe in the purity and worth of our mission. But all my children are fully exposed. It was never my conscious intention to jeopardize any of you. I admit the String's construction was conceived by a madwoman. Once we began, there was no way back. And more than that, its purpose seems to restore all who occupy a role. Do you believe in any of this foolishness?"

Peering out the giant bay window, Apple recognizes the tribal leader's plea. He appreciates the whole of it now and has made a final decision on how to go forward.

The lake shifts moods from black to emerald green as the sun breaks through incremental clouds, first against the cliffs' exterior, and then off the medicine woman's glass windows. It's at this moment Apple sees Mattie's indigenous traits exalted by lake waters and masked plumage. Courageously, his first love stands tall in her pronouncement. Apple looks to his grandmother.

"How long has she been waiting?"

"How long have you been gone?" asks the medicine woman as she admires Mattie's colorful proclamation. Hinmah appreciates her granddaughter's declaration and invitation. The old woman turns back towards Apple just soon enough to see the screen door bounce gently back in place. Hinmah goes about her business, leaving future events to Apple and Mattie.

Chapter 47-
BEMUSED PASSION

The slick rock shore is dicey. Great, thinks Apple, another barrier. Today, come hell or high water, he's going to catch Mattie and tell her how he feels.

Apple's deliberate effort makes it easy for Mattie to slip in behind undetected. He stumbles over glossy rocks and boulders to find the beautiful apparition seen from the cabin's window. Now, that very same manifestation mocks from behind. Apple turns, quickly splashing water as the ghost toys with him. His jerky reaction and subsequent headfirst tumble into the deep end of the lake makes Mattie laugh as she sheds her mask and dives in to pull her lover's quivering mass ashore. Goosebumps litter the city slicker's skin, and his lips turn a bluish purple. Apple looks like a loveable wet pup in a soggy flannel shirt and droopy mustache.

Mattie lures him back to her tepee. She works to strip away his wetness. He stands nude before her. Drenched, she quickly sloughs off the remainder of her wet apparel. Warmed by the fire, Apple shivers with chilled admiration as she disrobes. His hand slides through black damp hair as he tugs at his mustache with a look of rapture.

Mattie circles Apple in appraisal. Her fingertip traces his less-than-defined but still slender posterior before pulling him back into the soft confines of her makeshift bed. Early-morning desire takes the couple back and forth from passion to placid slumber. Eventually, the two famished devotees submit to hunger. The scent of smoked salmon, cream cheese, and crackers emanate from a small backpack. It beckons the ravenous lovers.

"I know it sounds silly, but this is a magnificent feast," declares the high-spirited lover from Washington, D.C.

Amused, Mattie folds used wrappers and returns them to the pack. She busies herself with various minutiae, hoping to make this moment last.

The conversation dries up as Apple pulls Mattie to him in one last attempt to avoid what looms ahead. He wants more before broaching the tricky topic. She folds herself into his neck, enticed by the pureness of his scent. Finally, regretfully, Mattie moves forward with the dreaded question.

"Between family matters and the investigation, you know a great deal about the String's progress."

Apple turns to grab his half-wet garb but hesitates to put it on. Mattie smiles at the urbanite, throwing her damp clothing on without hesitation and then watches as a solemnity envelops Apple's face. She watches his black eyes go darker as he searches for something resolute. It's the last question she expects.

Apple Tamer Gray, shivering inside his damp attire, bends down on one knee and asks Mattie to marry him.

Chapter 48-
THREE LEGS OF JUSTICE

The armory is divided into three tiers. At its center is a full-sized basketball court. Small communities like Helena use their armory for varying purposes. If a division of the Guard is called up for duty during inclement weather, the court acts as an indoor parade ground where families say one last goodbye before their loved ones depart.

Today, this space is dedicated to the reconnaissance and information technology command center, aimed at the arrest and seizure of the environmental activists who raid hunting camps.

The newly established task force is comprised of a small team from the Federal Bureau of Investigation, the Department of the Interior, local law enforcement officers, and a very frustrated Montana National Guard component.

From the beginning, the designated task force, named Finch888, falls to the inexperienced but proficient Special Agent Joyce Kingston's FBI unit.

The governor's political cadre works alongside the National Guard, led by Bridgette "Gig" Robbins. The Department of the Interior Liaison Beggs Cooper, a Welshman from back East, is charged with predictive analytics.

Kingston has determined that all of Cooper's cards aren't on the table. He's tall, blond, and incredibly urbane. In short, he doesn't meld with the team. Gig Robbins, on the other hand, is strong, confident, and a very competent asset.

Early on, Kingston decides to make Robbins her first meet at the armory. Joyce locates the office of the joint chief of staff buried deep in the daylight basement of the old building.

Out front sits the professional thirty-something company grade officer tasked with completing all and any duties mandated by the joint chief. Upon Robbins's return to the office, the officer salutes his boss and then notifies her of the impromptu visit. Special Agent-in-Charge Joyce Kingston verifies her identity with a quick flash of her badge. Commander Robbins greets Kingston in full uniform.

"I was expecting a visit. Please, come in, and have a seat."

Kingston follows the joint chief into a typical government office, nondescript and without excess. Pictures of various aircraft line the cinder-block walls, and the furniture is standard metal-gray military issue. It's evident to the SAC that Robbins doesn't blow her own very accomplished horn.

"Please call me Gig. Corporal, can you get us a… What do you drink, coffee?"

Joyce immediately feels at ease with this capable woman. "Yes. Coffee, please, and just a splash of milk, if you have it. I'm afraid I was out late last night on a team development mission."

Gig walks to the doorway, past the now-seated FBI agent. "I, too, had a difficult mission last night. I'm afraid General Markay is displeased with his rather indolent command."

The hot coffee and milk arrive as Gig hangs her uniform coat on the back of the door. The Corporal pours two cups of coffee and then asks whether the women need anything else.

Gig signals his dismissal. "Thank you."

Joyce Kingston takes a sip.

"I'm here because I think we can help one another. I'll be as honest as possible. I've never been in Montana, my team is new, and I have no interest in creating more problems for myself."

Gig sinks into the chair behind her desk.

"Well, I appreciate your candor. In turn, let me confess that these riders have been at least one step ahead of us at every go. They have support, serious support, like advanced technology, financial backing, and public admiration."

The two women take a minute to enjoy the unusual frankness.

"What can you tell me about the third leg of our task force? I can't seem to get a read on this Beggs Cooper. What kind of name is 'Beggs' anyway?" asks the indignant FBI agent.

Gig chokes on the coffee, laughing at Joyce's frankness. "I believe it's Welsh and, yeah, this guy gives us just enough information to keep us guessing. Don't get me wrong, he knows what he's doing. But there's something else going on, and I don't have a good feel for what that might be yet."

A commotion just outside the joint chief's door spills over into her office.

Chapter 49-

THE PERFORMANCE

"**W**ell, if you'd order this man to stand down, I might be able to clear a few things up," offers Cooper from under the corporal's firmly planted hand.

"Corporal, please. It's fine," says the amused commander.

The well-dressed Beggs Cooper swishes in with a flurry and then makes himself at home.

"Oh, good, I see you two are coffee drinkers. I took the liberty and brought you ladies a latte from a great little place on the gulch."

Cooper besieges the two women at length while he makes himself at home on his computer. Gig grins through the entire performance, but Kingston is far less impressed.

"I know you've been flooded with a vast amount of intelligence. I'm afraid it was the raid on Secretary of State Tully that has prompted this disproportionate response of which we're now all a part," elaborates the dramatic Welsh man.

Kingston can't take any more.

"I beg your pardon. Based on the governor's briefing, you should at least grasp how these disturbances have significant financial consequences, let alone the dangers they present to the public."

Cooper enjoys twisting the young agent around a little too much, so Gig intervenes.

"It doesn't appear that these raids follow any set pattern," she says, pointing to the whiteboard directly behind her. Let me provide you both with our packet of descriptors containing a vast array of intel to include a timetable of itemized events and areas of insurgency, along with each cold trail.

"We've determined the raiders' purpose, but not their stratagem. As you know, based on the command's presentation, an insignia is left behind at each completed coup. I refer to these raids as 'coups' because the emblem conveys a Native American postulate. Beyond that, these attacks feel like a distraction, although this is mere speculation on my part. Let's call it instinct."

Cooper immediately recognizes Robbins's ability to comprehend crucial evidentiary detail. She won't be diverted easily. He concludes she's an asset far too risky to alienate. He quickly shifts gears, sharing vital intelligence with both women, counting on the joint chief to keep the younger FBI agent in check.

An authentic Beggs Cooper emerges.

"I've been authorized to inform you that we have an undercover officer embedded inside this criminal faction. Obviously, I cannot divulge the identity of this informant, but the intelligence provided thus far confirms your suspicions, Ma'am. Please forgive my glib behavior; I find it helpful to do a little reconnaissance before tipping my hand."

"I hope we passed your test, Mr. Cooper," smiles Robbins.

A very serious Kingston explodes.

"I don't know how the joint chief feels, but I have little time for silliness. Rest assured, the FBI has full jurisdiction here, Mr.

Cooper. Failure to share information, critical or otherwise, won't be tolerated."

Beggs the performer reappears.

"Duly noted, Ms. Kingston."

"That's Special Agent-in-Charge Kingston, Mr. Cooper," adds the fuming agent.

Beggs winks at Gig as he gathers the informational packet on his way out.

"Thank you for the information."

Robbins nods at Cooper, adding, "If nothing else, I'm sure working with you will be entertaining. Please give my regards to your entire team."

Robbins watches as Cooper sashays down the hall. The seething Kingston goes into a tailspin, leaving Robbins to calm her.

"Just who is his team leader, and how many people are we talking about?"

Chapter 50-

COOPER'S CALLING CARD

The Seeker waits at the base of the stairs and can hear Kingston railing against Cooper.

"From the sounds of things, you left your standard calling card."

"How was the meeting?" asks an amused Samantha Cherchez.

All business now, Cooper checks his notes.

"Just as you anticipated, both women are competent. Special Agent Kingston is young, spirited, bright, and very ambitious. I can use that. Bridgette 'Gig' Robbins might need a little more attention. She's the whole package. Her experience is diverse. She's highly adept and likable; I suspect she'll take a bit more of our time. It won't do to bullshit her."

Sam rolls her eyes.

"No, really, this lady is intuitive. As per our prior agreement, I notified them that we have an Ink Prayer insider. The civil/military campaign is struggling with number detection. This target is savvy. It's incredible. The data challenge is enormous. Now, there's so much noise that everyone's digital surveillance software is struggling to find a single practical signal," says a confounded Cooper.

"Two weeks earlier, I nearly went insane looking for a single aberration. Today, the field is flooded with millions of potential indicators, but all proved dead ends. Now, it isn't that we can't find an aberration; it's that there are so many, it takes the bulk of my time to determine whether it's a decent lead. My best guess is that our little three-pronged investigation may have prompted this turn of events. The change in course makes me extremely suspicious. Do these eco-terrorists have an inside informant?

"Whoever is in charge appears astonishingly talented." The Seeker ponders this as her IT specialist vents.

"I'm forced to reduce the scope of this investigation. The state of Montana's overall operation isn't as significant as, say, Utah. Montana's governmental operation manipulates roughly 500,000 transactions per minute attached to countless data points per transaction. These copious datasets make for a complex analysis," concludes Beggs.

Sam and Beggs arrive at the smart house. The Seeker prowls in front of the state-of-the-art computer system, contemplating the multitude of transactions flashing over multiple monitors at light speed.

"Let's take a risk and change the data surveillance. Our present process is way too time-consuming. It's important to stay ahead of the civil-military campaign at the armory," determines Sam.

Cooper pulls at his brow and then offers an idea.

"I have a private sector contact who specializes in electronic fraud designs. She builds algorithms that can distinguish obfuscated aberrations. She starts her investigations with irregular nonentities. I could run her jacked-up algorithm to expedite the process. It's a gamble, but we could get lucky. It supports Betty's notion that the illicit financial transactions are probably funneled through Tall River Casino."

"Whatever we do, it had better happen soon. The FBI's counter-intelligence operation is well-organized. The governor has directed everyone to focus on Fish and Game revenues, but this thing feels bigger to me," declares the very competitive Sam the Seeker.

"We need to narrow our pursuit, but I'd start with the Wildbird/Lund connection. It's evident that Crebo hates Mattie. The thing is, she doesn't care."

Sam thinks about that for a moment before continuing. "Anyway, the gang at the armory doesn't enjoy access to your friend's version of software on steroids. I suggest you use her shortcut to stay a step ahead."

She looks directly at Cooper.

"Dig it out first, Beggs, and dinner with our new director is on me!"

Cooper smiles.

"Incentives. You know such things tend to motivate me."

Chapter 51-
THE INEVITABLE CLUSTER

P ete Holdsclaw's heart feels as if it might explode. His run
through the eastern interior of the tunnel system is extremely
demanding. Henry shouts directions through Holdsclaw's headset
and attached GO camera.

"A hundred feet, veer left. You have an eighth of a mile to
the jam. Kick it in the ass, Pete, or they're going to beat you to the
entrance."

This hasty pace takes everything Holdsclaw has. As a mugger, one must be quick at getting in and out of dangerous positions
swiftly. The race to the tunnel's breach is yet another yardstick of the
mugger's fitness.

Pete can utter just one word:

"Creekbaum."

The giant at control shouts back,

"She's in position, but it takes time to set up. Get there, or
we're busted!"

The National Guard has all but homed in on the riders. The
furious pursuit unknowingly forces them directly towards the
jammed cavity.

Henry switches his attention back to the chase. Today's lead rider, Jim Tarkio, signals for additional separation. The riders break into threes, making the National Guard's frantic chase even more complicated.

Bailey Hester, who volunteered for the Ink Prayer just two months earlier, now takes charge of the easternmost riders. Fully vetted, she and her sibling are more than just capable riders. Henry switches frequencies to act as eyes for the three riders in the greatest peril.

"Break single at the next hazard, Bailey."

Everyone diverts in opposite directions. Bailey fully garners the guard's focus.

Henry can't believe his eyes. It will take only minutes before the pursuers are directly upon the exposed cave entrance. His plans are to divert Hester in an opposite direction from the rest of the riders.

Suspiciously, Henry tells Winslow to use the surveillance system to look ahead. "It feels like the guard is deliberately herding this rider towards an entrance they don't even realize exists. There must be a reason."

Henry sifts through cameras further up the ravine. He spots a group of soldiers rushing to construct a large flex-net.

"Crap, they mean to capture a rider!" shouts Henry.

Pete, now on scene, lurks just inside the cave entrance 150 yards east of the guardsmen. He tries to suppress his breathing and forces himself to concentrate on the jam. Rock has fallen from above. Haplessly, stone fragmentation has lodged itself at the apex of the door's opening. The riders are within sight. The pursuit isn't far behind. Pete grabs a rock hammer from his satchel and slides along the opening in search of a foothold. He fashions a patterned strike, picking at the lower surface of the lodged rock to weaken and finally split the wedged stone into pieces. The coyote trickster dangles without sound or motion as the riders are nearly upon him. Henry redirects Bailey. Against orders, Bailey's younger sister, Jodi, circles back towards the pursuit.

Creekbaum's faint audio breaks into the fracas.

"We're up," she whispers to control.

"Pete, stay perfectly still," announces a soft-spoken Henry.

"The guard's right on top of you."

The FBI's munitions expert, seated beside Colonel Clarkson, shouts over the noise of the Humvee.

"By God, I think we have ourselves a rider. Your command's going to net a terrorist!"

"Yeah, and the governor will have to eat crow for dinner," smiles the frustrated guardsman.

The colonel hits the remote to mechanically draw the heavily constructed netting. Bailey Hester reins her horse in sharply to avoid striking the net at full speed as the Humvee flies past the cave entrance without a second look.

Anne Creekbaum's illusionary limestone rock outcropping and ground cover save the day as a nearly exhausted Pete Holdsclaw discreetly drops from the ledge and back into the dark opening. The focused guardsmen press the chase deeper into the ravine without recognizing the hologram portico.

All good news for the String.

Two problems remain. Bailey Hester is trapped at the top of the gorge with nowhere to turn. Jodi comes from the west in full stride. She leaps over the passing Humvee from a small ledge above the chasm's narrowing channel and then rounds her ride directly at the Humvee, hoping it will swerve and miss. This gives both riders a lane to escape.

After months of accumulated vexation, the colonel fails to consider anyone's safety. He floors the vehicle headlong into his prey. Bailey's ride manages to get out of the way of the Humvee but collides with the canyon walls. The rift is too narrow. Both horse and rider go down. Bailey Hester is at Jodi's side before the National Guardsmen surround them.

Dagmar Eiksund arrives at command just in time to witness the Hesters' arrest. Henry is busy notifying the absent PERT team members via burner cells. News of the exposure and capture of two Ink Prayer riders hits the inner circle hard.

Both female riders are escorted to the local hospital for a medical examination before finding their way to jail. News of their physical status isn't readily available.

The String's emergency tactical response is immediately implemented. Dagmar's first call goes to Drake Stoltz to request that the captured riders be protected from the media.

The Hesters come from a well-established family. Dagmar recognizes that mass media exposure is inevitable, but the inner circle needs time to execute a proper defense. Mattie cannot intervene, but Sheriff Stoltz can impede.

The situation doesn't appear to be salvageable. Everyone will have to wait to see what effect this exposure has on the String's overall operation. The next few hours are critical.

The old engineer pieces together what he considers the only possible rejoinder. He takes the headset from Henry.

"Anne, you and Grace get back to control as soon as you can." Next, he turns to Winslow.

"I need the chase's camera feed. Please collect as many angles of this pursuit as possible. Gracie will need them to create a video for tonight's newscast. I need multiple shots of the colonel running down that horse and rider."

Henry can't believe what he's hearing. Eiksund should be wigging out. Instead, this innovative engineer makes plans to design a social media silver lining. Dagmar simply smiles at Henry.

"What? You didn't think I'd have a backup plan to contend with the inevitable?"

Henry folds Dagmar up into a massive bear hug. By evening, a view of the chase is viewed by thousands and ends up on three national newscasts. Gracie's anonymously submitted video confirms horse and rider purposefully run down by the National Guardsman. The colonel's violent actions are copiously exhibited for all to witness. His ferocious conduct makes the chase seem heinous.

Both Hester sisters' bloodied T-shirts assertively display the String's motto, "Join the cause before there's no cause to join."

News of Bailey's physical status verifies their wounds aren't significant. The byproduct of this terrifying engagement begins to take on a more positive tone.

———————•◆•———————

That evening, at Gracie's dinner table, Pete the coyote trickster makes it a point to tell Anne that they make a good team. Thanks to Pete's quickness and Anne Creekbaum's hologram, the cavern's entrance goes undiscovered. Anne moves to a nearby closet and returns with Pete's coup stick. Another notch has been slit into the hardened wood. Pete's eyes widen with the symbolic gesture as Gracie leans under the table and gives Anne a knee squeeze.

Chapter 52-

DEEP NET INFORMER

Acting as a wingman, Beggs transports Apple to the armory. It's a meeting that the DOI's deputy director would like to avoid, but circumstances require that both men attend.

The heavily waxed floors and abundantly starched uniformed officials add to Apple's discomfort. It reminds him that an extremely disciplined and coordinated system surrounds Hinmah's clan of eco-warriors. History hasn't changed. The old medicine woman's entire crew is undermanned and woefully under-armed.

Beggs points the way through a maze of corridors, past a small gathering of four FBI agents huddled outside a half-lit media room. A clustered faction of this smaller counter-insurgency operation reviews a handout provided by a short but meticulous man without nametag credentials. Apple turns an ashen white. He's seen this guy before. Hinmah's cavern has been infiltrated. Beggs pulls Apple past the assemblage.

"Are you okay? Do you know that guy?"

Before Apple can answer, the meeting is called to order. Apple looks for the man who disseminated the handout. He has artfully vanished. Mattie and Hinmah must be warned that a double agent has penetrated the inner circle.

"This game is played in the dark," announces the overly aggressive FBI agent who conducts the presentation.

Apple has worked alongside ambitious women like Kingston in the past. In a male-dominated world like the Bureau, women either flame out or excel. This Special Agent-in-Charge is just that: in charge.

Five principal members, heavily invested in the task force, albeit with varying agendas, occupy the room. This heavyweight investigative group is Kingston's protection against further leaks.

Everyone at the table recognizes that an insider has wreaked havoc upon previous attempts to capture the riders. This reduced faction significantly diminishes the potential of betrayal.

The FBI's IT specialist signals the ready, and the room goes black. A gigantic screen blanketed by an unusual and alien meshwork surrounds the room's occupants. The specialist begins.

"This informational labyrinth represents a behemoth information frontier. Presently the FBI is at a philosophical loss. Does the government intervene and attempt to control this technological network? Should we regulate, participate, or step aside entirely?

"Perhaps this is the first time you've peeked inside what is called the Deep Web. To give you an idea what we're up against, the Internet facilitates hundreds of millions of users each month, and that number continues to grow exponentially due to social media websites.

"Most people use what's referred to as the Surface Internet. Access to this portion of the web is gained with the help of search engines like Google. The larger part of our population fails to realize that an even greater entity called the Deep Web exists. This portion of the Cybernet cannot be penetrated using a regular search engine. Simply stated, we can go from the Surface Internet to the Deep Web by incorporating a distinctive apparatus.

"From this point in cyberspace, we leap to an internal feature of this Deep Web. It's named the Dark Net. Is everybody following me?"

The IT specialist looks around at the small audience for confirmation before he moves on.

"Cyberspace's Dark Net is deliberately concealed and not available through standard web browsers or search boxes. Using an onion router, this portion of the net employs thousands of relays to conceal its users' identities. Remember, the Dark Net allows total user anonymity."

The CIA cyber-trespass and theft specialist enters the fray.

"We must think of the Dark Net as leading edge, full of good and harmful possibilities. Experts liken it to the Wild West. We at the CIA, in conjunction with the FBI, have long developed a presence inside the Dark Net. The question is how this might help our present investigation."

The joint chief jumps in.

"I guess that you're tracking any activity related to the raids."

"That is correct, Commander Robbins. It's ironic: The Dark Web offers us the same privileges as it does conventional villains. Others can anticipate our presence, but we're every bit as invisible as the next guy.

"Both the CIA and FBI provide enticements to lure potential targets. Trust me when I say most criminals feel a need to boast.

We tempt these braggarts with communal platforms. As you might imagine, these felonious pools provide insight to various nefarious mindsets."

The CIA agent takes this opportunity to present further investigative evidence.

"Let's get back to the two developments we discussed earlier. Remember, both good and bad players populate the Dark Web. For better or worse, a digital wallet has been created called Bitcoin. Rumored to be the new-age currency, Bitcoin applies a cryptocurrency that contains a proof of work algorithm. It's popular, cheap, doesn't use the centralized banking system or any middleman. Most importantly, it's anonymous.

"In short, anyone who wants to purchase anything can do so without the transaction being linked to an individual identity. Why is this of interest? Early this morning, a signature-less whistleblower provided an encrypted message to the Central Intelligence Agency. It's Deep, not Dark Web-initiated, and potentially traceable. The dispatch afforded two words, 'Triad Realty.' Ladies and gentlemen, this is a treasure trove."

Utter exuberance tumbles off the SAC and her team.

"It appears that the Holy Grail has fallen into our laps. We can promptly investigate Triad's books with minimal difficulty via a court order."

The thrill of such a hit energizes Kingston.

"Triad Realty is owned and operated by Henry Wildbird in alliance with some very powerful silent partners. It appears Crebo Lund and his Lieutenant Governor act as Wildbird's associates. All three are directly tied to the Triad consortium."

The media center whirs with amazed disbelief. This partnership makes little sense. The political fallout is more than controversial, and the implications of this disclosure are extensive. The inner task force reels with a broad range of inferences.

Gig Robbins brings everyone back from the edge.

"We can't jump to conclusions. This investigation must move in unison to avoid false allegations and assumptions. The governor and his lieutenant are well-connected, upstanding public servants, with means. Unilateral action of any sort would be a grave blunder unless we have solid proof."

Beggs Cooper winces at the fact that the FBI/CIA workgroup made this discovery before he did.

"Kingston, has your team legitimated this revelation?"

The quick-minded FBI agent responds.

"Our link between Wildbird and the governor's office was delivered just moments ago."

The SAC's response confirms Apple's intuition that the man he saw in the hallway was the messenger.

"My team will immediately foster a credible computer-generated intelligence profile with complete analysis into Wildbird's affairs.

Once completed, we'll cross-check all overt references or identifiers that reflect links between the three men. A brief surface scan of Triad has already revealed some interesting material. This realty firm has a reputation for buying unique properties for little or nothing with robust revenue returns," announces the SAC.

"Umm," interrupts the National Guard's joint chief. "Before we go further, in the interests of transparency, I want to go on record that Greyson Chance and I have been close friends — no, more like family for many years. My parents took him in as a boy. As you might imagine, we have a history."

With a smirk, Kingston is quick to minimize this declaration.

"It can't run deeper than Mr. Gray's involvement with the Wildbird clan. His presence here is no less onerous. Let's continue and discuss these relationships later."

Kingston continues with the presentation as the IT specialist flashes multiple rundown of mug shots that consist of Henry Wildbird's known associates.

Chapter 53-

PERT

Gaining access to the String's PERT, or Program Evaluation and Review Technique, meeting isn't easy. The isolated location for this gathering is the primary challenge.

Today's fierce rain squall makes this remote terrain tricky. The joint chief arrives by distinctive means: She parachutes in. Her staff thinks this early afternoon skydive is part of the joint chief's recurrent survival training.

Gig Robbins, like the rest of the inner circle, has skin in the game. Her position as a National Guard insider means she's a valuable String affiliate. If Robbins's participation is discovered, it might be considered treasonous.

———◆———

No two people arrive at the PERT meeting at the same entrance or time. Today's gathering is climatic. The atmosphere is charged with emergent anticipation. All ten indispensable colleagues embrace one another as a family, anxious and elated. The culmination of this sacred environmental uprising has finally arrived.

This is the third command center activated since the Federal Bureau of Investigation's munitions team began their systematic probe of Bandy Hawk Plateau. The center's built-in redundancy is an added precaution. Dagmar Eiksund resourcefully implemented the backup control sites early on. His foresight has saved the String many times. Dagmar will always be recognized as the ultimate defender and fervent backbone of the operation.

Still, final programmatic objectives fall to the Wildbird clan. Much has changed since Hinmah shared her conceptualization of this aspiring ecological revolution. The String's original organizational structure was very basic, but time and complexity forced change. Hinmah and Delsin did their best to track its development, but time and events made that target frenetic. Frankly, the String's original five members were forced to find talented personnel to buttress expansion.

Naturally, employing and actuating risk in multiple arenas simultaneously required a greater range of genius.

Specified skills demanded various professionals with supplemental aptitudes. All these talents had to be orderly aligned to optimize the String's realization. This enlarged pool defines today's inner circle. As time passed, these new, dedicated associates seized control of the internal operation. In addition, a larger group of unwitting ancillary accomplices joined the cause.

Today, Dagmar's computer analysis actively predicts each supposition from start to finish. This state-of-the-art computer application safeguards personnel, resources, and events. Each campaign is administered and managed by Dagmar's brilliant self-designed algorithm. Regardless, even a phenom like Dagmar Eiksund would been considered criminal if he were known to collude with the Ink Prayer riders.

Over the past ten years, the String has charted forty-three milestones, correlating two hundred and eight activities, to include every purchase, scheme, deception, and raid. All these activities necessitate that crucial and subsidiary members are in place, on demand. Each of these principal characters steadily apply science and faith to codify this environmental revolution's workable dogma.

Incongruous to this claim is Sheriff Drake's involvement. His early warnings and diversional strategies act as last-ditch notice to survive pursuit.

Inside one of two intact cavern command centers, Dagmar begins.

"Congratulations to the entire inner circle of the String. We now arrive at PERT's summary evaluation. Before I turn things over to each section lead, I think it appropriate to honor the Wildbird family for the near completion of this miraculous ecological campaign. Tree and Isabelle Wildbird sing in the heavens."

Delsin's screams of elation echo off the stone walls of the cavern. At that same moment, Anne Creekbaum loses control of a champagne cork, barely missing Henry as it zings by in celebratory flight. Sheer elation breaks out. Relief is openly displayed on the gathered faces. After all, this treacherous mission, now nearly complete, has transpired without too serious a mishap.

Glasses brim with champagne, eyes overflow with tears, and a throng of emotion erupts within the cavern walls. This improbable cast briefly experiences profound happiness. The price of victory will be costly, but for this cause, all feel privileged to pay.

Henry, Mattie, and Hinmah can't help but yield to the merriment, surrounded by their jubilant extended family. They circle Delsin, wiping away the elderly giant's spent tears. Moments later, embarrassed by this singular show of emotion, he looks to his family and signs.

"Back to work."

The cavernous room erupts in more laughter. Hinmah calls her husband a tyrant. Delsin places the old medicine woman atop her computer desk, now acting as a throne. Entertained, everyone follows suit and finds his or her place at PERT's final assembly.

Chapter 54-
DEVIL'S IN THE DETAIL

Dagmar is all but dwarfed by Henry Wildbird in the middle of the command center. Jointly, the two men begin the meeting with a question-and-answer session.

Gig can no longer constrain her curiosity.

"In the past, I haven't asked. I mean, I understand that it's a need to know." The typically exacting joint chief finds herself looking for words. "I figured I wouldn't have to lie if I didn't really comprehend. But now we're so near an end, I'm more than curious about how we've managed to hide all this.

"The thing is, for more than a month, this country's greatest forensic accountants have been pounding away to discover a String end game. They reckoned the raids to be a distraction but can't find discriminatory pecuniary evidence."

Dagmar offers a prideful response.

"I've spent a great deal of time with Hinmah and Delsin to further excavate the principled reasons behind this cause."

Dagmar points to the enlarged map of the connective parcels that now comprise the new migratory thoroughfare that runs from

Montana's most northern border all the way to its most southern boundary.

The engineer looks to Hinmah.

"Time and again, you've asked me to minimize risk while pushing the chain of succession to its farthest limits. Early on, it was recognized that exposure was predictable. Your first act was to declare that all things be hidden in plain sight."

The engineer looks back towards Gig.

"Secure acquisitions have always been a Wildbird priority. As a result, many redundant precautions were applied. Recently, we flooded the state's financial accounting system with so many dead-end leads that forensic investigators faced millions of false indicators. Then we reversed our methodology by hiding capital in plain sight."

"So, you've basically produced so much statistical noise, all dead ends, that the exact means of our extractions are obscure?" asks the perplexed joint chief.

"In a word, yes, but it's slightly more complicated. Let's move forward with the PERT, and I think things will clarify themselves," declares Dagmar.

The engineer takes a bow, first in Hinmah's direction and then that of his section leads.

"It's no secret that Winslow and Anne are kindred spirits. The professor's three-dimensional imaging is muse to Winslow's non-detectable systems-implant. He linked this numerical entity to the state's SABHRS database. Let me turn things over to Winslow for further explanation."

The ex-CIA agent seated beside Creekbaum types a few commands into his own computer before standing. Uncomfortable, even before this family of friends, he holds a prop to enrich his explanation.

Creekbaum cajoles, "Keep it simple, stupid, so the rest of us can understand."

The modest man begins.

"There's not much to it, really. Money can't be missed if it isn't there in the first place."

The introvert presses on.

"After a good deal of thought to our primary objectives, I designed what I call a supernumerary bot."

The ex-DARPA displays the software's algorithm that he personally installed inside the state's database. Sharp then points out how Montana's Accounts Receivables consistently donates to the String.

"A bot conceals the statistical variance. Every time a technician records a receivable they inadvertently contribute to our cause. Each division, department, and business unit are indiscriminately tapped, in plain sight. At the end of the day, these figures accurately align because the missing money never hit the system."

Winslow waits for that to sink in.

"I got the idea from Creekbaum's hologram and a piece of software called Magic Leap. Its digital animation poses interference across real-world settings. I simply replaced the animation configuration with a financial cipher."

The CIA double-agent turns sheepish.

"Please know that it's with rectitude that I implement this machination. Once the String is complete, so, too, is this contrivance.

I recognize its potential harm and promise to destroy the bot from root to branch."

With that, the humble and very private man takes his seat. Everyone in the command center recognizes the sheer brilliance of this invention. The supernumerary bot has possibilities both wondrous and ruinous. Whole banking systems, governments, and industries critical to the world's economy could be raided as result of this impropriety.

A hush settles in as the inner circle tries to comprehend this revelation. Anxiety spreads over the room.

Henry mightily asserts, "If you want something you've never had, you must be willing to do something you've never done."

The cavern goes quiet. The inner circle pulls itself back from a place of trepidation as Dagmar moves the meeting forward.

"Let's get started with the PowerPoint."

The main flat screen displays the title *"GO BIG or GO to JAIL."*

Henry and Dagmar open with a description of each section leader's activity. One by one, the inner circle provides the group a full status report.

Robbins relays the progress made by the FBI and National Guard investigation. Tarkio conveys the FWP's legislative progress, astounding everyone with the improved financial news of the Ten Lee Ranch's bottom line. His personal ranch confirms that wildlife and landowners can maintain a cooperative synergy that perpetuates the String's usefulness.

Pete and Gracie Holdsclaw testify next. The two summarize raid activity and provide a Hester sisters status report.

Next, Pete describes how another of Winslow's technological inventions are up and running. Sensor collectors have been attached to a variety of herbivores inside the String's boundaries.

"Everything is collared, to include bull elk, rag horns, and spikes. It doesn't matter what type. We try to dart and tag anything that will provide a rapid digital alarm. These sensors warn us about increased carnivore activity. It's this proactive technology that gives us an extra jump on poachers."

Creekbaum beams in the background, full of pride for all she and her new family have contributed. Finally, Henry introduces the String's pecuniary specialist.

Marley Womack, poised and prepared, provides a financial account of the past decade's undertakings. She's comfortably absorbed in figures, sitting behind a computer console at the farthest edge of control. The tranquil accountant lights up several massive computer screens that display an overwhelming multitude of financial projections. Marley makes use of the state's GIS website. String volunteers have compiled a composite layover of both private and public lands that illustrate the new wildlife corridor. One by one, purchased parcels are illuminated. The String's campaign from north to south highlights inside one darkened swathe.

The control center erupts with bombastic cheer. The importance of this last darkened tract isn't lost on the group. It's the very place that Tree and Isabelle Wildbird fell victim to gun violence. In memoriam, it's lit last.

This spectacle is followed by a numerical depiction that reflects the String's earnings. Enormous sums of money, larger than ever thought possible, have been recorded. Methodically, Womack discloses the String's economic story. This improbable monetary tale is so unbelievable, it's hard for the PERT team to comprehend. The gentle accountant bounces charts, figures, and spreadsheets across at least ten of the fifteen oversized computer screens to back up her claims.

"Numbers don't lie," announces the demure CPA.

Womack follows with an up-to-date list of activities used to earn these significant funds. They include siphoned revenues from the lease of trust lands, dirty water storage from the Bakken oil field, even advertisement billboards on TLMD lands. There are stock option profits from the new drilling area, timber sales, grazing incomes, and forest improvement contract kickbacks. The dominant irony falls under retail sales from the numerous Ink Prayer rider paraphernalia, including coffee mugs, bumper stickers, wristbands, and masks. Gracie's marketing team exceeds all expectations.

As the presentation progresses, the comptroller speaks to the String's impeccable accounting procedures. She declares that all funds, honest and ill-begotten, are legitimately documented and properly reinvested. Astonished by Marley's fiscal flamboyance, the remainder of the inner circle sits in dazed reluctance, unwilling to disturb the incantation.

It isn't until Dagmar stands and thanks Marley for her concise explanation of the Ink Prayer's financial status that everyone realizes what has been achieved.

Chapter 55-
FORCE OF NATURE

H enry pushes on as Dagmar slips out of the cavern. "Although it's difficult to top this kind of financial news, we have much more to cover."

Just then, the old engineer returns.

"Dag, what the hell?" says a bewildered Winslow Sharp as he watches the team's PERT leader wheel in an old-fashioned chalkboard from the exterior tunnel.

Looking down his long Scandinavian nose atop wire-rimmed glasses, he begins.

"As you can see," Dagmar says, pointing with emphasis at the chalkboard, "the String has always worked to achieve multiple objectives. Our primary goal is complete, but ancillary is the exposure of 'bad' hunters who break the law, something no 'good' hunter can tolerate.

"Also, we continue our attempt to educate the general populace regarding FWP's internal financial fracas. Supplementary and alternate funds must be found to underwrite the agency. If hunting licenses are the sole sponsor, then that subsidy will have a disproportionate influence upon its overall philosophy. We must press the legislature to embrace this basic truth and make the appropriate changes.

"Now, let me draw your attention to the overhead screen." The cavern's lights are dimmed. The computer's soft whir fills the space as its occupants get comfortable at their personal posts.

Dagmar continues, "Please note the last pearl of land to be ceremoniously added to the String. It's the public land at White Earth. This parcel didn't cost one commercial dollar but is the most expensive."

Solemnly, the engineer submits, "This last piece of the String will be forever revered."

Henry smiles at Hinmah, and the venerated medicine woman feels a profound sense of relief. The dream has been realized.

"Today, we celebrate the implementation of a widely accepted scientific model. A significant prototype employing island biogeography is fully operational. Tarkio's Ten Lee Ranch is a real-life proven archetype," declares Eiksund.

The industrious engineer continues.

"This brings us to the Ink Prayer raids. We've had many conversations about the risks. The endless argument is that these perilous incursions overexpose the entire operation. I've cautioned the Wildbirds on more than one occasion about these superfluous missions."

Pete Holdsclaw's face whitens. The engineer ignores his emotional reaction.

"As a scientist, I grapple with any motive based on religious ethos. While I concede to the importance of sacred rituals, these raids remain a statistical liability."

The Holdsclaw clan remains stoically silent in the background, while Gracie throws an arm across Pete's shoulders in support.

Eiksund adds, "I need not remind you of the Hester twins' captivity. It was a wake-up call, not to mention an unexpected blow. The twins endured two weeks' jail time and have now been released on bond. According to Sheriff Drake, those two young women haven't divulged a single String secret.

"The Summer Olympics are just around the corner. To these brave individuals, I tip my hat," declares Dagmar. A round of applause echoes through the cavernous room.

"Look at this."

Eiksund holds up a box of Wheaties that displays the Hester twins regaled in shirts that read "Join the cause before there's no cause to join."

"This cereal box advertisement has garnered worldwide attention. The U.S. Olympic Committee provided the Hester sisters with the best legal representation money can buy. Being an Olympic competitor has its perks. This free public relations campaign depicts both riders and the Ink Prayer raids in a very favorable light.

"I need not remind you that these coups are the only uncontrolled segment of our operation. We gamble every time horse and rider go out. That's a statistical fact."

The sage engineer lets this last comment sit for a moment, staring directly at Pete Holdsclaw.

"Well, everyone recognizes my skepticism. Today, I concede I was wrong."

The cavern is filled with hysteria. Whistles, taunts, and laughter bounce off the rock walls. Gracie Holdsclaw turns her hat sideways and crosses her eyes as her lover Anne laughs hysterically. Pete Holdsclaw stands to genuflect in affirmation of the compliment.

Dagmar waves his arms to suppress the celebration. He points to the old-school technology.

"I'm sure you all recognize a chalkboard when you see one. This is my low-tech flag of surrender."

Another emotional explosion overtakes Dagmar, who nods to Henry. The young giant renders an oversized thumbs up. The usually shy Pete Holdsclaw jumps in.

"It turns out having the Hester twins behind bars is an asset, both from a public relations standpoint and on the retail side of things."

He liberally distributes T-shirts sporting the original logo followed by ball caps and coffee cups. The room's populace has all but forgotten about the incessant rain above ground. Eiksund calls for order with a thump against the chalkboard.

"We need to address the String's last and perhaps most delicate objective: a public demonstration of empirical evidence against Crebo Lund for the murders of Tree and Isabelle Wildbird. This must be unveiled at just the right moment, amid our final resolution."

The inner circle refocuses.

"How do we take down a murderer who, up until now, simply purchased the law? By the end of the month, Governor Crebo Lund will be behind bars. Gig will make a case to further demonstrate progress in this area."

Chapter 56-
TIME SEIZES ALL

Just as Gig stands, explosive water pierces the cavern walls. Electrical wiring, smoke, and steam fills the command center. Total collapse seems imminent. Bandy Hawk Mountain has suffered another major assault, but this time, the FBI has an active partner: the wet, raging storm.

An unconscious Hinmah bleeds from the forehead after a piece of flying debris blindsides her. The backup generator spills a faint red light over the entire cavern's interior.

Mattie Wildbird crawls to her grandmother's side. The lights short circuit and control goes dark. The excessive force hits the center's built-in generation system. It takes time, but Delsin locates Mattie and Hinmah in the darkness. He sweeps them both into his arms and physically carries them towards the emergency egress.

Just then, a second wave sweeps everyone off their feet as large pieces of rock fall from the cavern's ceiling. Three-quarters of the team have managed to escape the confines of the command center. An enormous boulder leaves the remainder trapped inside. Delsin, Mattie, and Hinmah are entombed within the interior of the cavern, just short of the exit.

Henry, Winslow, and Gig double back against the swell to reach their imprisoned loved ones.

Winslow grabs Gig. "You can't stay. Go and get help."

Dagmar and Creekbaum reappear. The professor reassures the determined rescuer.

"Gig, Winslow's right. Go, we'll get the rest out."

Gig realizes that time spent arguing is time lost extracting the trapped party. She hugs Anne and pushes herself through the waist-deep water rising fast inside the underground corridor.

The command's interior is saturated. The water level is at Mattie's shoulders. She's forced to swim in search of an outlet large enough for both Hinmah and Delsin to escape. Time is against them.

Outside the cavern, Henry has discovered a gap, roughly twelve by eighteen inches, a full body length from the interior of the cavern. He shouts over the sound of rushing water in hopes that his family is still alive. Mattie hears Henry and follows his voice to the fissure. Delsin pulls Hinmah to a nearby boulder. Thankful for his tremendous strength, Mattie momentarily exchanges places with her grandfather to hold Hinmah's head above water.

The cave is completely without power now, but the narrow fissure provides a ray of light. Delsin climbs the obstruction and attempts to enlarge the gap. Henry uses hand signs to encourage Delsin to work hard and fast, but the old giant can't enlarge the hole to encompass his bulk.

Now only feet remain between the cavern ceiling and the water table. Mattie thrashes to keep her grandmother's face above the surface. The giant signals for Mattie to pull Hinmah backward into the breach. A tearful granddaughter hugs Delsin as he straps the belt from his pants around Hinmah's shoulder blade for a tight hold.

Once again, the cavern walls shake. Another round of rapidly increasing water rushes in, but this time, it works in Delsin's favor. He launches Mattie and Hinmah through the fissure. Henry grabs the two small women from the opposite direction. There is no time to lament. Delsin is close to being swallowed by water and looks for another exit.

Dagmar, Creekbaum, and Mattie haul the unconscious Hinmah outside Bandy Hawk's interior. Henry and Pete stay behind in search of an alternate, larger access to the collapsed command center.

Chapter 57-
SHEER TERROR

Gig never cries, reasons Greyson, as he runs at full speed down the hallway of the armory and then bursts unannounced into Regal Markay's office.

"You have to stop the blasting; it may already be too late," sputters the typically calm lieutenant governor.

The adjutant general wheels his office chair around to find Greyson Chance in an unusual state. With effort, the old man scrambles by Greyson and shuts the door after a quick look down the hall.

"What the hell is going on?" demands Markay.

Rattled, Greyson cuts to the chase.

"You must have the FBI stand down. Halt the detonations. There are people inside the Bandy Hawk caverns," cries the lieutenant governor.

"How's that even possible? It's a crime scene," responds the general.

Greyson makes himself slow down.

"I don't have time to explain. Please, just call them off."

Markay picks up the phone.

"Get me in touch with Joyce Kingston immediately. Ring back as soon as you get through," orders Markay as he observes the visibly distraught Chance.

"Lad, when exactly are you going to tell me what's going on?" asks the sympathetic father figure.

Saddened by circumstances, Greyson Chance is more than prepared to confess. He has carried this shame far too long.

"General, sir, what we have here is a brain grenade."

Just then the phone rings.

"Ms. Kingston, I need you to stop what you're doing immediately. Yes, yes, I understand. So, the detonation caused severe flooding? Yes, I see. I appreciate that. Thank you, Ms. Kingston."

Markay turns toward the increasingly distressed Chance.

"It appears that things have taken a dangerous turn, Greyson. You need to start explaining yourself. How is it, exactly, that you know people are inside that cavern?"

Chance grabs the Commander.

"Please, General, I need to know if anyone is hurt."

Regal Markay stiffens.

"Son, what have you gotten yourself into?"

The adjutant general isn't going to let his captain off that easily.

Greyson slumps into a nearby chair.

"Innocent people have paid dearly for something that deeply shames me. I've spent the last decade trying to make amends for my weakness, but with each attempt to restrain this crisis, it proliferates. If that isn't bad enough, I've involved someone we both love and respect."

Markay looks squarely into his most trusted captain's eyes and is on the intercom in seconds.

"Get Gig in here right now," barks the general.

"The helicopter is inbound," responds the aide.

"How far out are they? How many injured? Never mind; I'm on my way to the medical center now."

Markay slams the phone down atop the intercom and points to Chance.

"Get your butt out of that chair, mister, and follow me."

The two men move through the armory's hallway at a clip hard to imagine, given the general's undersized gait. Markay's resolute cadence somehow bolsters Greyson as he falls in line. In short order, they're off to what Chance hopes is the final act of this Bandy Hawk nightmare.

The car provides security to its' confessor.

"Hell, where do I even start?"

Greyson rubs his chin and passes his ring hand through disheveled hair, looking for the right words to explain the unexplainable.

Markay drives as Chance reaches back into his past.

"It's been nearly a decade since that cake eater Crebo Lund approached me about his political ticket. That jerk declared that he needed a man like me to offset his flamboyant ambitions."

Markay laughs.

"That's a polite way of putting it."

A sullen Chance rolls his eyes before going on about how he had met Crebo Lund.

"In some sick way, I think that belligerent ass needs conflict. Anyway, I figured I'd seen the last of that condescending bastard after graduating from Yale. He was just a bad memory."

Chance takes a moment to reflect.

"Call it fate or whatever, but Montana's too small a place to hide from a man's own destiny."

The drive to the hospital takes less than fifteen minutes. Markay parks off-campus, forcing the decorated National Guard captain to finish his story. The two men drift along the grassy ridge used by hospital workers to reclaim a little sanity during breaks. The autumn day and its gentle warmth sooth both men as they look out over the scenic valley, trying to make sense of things.

Chance gulps for air.

"Once I joined the Army, life seemed to come together."

The Adjutant General waits a moment before asking.

"Did you meet Danielle at grad school?"

Chance nods as the two men plod towards the front entrance of the hospital.

"My wife is brilliant, and I love her beyond words, but she's driven. When Crebo Lund offered me a spot on the ticket, Danny wanted it. Hell, she needed it. I should have put a stop to it right then. I knew that son of a bitch was just using both of us."

Greyson swallows hard before the next declaration.

"It took me six years to get over my first love."

Regal Markay asks the unbearable.

"Did Gig end things, or did you?"

"She did, sir."

Another painful memory passes over Chance's face.

"Is our friendship really that problematic?"

"Well, I believe she'd do just about anything for you, and to be honest, my best guess is that she's done just that," declares the intimidating officer.

Chance stops to fully confess.

"I wish that were the weakest part of my character, sir, but it gets worse."

Two paces ahead, a red-faced Markay reels around before he checks his temper.

"That woman is the finest officer I've ever had the privilege to serve with. To be frank, she's like a daughter to me. If you've done anything that will harm her or her career—" Markay pulls back.

Chance knows he has this coming.

"Yes, sir, I understand. Getting Gig involved is a huge regret; trust me when I tell you it's one of my lesser sins.

In all honesty, I never intended to entangle her in this mess. I just needed a friend — you know, a sounding board, so I could figure a way out."

Both men work to curtail their emotions before Chance continues.

"I'm trapped, General, and the only way to make amends is to set things right with all those I've harmed. I played a role in an incident at Bandy Hawk Plateau years ago. It has permanently altered life for the Wildbird clan.

"As far as Gig is concerned, she has her own reasons for what she's done. Some of her intentions lay in a shared philosophy, but she had nothing to do with the Bandy Hawk murders. That lands squarely at my feet."

Regal Markay looks past the man into the massive Montana sky. He takes a moment to decide.

"Okay, Chance, the National Guard has hauled a man in from Bandy Hawk. You mentioned the Wildbird family. Delsin Wildbird was nearly overwhelmed by water in an underground cavern. It appears his son Henry worked with several others to free the elder gentleman from a flooded area due to an exterior explosion detonated by Kingston's munitions team.

For the life of me, I don't understand why all these people were there to begin with. I'm going to need some quick answers if we'll salvage anything from this mess."

A tearful Greyson Chance interrupts.

"Delsin's alive, then. Thank God."

Chance swoops in unexpectedly. The general finds himself fully embraced by an incredibly relieved Greyson Chance. This physical demonstration softens the old man's resolve, and he gives Chance a pat on the back.

"All right, son, it's not a habit of mine to leave any man behind. Let's get things back in order. Start from the beginning, and don't leave anything out."

Chapter 58-
A LIST OF CONTRITION

"Thank you for coming by again. Please come in. You know the way. Get comfortable," offers the tribal leader.

The medicine woman looks spent and acts oddly bewildered. There is a bandage peeking out from underneath Hinmah's hairline. She and her guest settle in. Sam takes notice of the old woman's forehead. With little formality, Hinmah pours tea and begins without ceremony.

"Race relations is a toilsome mess steeped in a history that spans the spectrum of humankind's existence."

Hinmah looks out on the lake, searching for something lost.

"I won't pretend that problems don't exist among my tribe, its people, or the white man, but that isn't what I've committed my life's work to."

More than a little unnerved by Hinmah's emotional state, Sam backs up.

"Please stop! I was told that Mattie would be here."

Hinmah goes on as if in an altered state.

"I sent her away. What I'm about to say might take some time. I hope I haven't pulled you away from anything important."

The Seeker quickly glances around the room. It's apparent that Hinmah has long since made the necessary preparations for this notable declaration. She's fully primed to show the huntress enough recorded evidence to resolve the undercover agent's case. The table is set with bread for the breaking, and a written confession lies atop the credenza.

The perceptive DOI undercover agent sternly declares, "Let me make it clear, I'm in no position to make promises. Before we go forward, I'll need to read you your rights."

"Child, please do what you must. I'll wait."

A more focused and serene Hinmah sips her tea as Sam completes the legal directives.

"Good, now, if you're comfortable, we can both seek a peaceful conclusion to Finch888," smiles the tribal leader.

Sam flushes with the realization that Hinmah knows the assigned case name and number of the classified investigation. Everyone was forewarned with the threat of imprisonment for leaking information. So much for security clearances. Sam feels exposed. She senses the medicine woman knows more about the investigation than she knows about the String.

Oddly self-conscious, Cherchez politely suggests, "Please, go on."

The tribal leader summons the courage to finish what she started so long ago. Now in full control, Hinmah reminds her guest of their previous visit.

"You're a bright woman and formidable opponent. Thus far, you're the only one to ask the right question, and this from the beginning.

"My son and daughter-in-law's premature deaths led me to seek a distinct purpose. Murder is a violent act; its deepest strains are vehemently connected to power. You made it clear that you planned to start your investigation with the Bandy Hawk murders. I'm anxious to hear your interpretation of the crime scene."

The Seeker slowly sets the teacup down. She looks straight at Hinmah with pure compassion but says nothing. Sam cannot afford to give this cunning individual an edge, no matter her fundamental benevolence.

The medicine woman reflects.

"I suppose their deaths somehow make for vengeful ambition, a minor variation of power. Outsiders will come to see the raids as that form of vengeance, but I'm too old now, too tired, to defend myself against such absurdity.

With age, one realizes that the onus for justice is heavy. Collectively, humankind has always promised to fulfill this responsibility, but more times than not, it's never achieved.

"I've tried to make sense of my son and daughter-in-law's deaths. None can be found. People often tell me that it took courage to survive such malevolence, but the truth is we had no choice.

"Our heritage made that leap easier. The Ink Prayer's spiritual beliefs are merely an extension of all native people's profound faith that every living creature is family, a part of the whole, joined in the circle of life."

The sun is at its crest now. Shadows dance off the canyon walls, reflecting lake waters imprisoned by rocky shoals. A glimpse of darkness creeps over the coulee's edge. Hinmah acts as a centurion in this space and time. After a considered moment, she goes on.

"Today, the Ink Prayer people's sacred conviction is wedded to science. This natural belief is incalculably relevant to the future existence of all living beings.

"Consider humankind's present course. We, the Ink Prayer, may alter or at least slow down the impending doom. I cannot think of a greater goal or more significant contribution.

"If the United States government deems our work terrorism, I cannot change its mind. What happened to my ancestors proves this point. We are and have always been ecological guardians."

The old woman stirs in her rocking chair and circles back to her original thought.

"Perhaps you've seen the photo of the five Native American chiefs sitting stoically before the white man's camera? Red Dog, Little Dog, Little Wound, Red Cloud, and American Horse are armed with nothing more than peace pipes. The caption reads '*Homeland Security since 1492.*' It's good to have a sense of humor, but there's a curious truth in the description."

Hinmah tops off Sam's tea before adding more to her own. Sam recognizes the incongruity of this moment, pleasantly laced in politeness. Out of deference, she doesn't interrupt.

"Working with and around state government affords the String the best possible outcome. Believe it or not, Crebo Lund's chaotic leadership has augmented our success.

"I pray each day the universe protects everyone involved on both sides of this heated dispute. In the end, I believe in this cause, but please understand that, as the source of the String, I'm wholly responsible for its aftermath.

"It's an honor to forfeit myself. The enforceable rules of justice must be followed. I'm happy to pay for any trust betrayed. This is of no consequence. As a tribal medicine woman, I have a moral obligation as a steward of these lands and inhabitants. There are worse things than imprisonment or death. One must live with purpose!

"Perhaps the Great White Father will see value in the String and leave it intact, regardless of the proscribed means harnessed to acquire each pearl of land that comprise the wildlife corridor."

The admission stuns Sam. The Seeker is forced to recognize an illegal land grab. Not one soul working the civil-military investigation has the slightest idea that such a crime has been perpetrated. Sam's admiration is amplified. The medicine woman and her team have effectively hidden this ecological rebellion from the entire United States government.

Hinmah's confession is made from a place deep within, and so is Sam's response.

"I'm sorry for the loss of your only son and his wife."

The tribal leader waves this off to circumvent all she feels. With a mighty effort, she moves on.

"I've reaped the rewards of great thought borne of this society. We all benefit from the free doctrine afforded by our Constitution.

"Early in its history, the United States government set aside land in every township across its vast countryside. This generous exploit was referred to as the General Land Ordinance of 1785. It granted that every sixteenth and thirty-sixth section of a township is set aside to fund education. Renewable and non-renewable resources from these properties still provide revenues and are overseen by a program called the Department of Natural Resources Trust Land Management.

"Properly administered, these public lands and their accompanying natural resources are invaluable to urban and rural schools.

The String takes advantage of these reserves and builds on them. Of course, we have applied novel approaches that might seem ultra-progressive or even heavy-handed to many.

"Our need to finance the String was immediate. With thoughtful preparation, a community and its government can indeed accomplish many wondrous things. Determined people in critical positions can alter outcomes. I admit that many of our methods are atypical, but cosmic thought rarely fits in a box. The inner circle of the String has worked for over a decade to create a dedicated migration structure to be used by all wildlife.

"This aspiration might be viewed as imprudent — no, that's too polite… as madness. I've never been accused of pragmatism. So, let this foolhardy delusion fall squarely on my shoulders. You'll find my confession on the credenza."

The old woman points across the room, now exhausted by the truth, but the whole of this revelation has lifted a burden from Hinmah's shoulders. She sits content across from the Seeker with vibrant eyes, full of integrity.

Sam stays silent for a time to consider the judiciousness of the tribal woman's confession. She discreetly thanks her host for the tea and glances sideways at the confession.

Humbled by the tribal leader's presence, the Seeker makes her determination, stands, and casually stretches before she departs. The medicine woman's extensive list of contrition is left to sit on the credenza.

Chapter 59-
WILDBIRD CRAZE

The Wildbirds' dark history devours Sam as she makes her way back down the craggy trail. A murky, unintelligible past has cast its spell on this investigation. Hinmah's reluctance to trust white justice reflects a past and present Native American narrative. Between historical injustice and Delsin's injury, it has become too much. Add to this the power players behind the infamous Bandy Hawk murders, and one can understand the tribal leader's need to protect what family remains.

Intensely enveloped in the Bandy Hawk incident, Sam churns through garbled, shadowy clues as she bunches her flaxen hair into a ponytail and tops it off with her favorite ball cap. With each lanky stride, she gobbles the rock-laden path purposefully.

Azure skies fall victim to evening's firmament. The roving shadows from wind-blown trees stalk the undercover agent, all vying for attention. As incremental darkness overtakes the trail, the Seeker reminds herself that professional apathy has never found standing in any prior investigation. Does this case require a special dispensation?

From somewhere behind her, a tiny misstep snaps the Seeker from her rumination. The trained ears of a well-seasoned huntress warn of another's presence. Now, the shadows have someone to occupy them.

Mattie's long black hair glides behind a gap in the nearby boulders. Sam stops. Is it just the shadowy light, or does the agent need to converse with a night ghost in Mattie Wildbird's visage? She shakes off the apparition.

The Seeker's probe into the Bandy Hawk murders reconvenes, from beginning to end. The investigation is clean to the point of perfection. The evidence is indisputable. Beggs's research team has surveyed the crime scene and created computerized re-enactments. All the evidence substantiates the investigator's findings, even the ballistics report.

An intentional bird-like warble reverberates, but this time, the Seeker wholly ignores the ghostly jab.

Both Sam and Cooper concur that a powerful political presence applied full-scale damage control to save reputations, perhaps even to cover up the truth. There's more to this story; the Seeker feels it. Mattie's missing arm. Lund's discomfort in the presence of any member of the Wildbird clan. All are signs of something larger.

An important piece of evidence is missing. Mattie Wildbird's account of her parent's death. The sheriff indicates the twins were present on this family outing. They left the immediate area on foot at the time of the shootings.

Sam hears another sweet reverberation but again dismisses it, keeping her stride consistent.

When the tribal police confront Hinmah shortly after the murders, she testifies that her grandchildren had not witnessed anything. Henry Wildbird confirms this statement. Mattie is allegedly too ill and disturbed by the loss of her parents to contribute anything of value. Mattie's missing testimony and arm can be seen as nothing less than a base misgiving.

It appears the shooter's confession suspends what could have become a more exhaustive inquiry, coupled with the strategic consideration given those people of influence.

Crebo Lund is cause for wariness. His testimony is unctuous and slick, just like the governor himself. Greyson Chance is uninvolved. This piques the Seeker's interest. The lieutenant governor's rectitude is demonstrable. Beggs's research corroborates Sam's sense that Chance is authentic but somehow ensnared.

In the end, the shooter's declaration in combination with the Wildbirds' mistrust of the white man's justice makes it all too neat and easy to dismiss further investigation.

Sam isn't about to share her suspicions or feelings with any member of the Wildbird family. Historic motives play a significant role in the Seeker's present case. Beyond that, she senses a deeper rationale. Beggs shares this analysis, yet until Hinmah's confession, the wildlife corridor hadn't been unearthed.

The capture of the riders is primary, but that's not the only consideration. How is that possible that the land grab went undetected given each investigative entity's technological superiority. It isn't until Hinmah explains the String's purpose that Sam recognizes the fiscal implications. Beggs will freak out when he realizes that the inner circle hoodwinked the government's best forensic accountants, never mind multiple private-sector software gurus.

Given all the distractions, Sam still thinks the Bandy Hawk cold case will resolve Finch888. She has no interest in Hinmah's confession. No, the Seeker senses a much larger target for her investigation — one both politically and financially conspicuous.

Chapter 60

UPSIDE DOWN

S am arrives at the trailhead where the Jeep is parked. It's there, but it now hangs suspended in the forest canopy some twenty feet high, upside down, with the doors wide open. This amazing feat is made even more so by sheer imagination. The Seeker breaks out into laughter.

Sam pulls her smartphone from a small backpack.

"Beggs, I need a ride. No, I haven't destroyed another rig; at least, I think it still works. I can't say for sure."

"Why?" asks the IT specialist.

"Because it's upside down hanging from a tree, that's why. No, I didn't put it there. Dammit, Beggs, just come and pick me up!"

Still amused, Sam hangs up, gathering her rain slicker and personal gear from beneath the dangling vehicle, all the while scanning the darkened forest.

"That's going to be hard to explain, never mind drive," remarks a delighted Mattie Wildbird.

The Seeker wheels around just as the forest ghost evaporates.

"I know you've been following me, chantonner. You sang like a bird all the way down the mountain. Thank you for the company."

Mattie stands fifteen feet to the south of Sam.

"I wouldn't want you to feel alone on my mountain." Again, she evaporates into the night.

Now, from behind: "I should thank you. At least you read Hinmah her rights," states the enraged night ghost.

Sam walks in the opposite direction.

"You must know by now that I'm pursuing something larger. There's no doubt that your grandmother has an honorable agenda. My hunt is for justice."

As a distraction, the lights and radio blare from the aerial Jeep. Further up the hill, as if invited, Mattie dashes away. Magnetic, the chase so appeals to Sam, she cannot keep herself from tracking the prey. The Seeker recognizes Mattie has an advantage, but this is of little significance.

She shouts to the wind, "This forest may belong to you, but I'll give chase until we both drop."

Unreservedly, challenged, the Seeker runs at full speed towards the last place her target vanished. Mattie is aware that the control center personnel voyeuristically hover over the scene. The earpiece she uses to communicate finds its way inside her jacket. The small camera used to support her escapes goes black. Mattie wants this game played without interference.

It's late. Inside control, Creekbaum takes the readers from atop her head and squints at the computer screen, all the while yelling at Gracie.

"Ah, crap, your girl's gone off the grid. Wake Dagmar. He's going to shit nickels once he finds Mattie has gone rogue."

Straightaway, the old engineer finds his way into the cavern. Drenched in the blue glow of one of the remaining Bandy Hawk Mountain command centers, Dagmar can't believe his eyes.

The National Guard and FBI munitions specialist have taken a heavy toll on the caverns. Bandy Hawk Mountain and its occupants are once again in battle mode. Gracie Holdsclaw smiles with pride.

"Seems our little bird wants to handle things on her own."

Creekbaum signals Sharp.

"Light them up, Winslow. This will be a hell of a show."

"Which route?" asks Sharp, as he taps several commands into his console to activate every camera he can near Mattie's last known location.

"All of them!" hollers a frantic Creekbaum. "I have no idea what this woman's intentions are, never mind the direction she's headed."

Gracie places a calming touch on Anne's shoulder.

"Hinmah's granddaughter has a plan. You must learn to trust her, just as you do the cause."

"I believe you, but it's obvious your friend is more than upset," smiles Anne as she lays an aged hand atop Gracie's.

Chapter 61-
EVEN DRAW

Mattie doubles back to sit just below Sam, who has stopped to listen for clues. Both women are drenched from the chase and struggle to quiet their heavy breathing.

The night's stars have all blown out, covered by frost-lined clouds and inclement weather. Mattie throws a stone into a nearby creek, moving closer to Sam. The huntress doesn't flinch or shift position. Instead, utterly motionless, Sam wills her quarry closer. The Seeker can sense Mattie but doesn't shy away. Instead, she tries to subdue the wild bird perched just outside her reach.

Fetid odors permeate the air. This one moment reels with an intense vibrancy linked to mesmeric femininity. Evenly matched, the two women have challenged one another beyond limits. Sam takes a moment to appreciate her opponent's skills before the next surge.

———•◆•———

The hypnotic forest swells with shadows. The chase deepens as a very determined contest unfurls. Beggs tried multiple times to contact Sam. At some point, he felt something had gone seriously wrong. He called the joint chief. Straightaway, Robbins makes air surveillance available, but not without briefing Greyson Chance about this latest incident.

Below, the Seeker and her prey dart in and out of the copter's illuminating beam until the huntress and hunted disappear entirely. The metal bird searches the forest floor, crisscrossing the arena where both stalker and stalked have gone underground. Robbins's airborne crew brawls against the wind just above the terrestrial skirmish. Robbins decides things have gone too far and determines to put boots on the ground before Mattie does something she cannot reverse.

———————◆————————

Surveillance is optimized with Winslow at the helm. Dagmar is glued to every move Mattie makes.

"Why doesn't she use our eyes? We can help her escape."

The engineer is acutely aware that a National Guard helicopter is in pursuit. Dagmar doesn't understand Mattie's motivation.

"Does anyone know what's going on? And just where the hell is Henry?" Wheeling around in search of answers, he looks to Sharp and Creekbaum.

To release tension, Anne replies, "If the ex-CIA guy doesn't know, I certainly don't!"

Just then, a human flash followed by a second streak wisps by camera 33p, positioned before a remote and dangerous cavern entrance known for its bad air.

"What's Henry doing out there?" asks Creekbaum.

Dagmar squints at the screen's camera image, now fully engulfed by Henry Wildbird in all his size.

"Sharp, can we look at this situation from a different angle?"

With a few adjustments, Dagmar watches Henry stealing into the darkness, carrying a limp body with long blonde hair. Creekbaum leaps to her feet.

"Crap, is that who I think it is?"

All that's left behind is a Montana State University baseball cap.

Chapter 62-
FORTUITOUS AND LUSH

Strident argument forces itself into Sam's consciousness, but she can't quite connect with reality. A female voice fueled by fury fades in and out. Secrets with consequences, roguish partnerships, and money laundering subliminally invade her subconscious. This vivid rendition of outrage overcomes her sleepiness.

Sam doesn't convulse or gasp. She physically stirs to the dark depths of Henry Wildbird's eyes. The quarrel is over. Henry holds her in his arms, where she's swallowed by his pronounced size, cradled tenderly against his stately chest. The Seeker wonders momentarily at the autumn red flecks in Henry's dark black hair before deciding it's Tree and Isabelle's Irish-Ink Prayer fusion.

Fresh air brings Sam back softly without a struggle. Now, it's Henry's careful attentiveness that immobilizes. Time doesn't stop but, rather, sojourns. She thinks, *why squander this opportunity?* Instead, the Seeker dwells inside this intimate space, appraising its worth.

The night, as always, becomes victim to the early break of day. The clock demands an explanation as morning light streams in from all sides. Sam regrettably abandons the lush comfort of Henry's arms. She tries her legs, looks around, and realizes she's in an unusual place.

The tree house is overgrown, veiled beneath the canopy of a giant evergreen forest. The shrouded dwelling matches Henry: It's a place of size and sturdy solitude. The giant watches Samantha Cherchez intently, but without sound. She slides her sensually elongated fingers over the smoothly lacquered woodwork, her eyes wide in admiration and wonder.

The multiple-room dwelling with a flow-through kitchen has an open floor plan studded with intricate animal carvings: Each base-relief is rich with detail. The Seeker is enthralled with the tree house and its serenity.

The giant detects a small quiver emanating from his pocket. He excuses himself and answers the cell phone. Sam pretends indifference but is grateful for a means of communication. When Henry returns, he offers her the phone.

"People are worried."

With that, the giant leaves Sam to make a call. She dials Beggs. The Seeker's eyes sweep the room to see if she is alone.

"Hey, I need to touch base. Yes, I'm fine. No, please call off the search. I saw the helicopter tracking me, but I had my hands full. No, nobody is in custody. No… No, everything is fine; I simply couldn't get word to you until now. I lost my cell during the chase. No, I can't talk now, but don't worry about me."

With little ceremony, Sam hangs up and finds Henry in the kitchen, busy with breakfast. She hands him his cell.

"Can you tell me how I got here?"

"Please sit and have something to eat. You must be hungry. I know from experience that my sister is a relentless competitor," sympathizes Henry. "Even after all these years, she still manages to outsmart me."

The Seeker frowns. Henry offers Sam a seat inside a snug nook. It's a special place, overlooking a dense grove, presently inhabited by squirrels busy at play. There's no sense of constraint in the small booth beside Henry: rather, an intimacy. Such confines typically set off five-alarm bells, but Samantha Cherchez is surprisingly at ease. Her senses betray. This proximity to the very man she intends to bring to justice is too great a compulsion.

Sam works hard to concentrate.

"Mattie didn't outsmart me. I was outmaneuvered, but only because this is her home court."

Henry spoons Sam a large helping of fresh berries and then offers his guest bagels with cream cheese, hot coffee, and scrambled eggs with turkey sausage and green peppers.

"Fair enough," concedes Henry. "I would imagine if Mattie had been in the middle of the Chic Chocs, things might have turned out differently. You two are evenly matched. Just don't tell her I said so," smiles the handsome villain.

Ravenous, the Seeker grudgingly gives into her seductive surroundings and all its trappings. She eats. The squirrels have visitors. Twin wapiti calves are intrigued with a nearby rabbit basking in the grove's liberal morning sun. Sam has never seen a rabbit so content, stretching on a rock, belly length, languid. The curious young elk are captivated, and so is Sam.

"It's a ritual," confides Henry.

"That rabbit beguiles anyone with a moment to spare. I've learned much as a spectator here in this peaceful glen. If I'm patient enough, these creatures teach me what is to be made whole."

Sam devours the bagel and berries without interruption. Nature's spectacle provides everything this insulated sanctuary needs to feel inclusive. She takes in Henry's proclamation. It's a rare and alluring perspective. She decides to like this man. He is rich and yet doesn't care for money, powerful but cautious with clout, reliable, yet tractable, and very attractive.

Chapter 63-

ALLURE

Cherchez yields to Henry's magnetism, seizing the moment.

"I'm sorry I've drooled on your shirt." She attempts to brush the off-color mark from Henry's blue plaid flannel. Her hand swipes his chest, and he pulls her in. Their lips meet in a slow but sustained, gentle synchronicity. Henry draws Sam closer as their tongues explore and caress one another. Waves of hunger give way to a tantalizing receptiveness as they kiss. She moans softly and gasps for air.

Henry clears the table in one sweep and lifts her on the flat surface. The brawl to disrobe becomes their latest contest. Of course, Sam wins. Unclothed, she sits comfortably, nude before the giant. Henry is overcome by her radiance. She poses as if sitting for a portrait. Henry's passion is transformed. It's this woman's self-possession that stirs.

Hungrily, they recognize that the splendor of this experience can never be repeated. Henry liberates himself as he lures the Seeker to him. The freedom of his delivery binds the two in a way not owned. It's more than a proclamation of their union; it's a declaration of a combined veneration.

Sam rises and falls in nascent rhythm, bending and rotating, spiraling and coiling, all to consume Henry completely. A half hour later, the two find themselves spent. Henry picks berries from Sam's opulent mane.

"This doesn't change anything," declares the Seeker.

The giant's fingertips lightly trace his lover's hairline, brushing against her furrowed brow. The Seeker recaps the chase.

"Correct me if I'm wrong, but I think your sister tried to kill me last night."

This idea sits between them for a moment before they chuckle openly.

"I'd say this brings a whole new meaning to the notion that my sister doesn't like my girlfriend," remarks Henry.

Both lovers laugh to the point of tears. Sam gathers her belongings, but her deep guffaws turn into a loud snort. This makes both she and Henry stop short, then fall deeper into their expressed amusement. Struggling to dress between belly laughs, the Seeker can only manage to administer two legs into one pant hole.

"It's pretty obvious that I've enjoyed this distraction," shares Sam, "but eventually, we must go back."

Ever the hero, Henry leaps into action. He assists his new lover's endeavor to maintain her balance, but this just makes them both fall into a new round of hilarity. So, the giant does what comes naturally. He embraces his lover, whispering, "I know that your pragmatism demands a resolution. I promise you'll have it soon."

Sam looks at Henry solemnly and then pushes herself from the giant's embrace.

"We need to get back."

The lovers walk in silence through the glen, over a small ridge. Sam's Jeep waits no more than a quarter of a mile from the treehouse. It sits upright, tidy, and fully intact, with the fuel topped off.

She smiles at the giant.

"I won't even ask."

Henry opens her driver's-side door.

"Good."

Sam buckles up and announces, "The String, it makes sense. I mean, it's more than significant. You should know, your grand-mother told me everything. That's why Mattie's so upset. She thinks I took Hinmah's written confession. I didn't."

The giant smiles a grateful confirmation. Sam moves closer to him and softly pleads her case.

"The thing is, I sense that a lot of this can be fixed." Henry falls deeper into silence, so Sam presses her argument forward.

"It doesn't take much imagination to see you mean to settle an old score. The question is, how?"

The giant's eyes shift ever so slightly to hide his conviction. Sam presses, "At least trust me enough to talk about your parents' murder!"

Deeply pained by the Seeker's interrogation, Henry doesn't reply. He merely kisses Sam's palm and turns to head back towards his tree house. Sam starts the engine and then shouts over the clatter.

"Vengeance is a dangerous quest, especially when the target of reprisal is Montana's governor. Let me handle things going forward, Henry, please."

The giant's long strides have taken him back atop the ridge. He turns to wave goodbye before disappearing. The sound of the Jeep as it heads south comforts him. For the first time since he pledged himself to the String, he staggers under its weight.

Triad Realty is just one reason he predicts an impending visit from his grandmother and twin sister. Things seem to be spinning out of control, and Henry's budding relationship with Samantha Cherchez will only confirm his family's fears. The pending and extremely awkward conversation is long overdue. Hinmah's initial trepidation about Triad Realty can be assuaged, but Mattie's fury will be difficult to overcome. She's her grandmother's great protector, and there's no doubt that Samantha Cherchez means business.

Henry anticipates the two women's arrival. This is his one chance to rebuild enough trust to finish off Bandy Hawk's murderous affair. He'll spend the next several hours bolstering the alliance needed to annihilate Governor Crebo Lund once and for all.

Chapter 64-
SUPER MOON CELEBRATION

This midnight revelry coincides with the Super Moon. Twinkling with a luminous glow, the Roe River's archetypal winds are held in a trance.

More than a hundred human shadows undulate down hillsides as others glide atop water like swallows in flight. Some arrive by feted horse; others hike into the shores of this sacred place, just as Hinmah's ancestors have for hundreds of years.

Dressed in fluorescent clothing, the String's volunteers aptly display their pride. Each pre-designated color depicts a skillset. They advertise the wearer's overall function within the campaign. Sam the Seeker's informant bears the lurid green worn by the techno crowd. Betty, like her cohorts, sports the shirt with dignity and is central to the celebration's activity.

From above, the Seeker edges in aboard one of the National Guard's soundless black helicopters. It provides the perfect perch to document the ceremony. Sam cannot help but feel admiration for the people gathering below. Their service to the String exposes each to a tentative fate. All could potentially lose jobs and face imprisonment. But for them, like so many others, this night celebrates a hard-earned state of grace, an accomplishment larger than one's self.

Betty acts as the perfect geek plant. Finch888 has been the most brutal and emotional case she has endured as a DOI agent to date. Still, she delivered critical clues promptly. Without doubt, this information furthered the ongoing investigation. Betty's undercover cohorts learned of the Super Moon ceremony via Pinterest, the same social media applied earlier to establish the Kumba-Cooper liaison.

The Seeker senses her friend's cues come from a mixed bag of allegiances. Fitted with a microphone and earpiece, Sweet Brown Betty stands in a place of privilege. At the center of this fluid activity, the DOI eavesdropper deciphers the purpose and meaning of each stage of the gathering with stilted narration. Oddly, Betty's voice is filled with a demonstrable measure of pride. The Seeker is caught off guard by her associate's trembling voice, thick with gratification.

While troubled, Sam has little time to reflect as the action intensifies. The whole of the congregation packs tightly upon itself, crushing inward to form a circle.

Inside the helicopter, Sam instructs the film and audio technicians to closely record as many faces as possible. "Please remember, the videotape will act as evidence."

Betty's audio testimony, presently muffled by the sheer proximity of those assembled, will act as corroboration. The Seeker gazes in amazement as the splendid Super Moon reveals itself.

In the center of the gathering stands the young giant Henry Wildbird. He proudly introduces his brother Apple. The DOI deputy director verbally vows to protect the String. Gone is the suit, tie, and stressed expression. Apple sports the same neon purple worn by the inner circle of the String.

Apple Tamer Gray stands tall with a firmly decided public pronouncement.

"I pledge to defend what has been accomplished to build and protect the corridor with all the legal know-how I can muster."

This show of unity is bolstered as Lieutenant Governor Greyson Chance moves proudly opposite Henry Wildbird. The two men exchange a bear hug in a sign that all past liabilities are forgiven. Greyson, an accomplished National Guard captain, breaks from the embrace and salutes all at the gathering. He sheds his outer uniform, exposing the inner circle's purple tee. Chance looks to the sky and then shouts, "Join the cause before there's no cause to join."

Astonished, Sam realizes that he's aware of her presence. His involvement with anything related to the String will create a hailstorm of public scandal. The lieutenant governor is fully aware of a predetermined fate. Sam considers Greyson Chance's status within the military. Indubitably, he'll be perceived as a turncoat. There must be an ancillary motive behind his apparent collaboration. It's hard to imagine someone more devoted to public service. His entanglement with the String poses a perplexing societal dichotomy, but this exclusive partnership only validates Sam's suspicions. Now more than ever she's determined to follow her instincts. Chance must have witnessed or, at the very least, suspected something truly unbearable happening at Bandy Hawk.

Suddenly, a wave of elation grips the crowd. The fervent circle tightens further in pulsing adulation. A throaty rumble overtakes the mass. Betty describes it with overwhelming anticipation.

"They're waiting for the lone masked rider whose emblematic stature defines the String."

The Ink Prayer's tribal leader has waited for more than a decade to see the actualization of the String. The tearful old woman looks to the moon in gratitude. She gasps when the masked rider arrives and then gracefully disembarks from the dancing steed, Virtuoso. Ceremoniously decorated, Hinmah modestly accepts the famed string of pearls.

"Grandmother, it is your resolve that made this day possible. Montana's wildlife has a marked chance to survive because of your vision.

"Each lustrous, spherical mass rooted within the necklace represents a hard-earned piece of land that links wildlife refuges, wilderness areas, and wetlands to national parks. Everyone gathered has contributed to the String. A select few have paid dearly, but none more than you," declares Mattie.

Chapter 65-
ANCIENT CADENCE

The hundreds gathered here fall into a renewed silence. At the edge of the circle, Hinmah swings gently to the sound of an ancient beat. The crowd shadows the medicine woman's rhythmic drift as they pulsate to a traditional cadence. Every step appears choreographed amid some primeval resolve.

Sam's artificial height provides clarity. Below, in organized pandemonium, participants form into a neon insignia upon the Roe's shore. From above, Sam witnesses the dynamic formation of the emblem left behind at each illicit hunting camp.

So magnificently celebratory, this congregation can be heard miles away: A collaborative human cheer stirs the area's wildlife into a revelry all their own. From above, as onlooker, the Seeker watches nature burst into its own flamboyant kinesis. Anxious geese take flight, muskrats rush from water's edge, and deer leap. Nature's broken trance affirms a precise symmetry.

Abruptly, the fabled spell ends. Once disturbed, the wildlife returns to a peaceful threshold. Human and creature alike retreat in preparation for an impending storm. The Seeker is literally left up in the air to decide which direction best serves the whole.

For the second time in as many days, she feels a need to reconsider. It's difficult to ignore dedicated heroism. The fact is these dutiful people will be labeled criminals, conspirators, and eco-terrorists. Sam the Seeker ponders what little can be done.

A tribute to Tree and Isabelle has found a home beside the fleeting river. Their bronze commemoration now acts as sentry beside the flowing Roe. Sweet Brown Betty broadcasts the inscription into the tiny microphone hidden on her person. "These devoted conservationists have served with distinction."

Betty looks to the sky in search of truth.

"There must be something we can do to make this right!" Betrayed by the light of the Super Moon, Betty makes a final plea. Reconciled, Betty Kumba decides. With utter amity, she speaks to Sam directly.

"Join the cause before there's no cause to join."

Once again, the acclaimed horse and rider emerge with a second steed. In one vast bound, the rider dismounts and lays flowers at the monument with tender homage. Mattie Wildbird sheds her mask, looking candidly into the night skies. Sam isn't surprised at this revelation. The leader of raids and keeper of the String, Mattie Wildbird glances proudly into the heavens.

Sam slants slightly outside the confines of the helicopter. The backlit full moon delivers complete exposure. She tips her invisible cap to horse and rider. Like Betty, the Seeker is enticed by both the String's source and mythological lore. The lure of this cause demands a zealous commitment and extreme devotion.

The question remains: Is the String a cult faction or incredibly prophetic? Sam considers all this and more as she orders the pilot to disengage. The Seeker has been invited. More than that, a respected peer and member of her professional clan has posed a valid question. Betty's missive is perhaps the purest invitation, given the two women's relationship.

Chance's stirring confession and Hinmah's ceremonial dance force the Seeker to reconsider many foregone conclusions. Has she become another casualty of Hinmah's madness?

What is the moral path forward? Should Samantha Cherchez conform or deviate from the law by joining forces with the enigmatic medicine woman? She admires Betty for the ease of her resolution. Her colleague and friend always exhibited great nerve, even if not the best judgment.

Has the eccentric medicine woman defrauded everyone or saved her corner of the environmental world? Perhaps Hinmah's version of what is right falls on the wrong side of the law, but the right side of humanity. Sam ponders all this on her way back to the base. Betty's choice is apparent. Honestly, her decision doesn't surprise Sam. But it will be difficult to explain to the very black-and-white Beggs Cooper. Betty is his touchstone.

Chapter 66-

3:00 A.M.

Three in the morning is either very early or very late, depending on one's perspective. Purely devastated by Betty's declaration, Cooper's mental state has deteriorated, and his fatigued emotional state has run him underground. Sam finds herself alone, poring over the videotapes that document each raid. Two pieces of the puzzle are in place. Not sure what she's looking for, Sam knows whatever it is will be buried in the miles of footage taken of the raids by National Guardsmen.

The audio is off. Instead, Sam repeats Vivaldi's *Concerto in D Major, Second Movement*. An avid music lover, the Seeker uses the classics to reduce stress and increase concentration.

Sam pulls her hair back into a ponytail and then rubs her temples. She's determined to resolve the riddle that is Finch888.

It's remarkable. The riders cover significant ground with such ease. Sam zooms in and out to find the clue that lingers. She enhances the view of several riders, then flips to another raid and back again. It's here, a small trace of evidence so close, it itches. Sam tries to overlay the videos just as Cooper does, but she lacks his technological deftness. Sam wants a better perspective of the surface area covered by the riders from the time the raid starts until they literally disappear.

After a few tries and more than a little bad language, she moves to her Cooper-assigned, over-stuffed chair to think. The Seeker ponders the notion that it's not one thing but several. The masked rider who spearheads the raids is always present. Sam thinks the main group of riders might, in fact, be several teams that switch out. It's not terribly noticeable because the lead horse and rider command all the attention. The videotape continuously follows the lead, so it's difficult to see how and what the other members do in reaction to the chase.

That's another thing: The lead rider is readily identifiable, yet everyone pretends not to notice. Masked or not, it's apparent that Mattie Wildbird is lead. Repetitive examination for a hidden clue grows into mounting frustration. The damned computers make Sam buggy in the light of day, never mind the middle of the night.

Stymied, the all-powerful Seeker sits within the confines of her pre-defined Cooper space and breaks out in laughter. When did she lose control of everything, including her heart?

Add to this Betty's newfound commitment to the String. Betty is family. The Seeker cannot protect anyone from the law, not even a sister.

Cooper's latest meltdown is the direct result of Betty's unlawful choice. The Super Moon videotape confirms his best friend has traded sides. Beyond this obvious concern, Sam can't shake Betty's invitation. She watches the video playback for what must be the twentieth time. With each reiteration, Betty's betrayal tugs at Sam's heart in surprising ways.

Just then, a withdrawn Cooper walks in with Sweet Brown Betty at his side. Anger floods the space between Sam and her old friends. Tears have been shed; that's apparent. A pale-faced Cooper pleads for a chance to make things right and does so with nothing more than his pathetic red eyes. Betty, on the other hand, stands resolute, her arms crossed, ready to accept things as they are. Betty Kumba's prodigious, perfected stubbornness will someday eat them all alive, and today may be that day.

"Ladies, if you'll allow me, I have an idea," begins Cooper.

"Betty recognizes the sin she has committed, which suggests she can redeem herself."

Chapter 67-

AMEND AND ALTER

Cooper looks nervously back and forth between his two best friends. He senses danger and stiffens.

"Think about it. Betty is better with these computers than me. Let her go back to D.C. ahead of the team. She can get Painted Rock back up and running."

Betty's physical stance hasn't changed. Her pure mass and dark eyes mock, taking Sam in whole. The Seeker sits with long legs folded against her chest. Neither woman has taken her eyes off the other. The discomfort is palpable.

Cooper tries again.

"You guys are the only family I have. Please, don't let this destroy us!"

Betty caves. She can't tolerate Cooper's pleas for reconciliation.

"You should know right up front. This isn't about us three."

Betty talks as much with her hands as her mouth.

"I never imagined I'd see the day when we'd be forced to choose. I mean, we've always been righteous, you know, the good guys."

Betty maintains a sense of scrupulous equilibrium; that's why Sam hired this complicated woman in the first place.

"I know I've let you down. You probably even think I'm disloyal, but this thing is bigger than you and me," declares the willful woman with open palms.

Sam the Seeker sits motionless. Translation: There's much cause for worry. She exhibits the uber-attentive trance of a wildcat, senses finely honed, in an entirely static pose.

The feline's quarry perceives an eerie demise but knows not from which direction it will come. Courageously, Cooper stands between the predator and her kill, ready to intervene.

Sweet Brown Betty deploys her last and best means of protection: honesty.

"I love and respect ya, but the String makes my insides swell with justice. And if I ain't genuine about this, I ain't going to be good to nobody. My heart won't hold out."

That said, she awaits judgment. What will come of this terrible event: brutal retribution or graceful absolution?

In the background, the video unceremoniously loops back at the place Betty stands beside the masked rider. Sam watches Betty onscreen and redirects her line of sight to the masked rider. Her focus returns to the present. Once again, Sam makes the video her focal point.

"That's it!" announces the Seeker excitedly. "Everyone knows Mattie Wildbird spearheads the raids, but they look the other way. Why? Bandy Hawk! That's how Mattie freely directs these raids without obstruction. She's untouchable."

In one fluid motion, Samantha Cherchez grabs her car keys and rushes to hug Sweet Brown Betty. This revelation floods the undercover agent with renewed zeal. Sweet Brown Betty smiles broadly with relief. She recognizes that Sam has put the entire puzzle together — something even Betty has yet to accomplish.

The frenzied anger evaporates, and a truce is sealed by the Seeker's gentle kiss on Betty's tear-stained, oval face. The two fearless females have come to some tacit agreement, which Cooper can only guess. Sam the Seeker has regained her balance and shouts orders on her way out.

"Cooper have the pilot get the plane ready for departure. Betty, if you want this thing to turn out, Cooper must understand every-thing. He's going to need help to decipher the means used to build and hide the String's finances. Gather the proof we need."

The Seeker turns sternly.

"It's time to provide a complete list of everyone inside the String's inner circle. You've known their identities for some time. Oh, and by the way, you make a lousy turncoat. Don't hold back, because if you do, I can't protect these people."

Before Sam can get out the door, Sweet Brown Betty runs at her. The teary-eyed woman swallows her boss up in grateful arms. With that, Sam the Seeker heads for the nation's capital.

Beggs concentrates on the boss's orders.

"Contact Tamer Gray. Tell him to head to D.C. and bring everything he can to defend his surrogate family. Then let Director Mac know I'll be in D.C. late this afternoon. He needs to set aside some time for us to speak to the president."

Chapter 68-
EXPERITUS WAVE

The formidable DOI undercover agent is out to rectify and amend. Cooper and his best friend are left standing in the wake of relief. Neither knows how to react. Once dressed in gloom, the room feels kinder, lighter. The two breathe through waning trepidation. Betty cries out, "Let's get to work. There's a crapload of evidence to gather. Apple will verify members of the inner circle if Sam makes a promise to protect the whole lot of them. Riders, scientists, professors, even that tender little bookkeeper who keeps track of the cash can be pardoned. We're gonna pull together everything that Sam needs to exonerate those folks' reputation."

The hour and stress have taken a toll. More than a little grumpy, Cooper looks at Betty accusingly.

"How long have you known these insiders?" questions Cooper.

"I told you over coffee you wouldn't find anything hidden. That's because these people aren't thieves; they're just creative," explains Betty.

"Besides, I have a right to protect those I love, and I love you more than just about anyone," smiles a wholehearted Betty. "If I'd let you in on things, you'd be guilty as me!"

Betty's last declaration thaws the city slicker's anger. Cooper shakes his head and walks to the sink. He plunges his thick, bronzed hair under the cold-water faucet. All Cooper can muster is a good sneer.

After coffee and a quick bite of breakfast, the two DOI agents settle in. Beggs doggedly focuses. He promises himself that by day's end he'll realize just how the String's inner circle managed to fake out the best criminological minds in the country.

Computers hum. The heralded team of two plows ahead with renewed vigor. It turns out Cooper's prized, state-of-the-art fraud software did its job.

"We discovered exactly what the accused intended. The multitudes of incongruities were designed to lead investigators to a dead end. This was part of the String's scheme, right, Betty?"

"That's correct. They generated so much information that it confused the entire investigative pool, to include the FBI," smiles Brown Betty.

Sheepishly, Beggs admits that someone's highly creative technology outgunned him. He questions, "How did these people manage to generate so much of nothing?"

"That's easy," laughs Betty, "far-sighted genius. That, combined with an inside understanding of the state's daily accounting functions, made the Ink Prayer a formidable lot. On top of that, these folks have a profound knowledge of forensic audit procedures."

Betty commiserates with Beggs.

"I know how you feel. I couldn't make sense of anything. The truth is, until Mattie told me about her ex-DARPA expert, I was totally lost. According to her, he created an exclusive algorithmic feature. This guy calls his invention a super-numeracy circuit. As near as I can figure, it combines nature's own numerical demarcations with a systematic software application hidden inside the state's database. If someone buys an out-of-state deer license for $303.50, an invisible sequence of gyratory numerals takes a fractional fee from the procurement. The percentage subtracted by a fraction is never the same due to a patterned spherical rotation."

An animated Betty admits that she doesn't comprehend a lot of what that DARPA guy did.

"All I know is that every monetary credit paid into the state's coffers triggers an undetected donation to the String. I gotta admit that this super-numeracy circuitry device is over my head.

"Who woulda guessed a network of so-called outlaws would have such prominent participants? They come from all walks of life, private and public. It's a diverse and educated population. Imagine, a spook works for 'em," finishes Betty with a flourish.

"Wait," demands an incredulous Cooper, "are you telling me somebody from the CIA has a hand in all this?"

"Well, yeah. Besides this DARPA guy, Mattie has a CIA contact sympathetic to the cause. Like I said, for criminal types, they enjoy an awful lot of brainpower. These people ain't your average felons."

Chapter 69

THE STORYTELLER

As morning becomes midday, Sweet Brown Betty continues her story. She tells Cooper that the String comes from a place of darkness borne unto light. Betty exposes Mattie's version of her parent's demise. With exuberance, the undercover agent describes the String's purpose. Her softened eyes ardently express her commitment. Cooper has not seen Betty this passionate about anything, and that says a lot given the woman's fervor.

"Turns out the judge's decree was beneficial to our investigation. My job at FWP explained some things. Eyeing invoices can paint a wide-ranging picture. The story walks right in the door. Hunting applications, inbound receivables, hell, even rentable income pass through the mailroom. I date-stamped each item and catalogued everything for our investigative purposes. The funny thing is that I thought I was collecting evidence to take down the bad guys. Turns out this collection demonstrates the String's innocence.

Within days, I obtained a rather unusual set of numbers, attached to a rather peculiar list of land acquisitions. I couldn't make heads or tails out of things. I employed the state GIS software and cross-referenced land assets."

Gesticulating as she talks, Betty continues.

"I was perplexed, so I thought I'd just go ask. That was a big mistake," smiles Betty.

"Right up front, Mattie told me about the String and that her group knew I was a DOI undercover. The inner circle of the String deliberately planted the evidence on the mailroom computer."

Beggs jumps in. "What? How the hell did they figure out you were covert DOI?"

"Apparently, these people investigate anyone who comes into direct contact with the String's inner circle. As soon as Sheriff Drake introduced me to Mattie, they applied appropriate counter-surveillance," nods Betty.

"My identity surfaced on a financial statement. You and I both know those people really had to dig hard to unearth my real identity. They're shrewd, Beggs."

Cooper bows his head in agreement.

"Are you telling me that Sheriff Drake is part of the String?"

Betty spreads her hands, palms open.

"Yep, but Drake and his group can prove every dime the String attained has reverted to the state of Montana in the form of real-estate proprietorships along the eastern Rocky Mountain Front. To tell the truth, it was Mattie's blatant honesty that won me over."

"Yeah, and her candor is the cause of your most recent difficulties with a determined Sam the Seeker," declares a still-very-skeptical Cooper.

"Hell, man! These people aren't buying condos on Flathead lake. They have endangered themselves for a noble pursuit," proclaims a passionate Betty.

It's been a hell of a day, and the two DOI agents have been at it for nearly twenty hours straight. Another round of fatigue hits Cooper, and he barely affords a tiny smile.

"What the hell are you so happy about?"

"The fact that Sam has joined the cause gives us all a chance," declares Betty.

"Wait a minute," intervenes a weary Cooper. "I don't want you to get too far ahead of this. Not once did Sam express, she believes in the cause. For all you know, the Seeker is out there now, detaining Mattie and Henry Wildbird. One thing is for sure. The shit's in the hat, and the fight is on!"

Betty moves toward him with pronounced agility.

"You're right. That just means I need to demonstrate the facts. Pitiful child, you must be dead tired. Why don't you go lie down on that couch and get some rest? I've put you through a lot, and you can't think when your clothes are all wrinkled." Betty waves her hand at Cooper's rumpled duds. "Take a breather. I need you fresh by morning."

Cooper leans heavily against his friend as the two-walk arm-in-arm to the leather sofa. He falls into it, pulling Betty close enough to hear him whisper.

"You need to promise me something: Tell me you'll never use our family like some two-bit poker chip thrown in the pot to let it ride. I can't love someone who doesn't cherish real friendship as much as I do. It'll slay me."

Betty helps Beggs shed his shoes and covers her drowsy companion with a blanket.

"I promise," smiles Betty with tenderness.

Moments later, Cooper's snores fill the room. Sweet Brown Betty gets back to the all-important fiscal trail proving the String's integrity. By late morning, Cooper stirs.

Chapter 70-
CO-MINGLING

Betty launches a nearby couch pillow at her old friend. "It's time to get your crinkled little butt in the shower. Take care of the essentials. You know, make yourself all pressed and sweet-smellin'. Everybody knows your delicates have to be in order before you can work."

Cooper moans something unintelligible. Thirty minutes later, he looks like himself again. The quantity of information his partner has gleaned from the state's computer system doesn't surprise Cooper. That's just Betty being Betty.

"Damn, these people are inventive," admires the computer wizard. She begins.

"As you know, governmental accounts run the gamut. Agricultural leases; oil and gas leases; cabin and homesite leases; oil royalties; timber sales; coal leases; grazing leases; public facilities; communication site leases; licensing of all types to include hunting, fishing, and individual use licenses; gas royalties — the list goes on.

At the end of each fiscal year, a check is drafted from the Trust Land Management Division to the Department of Revenue. The funds are then reapportioned. For example, the legislature gives Trust Land Management operational monies for the next fiscal year.

Dollars collected from the previous year, above and beyond operational costs, are dispersed amongst school trusts, thus meeting the legislative mandate to assist with education expenses.

"The String siphoned undetected monies from everything. Each triggered receivable was fractionally redirected until the sale sum for a piece of property was collected. These acquisitions look like any other. That's when that little trust land comptroller steps in. She buries these acquisitions into the Land Board Commission meeting minutes. If an auditor comes across a suspicious purchase, the Land Board transcripts act to verify the purchase. If an auditor gets more than just curious, they wouldn't find a misspent nickel."

Cooper leans back in his chair and laughs with incredulity. In the brief time it takes for Cooper to sleep off his emotional hangover, Sweet Brown Betty has compiled ten years of accounts receivables, each fully documented. She walks Cooper through the simplicity of the String's deception and then taps into the GIS Kestrel system. Betty matches the property coordinates with the financial properties of each real-estate acquisition. She then displays that specific piece of property on the overhead computer monitor. Cooper can't believe his eyes and spews unintelligible Gaelic.

In full Welsh brogue, he exclaims, "You can't even trust crooks to be crooked anymore!"

A gentle smile lights Betty's face. She smothers her man friend with love.

"Come close, my little Welsh pup. It's a pisser to get outsmarted, ain't it? You'll see the beauty in their scheme once the rage subsides."

Chapter 71-

ROSE GARDEN FIX

The DOI secretary requests an inbound over-flight and landing clearance into the Arlington, Virginia airport. The chief of protocol directs Reilly Geo Mac and his deputy from the jet to the presidential helicopter personally.

Marine One's VH-60N White Hawk lands on the south lawn minutes before Samantha Cherchez arrives on the north side of the White House.

———————◆———————

There's urgency in the administrative aide's voice as he directs Cherchez to the Rose Garden.

"Secretary Geo Mac is on site, but the president has been delayed. Please follow me," adds the perky assistant.

The walk through the West Wing is brisk. Samantha Cherchez doesn't wear a nametag. She is, after all, undercover.

Washington, D.C. is called "the Foggy Bottom" for a reason, but this autumn day challenges that nickname. The Rose Garden is groomed meticulously. The tea roses in full bloom are coupled with Queen Elisabeth's, all sheltered by Katherine Crabapples and Little Leaf-Linden trees.

Sam's escort takes her to a great white awning just off the West Wing Colonnade. Inside, the enclosure is peppered with tables and chairs, four separate bars, and a variety of barbecues. Opposite each barbecue is a large washtub stocked with cold beverages sunken in ice. The subtle smell of mesquite permeates the tent. Two men lean against the far end of the bar. DOI Secretary Reilly Geo Mac and Apple Tamer Gray are deep in conversation.

The young deputy director looks comfortable. Beggs forewarned Sam that Apple and Mac have spent time cloistered over the narrative that is Finch888. The Seeker feels off balance and doesn't know what to expect. Still she commits without hesitation. Samantha Cherchez walks towards the two men with her usual conviction.

"Gentlemen."

Both Mac and Gray greet her in a curiously friendly fashion, considering their present predicament. The Secretary turns to Cherchez with an ample smile.

"Samantha, as ever, you've proven yourself to be golden."

Gray can't contain himself and hugs the Seeker as if they're old friends.

"Please, join us. Can I get you something to drink?"

Mac signals the barkeep stacking tall pilsner glasses into a double-decker freezer at the opposite end of the bar.

"I can't tell you how proud I am of you and Gray here," begins Mac.

"Your associate, Beggs, filled me in on the task force details. That Cooper is quite a character.

"Anyway," continues Mac, "I think the president will be very pleased to hear about your plans and ultimate endgame. Mr. Gray has clarified the String's purpose. While I don't approve of the methodology, I embrace the cause. It'd be an extraordinary ecological feat if we could manage to maintain the integrity of this so-called String of ecological pearls."

Sam curiously glimpses at Apple as the president of the United States walks beneath the sprawling tent. The bartender hustles to serve Andrew Delahunt his favorite pilsner. POTUS shakes hands with Mac and Gray and then turns to Cherchez. "Well, Sam the Seeker, it appears you got more than one man this time. Let's grab a table so you can tell me how this environmental rebellion will end."

The president takes his cold beer and heads to a quiet area. The threesome joins him at a select table.

"I have to say, meetings with you people always entertain. Ms. Cherchez, please tell me what's happening."

The president takes this moment to take a gulp of cold brew. Sam is seated to his right, while the other two men settle opposite. Cherchez is dressed in a stylish business suit. The peach, black, and aqua scarf makes her eye color shift with interchangeable expressions.

The undercover agent looks directly across at Apple before she starts.

"This assignment has been more than a challenge. My team, to include Mr. Gray, has detected and analyzed compound transgressions, ranging from misdemeanors to felonies. Misconduct spans a broad spectrum of society, to include a felonious Governor presumed responsible for the murder of two public servants. You see, I start with these deaths because that event precipitates the outcome of our investigation."

The graying POTUS stares at Cherchez incredulously and then looks to the DOI deputy. Apple sits before the leader of the free world calmly, without a tinge of emotion.

"Well, Mr. Gray, do you agree with Ms. Cherchez's analysis?"

Apple sits back in his chair, fronted by a cold mug of beer. "I do, but with a butterfly-effect addendum. The murders placed my surrogate family into a state of immediate mayhem. They reacted to their agonizing initial condition with a protracted and anarchistic response."

The Seeker jumps back in.

"You see, the raids are just a distraction. These diversionary tactics hid the purchase of specific properties along the eastern Rocky Mountain Front. Illicitly procured pearls of land stretch south from the Canadian border all the way to Yellowstone Park.

"Today, this String of Pearls comprises one continuous loop. This biological phenomenon spans more than four hundred fifty miles north to south and links two major national parks."

Mac follows up.

"If I may, there are several complexities attached to this narrative. I'd like to sketch things out and have these two-" the Secretary points at Sam and Apple, "-jump in when necessary."

Mac pulls a pen from his tweed jacket and flips over a nearby cocktail napkin. A quick rendition of the situation is outlined and handed back to the president who, in turn, studies the rough copy.

Andrew Delahunt turns to further scrutinize Cherchez and then Gray. The two unobtrusively wait while Mac fills in the many gradations that comprise the String. At the center of the napkin are the Bandy Hawk murders. The president takes a moment to digest as much information as possible. He gulps his beer and then adds, "Let me get this straight. Mr. Gray, did you witness the murders?"

The typically detached Apple Tamer Gray struggles here; his poker face wanes.

"I can only confirm the massacres secondhand. Mattie Wildbird witnessed the murders from atop Bandy Hawk Ridge."

Sam chimes in to give Apple emotional cover.

"Sir, the most astonishing fact is the composition of this criminal group. It included Montana's fledgling future Governor, Crebo Lund."

POTUS simply nods.

"I suppose I should be shocked, but I've been in politics too long to think anything atypical. Besides, this isn't the first I've heard of Governor Lund. Power speaks to ego, and unrestrained ego contaminates everything within its reach."

A perceptibly distressed president looks to the bartender and signals for a second round.

"Ms. Cherchez, what can you tell me about the labor force behind this environmental crusade?" asks POTUS.

The consummate professional dabs her beer-laden lips with a linen napkin.

"Sir, as discussed earlier, Finch888 has presented many challenges. Today, we can provide a detailed list of the String's entire workforce, but it's very late in coming.

"I embedded an undercover agent early on. This agent determined that the inner core of the String is relatively small but acutely disciplined and technologically innovative.

It appears that, over a decade, the Wildbirds recruited some very talented people. In addition to this, a larger volunteer pool exists, numbering in the hundreds. The raids have gone viral and with each successful raid, that figure swells."

Samantha Cherchez reaches for a T-shirt from her briefcase adorned with the String's insignia. The catchphrase reads: "Join the cause before there's no cause to join."

"Practically everyone in the Northwest owns one of these shirts. You can't walk down the streets of Seattle without seeing this logo. Turns out 10 percent from all paraphernalia sold to local environmental organizations was used to purchase land. The Robin Hood Syndrome is vigorous."

The second round of drinks arrives. POTUS asks Secretary Mac for a private word.

"Ms. Cherchez, Mr. Gray, please enjoy another beer, and excuse us for a moment."

Gray stands as Delahunt and Mac walk outside the tent into the Rose Garden. The tidy landscape offers serenity as the two men confer.

Mac starts.

"Well, it has become evident that Neff stumbled into a hornets' nest. Looking back, it seems Tully's drunken hunting party is merely recurrent history."

Chapter 72-
FULL DISCLOSURE

Cherchez closely watches the two men as they review the facts. The president's conversation, as conveyed by hand gestures, is involved. Sam considers this before looking to DOI Deputy Director Gray.

The Seeker stares at the talented young man opposite her. "Things are going as planned so far, but don't get your hopes up. This situation can go sideways in a millisecond. Did you bring both sets of books?"

"I did, and they're in the hands of the White House counsel as we speak. Before the president returns, I need to know something: Why are you doing this? Exactly what made you deviate from your standard investigative practice?" demands Apple.

Her eyes glistening with integrity, the blonde woman grins.

"'Veracity,' Mr. Gray. There is no substitute for truth. Your family's work is admirable. But more than that, it challenges all of us to rise above our baser selves."

Sam lifts her pilsner in a toast. Apple tugs at his mustache and then hoists his glass.

"In honor of the Wildbird clan."

Apple's ridiculous smile hits the Seeker hard.

"All right, what's behind that smirk?"

The DOI deputy enjoys this moment. He leans into his beer to hide a deepening smile.

"You don't know, do you, about the CIA agent? This feels great: For the first time since this investigation began, I actually know something before you."

"Well, do you plan on full disclosure, or do I have to guess?" criticizes the very competitive Samantha Cherchez.

"I attended a meeting last week with your man Beggs. This glossy city type cornered Special Agent Joyce Kingston. Immediately afterward, the FBI announced that Internet surveillance linked the governor to Henry Wildbird. This is when I first learned Henry is partnered with Lund and Chance. Naturally, that blew my mind.

"The man who delivered this bombshell looked familiar but abruptly vanished. It took me some time to put the pieces together because I'd taken a pretty good blow to the head. I recognized he's a String insider. That's right; he's part of the inner circle. Turns out this guy, Winslow Sharp, used to work for DARPA and faked retirement. He serves the president and is on temporary assignment to the FBI. Hell, Winslow Sharp is a double agent.

"According to Mac, Crebo Lund garnered the FBI and CIA's attention inside the Dark Web. This all transpired during his first political campaign. Lund's an ambitious ass, but an unlucky one. Turns out, he lost both his profits and original investment in the Bitcoin crash. Apparently, he needed funds to promote his Senate race run.

"The CIA, using a false identity, followed a third-world bureaucrat in search of military-grade munitions. A backwards trace tagged Crebo Lund as the seller, but they needed proof.

Winslow was the man who discovered the original arms deal. Today, he works both sides of the investigation. Mattie recruited what she thought was an ex-CIA agent. The String's urgent need for a surveillance and techno wizard meant taking a risk. Turns out, Sharp was CIA and now FBI."

Proud of himself, Apple tugs at his mustache and then slurps down his beer.

"Are you telling me Delahunt has known about the String from the onset?" asks the astonished DOI agent.

"God, this feels good," declares Apple.

"My guess is the CIA approached the president about Lund's weapons sales and didn't know what to do with the information. Delahunt needed a trusted source inside the FBI because the CIA has no authority to operate inside the United States. Sharp is the president's informant.

"One thing did happen that no one counted on. This guy Sharp fell in love with Mattie and the idea of doing good. Apparently, he got carried away. Mattie has that effect on people. This brilliant techno-geek gave the String its financial legs. You understand Sharp's choice to back the String puts POTUS in a rather tenuous situation. Of course, it's not a bright idea to force this fact down the president's throat."

The surprised undercover agent mulls over the latest information and breaks out into her own silly grin. Apparently, Sam the Seeker isn't the only one whose staff made the decision to change sides.

Gray rises as the Delahunt and Mac return to the table. Reilly Geo Mac looks confident.

"I've given this situation some thought. Mac and I believe the String is an honorable and widely held popular environmental action. Wildlife stewardship is often a last consideration," the president laments.

"Tell me," remarks POTUS, "is it possible to meet this medicine woman? I find her crusade intriguing and would be delighted to visit one of these remarkable command centers before our fledgling FBI agent blows them to smithereens."

Both Sam and Apple smile in recognition of this prospect. "I'll pass on your request. I'm glad to arrange a meeting," declares Apple.

"Ms. Cherchez, please summarize what business is left to conduct," requests Mac.

Sam directs her attention to the DOI secretary.

"We plan to return to Montana and assemble the principal members of the String, at which point we'll await your directives."

"That easy?" interrupts the president, looking straight into the eyes of the resolute Apple Tamer Gray.

Apple replies confidently.

"My grandmother and her legion have understood the risks from the onset. Believe me, I've pressed her about the inevitable. She accepts full responsibility, and I know the others will stand with her, whatever the outcome."

Apple Tamer Gray slips his hand inside his coat jacket and sets a sealed envelope on the white linen. Mac's eyes widen as he holds up his hand.

"Let's not get ahead of ourselves, Mr. Gray. I would expect your resignation, had you been to blame."

POTUS takes up the torch.

"To be honest, we took advantage of your familial status in hopes of finding the underlying cause of things before someone got hurt. I understand the need to protect family. Please, wait. You see, I have a few creative ideas myself, and it won't come in the form of a legislative treaty. This government has broken enough of them already.

"In the interim, I'd like you and Sam to head back and stabilize the situation. The secretary and I will break away as soon as possible to settle this thing once and for all."

Apple slides his resignation letter back into his coat as both agents agree. The two DOI employees exchange quick handshakes with Delahunt and Mac before excusing themselves.

Chapter 73-
ZENITH LOOMS

The pursuit begins in earnest. National Guard handheld radios blow up as the String's command center systematically foils every effort made by the Guardsmen to capture Mattie.

After Henry's ceaseless attempt to persuade his sister to stand down, Mattie asserts herself as a lone fugitive. She's convinced that Delahunt's proposition is a hoax.

"I don't trust this government. How many times must we learn this lesson?"

———————◆———————

A woodland-patterned battle dress uniform is made available from Crebo Lund to the assassin. Dennis Ciske dresses surreptitiously as a National Guard private. He melds in on this latest pursuit. The uniform's newness is noticeably incongruous. Dennis remedies this by sliding down a dusty hill on his behind, hoping to acquire that grungy look. It takes four runs before the guise takes hold. Hidden within the troops, the counterfeit guardsman focuses on finding his targets: Mattie and Henry Wildbird.

The ex-con recognizes the irony. There's an odd symmetry at play. Dennis Ciske did time for the murders of Tree and Isabelle

Wildbird. The actual shooter handsomely recompensed him. Ciske honestly thought the money would change his life. He was right; it did. The prison sentence outlasted his marriage. Afterwards, decent work was hard to come by, particularly given his violent criminal record. Before Dennis was released, his wife remarried. He knew better than to fight for his kids. No court would give him custody, not after Bandy Hawk.

Just like Crebo promised, Dennis's release came early, accompanied by an enviable bank account. The day Ciske left prison, he did three things. First, he took a draw from his Bitcoin account to buy a Harley Davidson. Next, Dennis sent a check to his ex-wife for his children's future education. Hell, he owed his kids that much. All that was left was to purchase a sleeping bag to tie to the back of his motorcycle. The ex-con planned to take a short break from life's realities. Ten years later, Ciske had frittered away the remainder of his take. Afterwards, the drifter tussled through a dozen or so no-account jobs, serving two more jail sentences before languishing alone in Los Gatos. That's where Crebo Lund found him. Today, if all goes well, Dennis will be drinking gin on the Costa Rica coastline. Before the hunt, he checks that a cool million dollars is in his Bitcoin account. That kind of money goes a long way in Central America.

The lone fake guardsman works hard to stay close to his prey. Ciske stumbles onto a couple of agents from the DOI. He listens from across the gully.

"She's toying with us," hollers Samantha Cherchez. A confident Mattie Wildbird is three hundred yards to the left.

"It's like playing chess: She moves, we react. Her advance is premeditated. The damn hologram," complains Sam.

She looks down at Apple. Habit makes him pull at his mustache, sheltering the small grin. Each time, Mattie circles back, then vanishes, then reappears further ahead, Apple experiences a sense of pride. After all, Sam the Seeker is a famously skilled tracker. Eventually, the National Guardsmen will corner Mattie Wildbird. There are too many soldiers, hologram or not.

Most importantly, the proposal between Hinmah and the president must take effect, regardless of Mattie's mistrust.

Apple recognizes that five hundred or so broken treaties don't help his cause, but it's critical that Andrew Delahunt's inspired initiative be given a chance. There's just one problem. No one knows what that looks like. The DOI deputy recognizes one thing: A deal must be struck, or everyone attached to the String will be incarcerated.

"We have to split up. You stay close to Mattie," whispers Sam, slipping behind a stone outcropping.

Apple climbs hard to the last place he saw Mattie and sinks into the soft pine needles blanketing the ground beneath a pair of giant fir trees. He tries to quiet his breath. Hiking these mountains is sheer delight unless you're a smoker. Chasing a woman who habitually runs the ridge is agonizing, even if one is in decent shape.

Mattie rarely underestimates her competition. Apple thinks about that for a moment before he simply stands to announce what's on his mind.

"You know this entire Delahunt deal is predicated on every one of Hinmah's inner circle's confessed involvement. Cherchez won't stop until she apprehends you. And neither will I."

Five hundred yards straight up and to his right, Mattie mocks Apple. Upright, standing in all her glory, she's an affront to her pursuers.

"You've lived in the city too long. Slow down, you are out of shape," replies Mattie, leaping from one boulder to another effortlessly.

This unforgettable moment mesmerizes Apple, who's captivated by the pursuit's sheer splendor. He struggles to focus and finally collects himself.

"I'm not the one you should worry about!"

Clambering forward, he's short of breath. Mattie watches from above.

"Calm down, or you'll drop over dead. Don't you want a cigarette?"

Mattie is now just five feet beneath Apple.

Apple stumbles. "Shit."

He throws himself at her, and just that swiftly, the real Mattie is ten feet to his right, dashing towards the hilltop, totally amused.

Chapter 74-
CLARITY

S am the Seeker sits, silently watching this game unfold. This new perspective provides lucidity. She has recognized Apple's emotional attachment to the Ink Prayer people, but his affection for Mattie runs deeper. He's in love with her. Of that, Sam is now confident.

The Seeker can see something else from this vantage: Creekbaum's hologram gives Mattie an edge, but it's not foolproof. The projected, three-dimensional illusion floats on haptic points and emits small, nearly undetectable flecks of light. This makes it possible to segregate the actual Mattie from her mid-air apparition.

Anyone able to distinguish the non-artifact could take a clear shot. Still, from afar, a three-dimensional, life-sized Mattie with absolutely no physical limitations can be anywhere and everywhere. No wonder the National Guard failed to make a capture.

"I know where you're taking us," yells an indignant Apple.

"That may be, but I don't believe you or your undercover agent can catch me," responds the annoyed woman, now near the crest of the mountain.

"I'll tell you what; the both of you can take the president's pledge and lay it on the Trail of Tears."

With this forceful declaration, Mattie twists off her artificial limb, folds all but the middle finger of the fake appendage downward, thrusts it in the air, and then throws it at Apple.

"Give that message to your boss."

The prosthetic just clears Apple's head. He stops to pick up the fake arm and, after closer examination, breaks into laughter. Apple is done with the chase. He heads to Bandy Hawk Lake.

Sam is left wondering what just happened. She spots movement in her peripheral vision. Someone is shadowing Gray. A National Guardsman armed with an M1 Thompson rifle isn't far behind, mirroring the DOI deputy's every movement. Motionless against the forested backdrop, Cherchez observes the dubious onlooker. She leans undetected against a boulder. Sam concentrates, trying to put the pieces together.

Then, like a thunderclap invading the forest's calm, she recalls something Hinmah said: "*Tradition and faith signify everything to my people. We live the circle.*"

"That's it!" declares Sam. "Mattie lost her arm at Bandy Hawk Lake!"

Quickly, the Seeker pulls out her GPS and enters that destination. A moment later. the handheld locates the necessary coordinates displaying the quickest route. She prays she won't be too late.

———————◦ ◆ ◦———————

Henry Wildbird is aware of his sister's deliberate attempt to stonewall the presidential negotiations. The command center video surveillance acts as reconnaissance.

Confused, he thought he had convinced his strong-willed sister to accept the agreement. Why, then, is Mattie involved in another dangerously unrehearsed chase?

Everything had been going as planned: The String's inner circle surrendered in exchange for Hinmah's pardon. The entire group unanimously agreed to concede. Hinmah's freedom is dependent on the entire group's concession. This prearranged visit includes the FBI's tactical squad, the National Guard, and Sam the Seeker's operatives.

Henry's immediate concern is the lone National Guardsman shadowing Apple.

"What is that simple bastard up to, Dagmar?"

The elder engineer watches the long-legged private tracking Apple and considers the possibilities.

"The only explanation I can think of is that this guy thinks he'll jump the ranks with a single-handed apprehension."

Henry asks Winslow to zoom in on the guardsman's face. The magnification sends an immediate chill down Henry's spine. He bolts from the center to re-enter history.

Winslow looks to Dagmar.

"What the hell... Look at the M1 Thompson. There's only one reason for the handler to customize that gun with a Hawkeye borescope."

The Command Center leaps into overdrive. Creekbaum yells, "Keep every camera we've got on that wicked son of a bitch, Winslow!"

"I'm calling Gig," relays Gracie Holdsclaw.

Dagmar's reaction is typical. Calmly, he tells everyone to settle down.

"If ever Mattie needed us, it's now."

Chapter 75-
LAKE SWALLOWS BIRD WHOLE

Hinmah straightens her husband's tie atop his stayed Italian shirt with eighteen-inch collar. Delsin's black eyes, full of reflection, scan the lake as his mate works towards a final, genteel finish.

This couple has endured more than their share of tragedy. One day, fate visited the Wildbird family and, with it, calamity. These two forces fostered a deep heartbreak that, in the end, created an involuntary sagacity that the old medicine woman still describes as "insanity."

Today, fate will once again expose Hinmah's clan. The old medicine woman prays for a peaceful conclusion to this tumultuous circle of events. She stands back to appraise her work.

"You look very refined, my husband."

The giant delicately lifts his wife's tiny hand and kisses it and then gathers the old woman in a massive embrace. She brushes her hair back into place and fluffs the wrinkles from her dress.

"We must go. It won't do to be late."

The giant pulls at a hardback copy of *The Theory of Island Biogeography*, hidden in plain sight with other noteworthy reads inside a nearby bookcase.

Hinmah and Delsin back away from the table, chairs, and carpet that they roll upwards. The floor automatically lifts, exposing the hidden entrance to the underground tunnel. Hinmah slips down the staircase into the well-lit passageway and waits as the Delsin folds himself into the dark shaft. From below, Hinmah hits the tunnel lever, and a series of pulley mechanisms reverse everything to their origin. Should someone walk into the cabin after the lever is drawn, they would have no idea the passageway exists. Thus, demonstrates the brilliance of Dagmar Eiksund.

The old couple's fine apparel gets little attention inside the command center. They stand in the background, tucked out of the way, frozen in time. The tension is palpable. Hinmah's keen intellect quickly makes sense of the activity and immediately perceives the impending danger. She instinctively focuses on the National Guard private and mutters, "Ciske."

The old medicine woman moves to Winslow's side as he manipulates every camera in the area. It's then she recognizes Mattie's pursuer is armed.

"Dagmar... who do we have out there?"

"Your grandson left just minutes ago," volunteers Creekbaum.

Dagmar attempts to calm the elders.

"What we've ascertained from surveillance is very sketchy. It seems Mattie is having second thoughts about the proposed meeting. Winslow, please play the recorded video from a few moments ago," requests Dagmar.

The elders watch as Mattie throws her prosthetic arm at Apple, condemning the president's promise as preposterous. Fate settles in on the woman with unimaginable clarity.

"Oh, my God, Mattie is headed to the lake," cries Hinmah. "This can't happen again."

Delsin scrambles into a nearby four-seated Honda Pioneer 700. He means to kill Ciske.

———◆———

An Air Force Lockheed C-5 Galaxy lands at Great Falls International Airport. One of the HMX-1 Squadron's eleven covert Sikorsky VH-3D copters rolls out the nose of the behemoth cargo plane and is made ready for takeoff.

Regal Markay, Adjutant General and trusted Pentagon advisor, sits beside the president, presenting detailed intelligence regarding Governor Crebo Lund's financial acquisitions. Markay's military reputation is impressive, but more importantly, his historically professional standing makes POTUS comfortable.

"Our finest forensic auditors have verified Greyson Chance and Henry Wildbird's declaration. Every dime obtained from Triad Realty was used for land purchases on behalf of the String," confides Markay.

"This includes Crebo Lund's share. In short, the scammer got scammed. Lund's account tallies over five million dollars. These funds purportedly vanished in the Bitcoin scandal. In fact, Wildbird fleeced everything."

Delahunt chuckles.

"I've got to meet this Henry character. So, Lund has no idea he's been taken by his partners?"

"That's right. Wildbird set up three separate Bitcoin accounts for the funds gleaned from Triad Realty holdings. Henry subverted all three accounts using a backdoor cryptosystem. In short, he bypassed the typical authentication process that secured these personal Bitcoin accounts. When Crebo Lund paid a well-established computer hacker to substantiate how the accounts were leveled, Greyson Chance intervened. He simply paid Lund's hacker more to look the other way. The best part is that the hacker got paid twice — and with Crebo's own funds," laughs Markay.

"The raid on Tully Neff's camp was a second blow to Lund's self-esteem. He went off-shift. His over-developed hatred for the Wildbirds swelled.

"It's been reported that Lund has fallen far into the bottle, sir. A vengeful man like Crebo is dangerous after such humiliations," adds Markay.

"That's exactly why I mean to act fast. What I find fascinating is that Lund unwittingly contributed to the String," verifies an astounded president. "Does he know? That fact alone could send any self-aggrandizing jerk over the edge."

"Precisely," adds the pensive adjutant general. "Frankly, I could never figure out why Greyson Chance put up with that pompous ass."

Familiar with Markay's direct but compassionate attention towards the rank and file, the president states, "Tell me more about Chance."

"Sir, he's an exceptional officer who served his country honorably with two tours in Iraq and Afghanistan. Chance is one of the few true gentlemen left. I'd trust him with my life."

The President sits back against the leather commander's chair of the Sikorsky helicopter and looks out the main cabin's window.

"Well, then, let's offer Chance and the Wildbirds a ride to the Seeley Swan. I mean to see Lund face justice before things get deadly."

Chapter 76-

BANDY HAWK ECHO

Mattie has increased her lead to the lake but hasn't lost her pursuers. Technology and familiarity level this chase. Apple is already at the base of Bandy Hawk Mountain, and his shadow, Ciske, has looped to the right, remaining out of view.

The GPS gives Sam an advantage over Apple. Its coordinates take her into Bandy Hawk at a higher altitude. This upper elevation allows Sam an unobstructed view. She's particularly leery of the trailing National Guardsman. Tracking Ciske in camouflage is difficult. Sam keeps an eye on Apple, correctly surmising that the private stalks Mattie.

Mattie reaches the narrow shoreline of Bandy Hawk and sits on her haunches for a better view of her trackers. Two forms, barely detectable, are shielded by forest. She assumes Apple's escort is Samantha Cherchez. This assumption may be fatal.

Sam concentrates on the woods, but its density makes it nearly impossible to detect the camouflaged assailant. Two shots echo through the canyon simultaneously. The first belongs to Dennis Ciske.

———————◆———————

The race to Bandy Hawk Lake is challenging. Enveloped in terror, Henry has made his way to the lake. This resilient man cannot fathom such a recurrence. Everything accomplished will be destroyed if Mattie dies at the hands of Lund's hired gun. A lethargy consumes Henry's legs. It takes every bit of internal strength to compete with the sound of the bullet. He consolidates all his might into a forceful leap.

Time is no more than an artificial pretense. Native Americans measure this superficiality not with a clock but natural phenomena. The circle of life holds all truth. Spherical fate is forever the final yardstick.

Mattie senses Henry's presence. His coiled mass knocks her into the cold depths of the lake's water. This chilled shock is all too familiar. Mattie doesn't struggle as Henry pulls her to the bottom of the lake. Trusting her twin brother is inherent. Mattie's lungs scream with agony as consciousness dims.

The water's force builds against Henry. He looks for the light and drags Mattie towards it. He begs his mind to concentrate on the task. There's the light. Henry trusts in its brightness and rallies towards its heart.

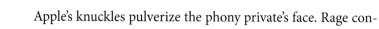

Apple's knuckles pulverize the phony private's face. Rage consumes Mattie's lover. It's not until Sam pulls the furious DOI deputy from atop Ciske that some semblance of sanity is regained.

"Hell, Apple, if I wanted this guy dead, I would've handled it with my shot. Stop! We need to ask this fool why he took a shot at Mattie in the first place," reasons the Seeker.

Dennis Ciske lies atop the soiled surface of the mountainside. There's a lot of blood. Sam deliberately avoided Ciske's brachial artery. Her precision was intentional. It wouldn't do for the private to bleed out. Apple's fury is less exacting. The DOI deputy grabs Ciske by the lapel, dragging him to an upright position against a nearby boulder.

Just then, an off-road vehicle screams to a halt. Delsin leaps out. Real fear pulses from Ciske's bloody face. The angry giant leaps from the driver's seat. Apple intervenes.

"Who told you to take that shot, private?" asks Sam.

Delsin breaks loose of Apple's grasp long enough to sign, "Dennis Ciske! Dennis... Ciske."

Sam looks at Delsin with renewed recognition. She turns back towards the National Guardsman and slugs him with all her might.

"Tell me what I need to know right now, or I'll let Mattie's grandfather tear you apart."

Henry Wildbird surfaces with Mattie in tow. Fretting, Hinmah lingers atop the interior cavern's shore. Dagmar, Winslow, Creekbaum, and Holdsclaw position themselves next to the medicine woman. The wait seems limitless. It isn't until the old woman recognizes Henry's shadow against the iridescent green of the lake that she realizes she's holding her own breath.

Finally, the oxygen-deprived twins claw their way to shore, gasping but without the slightest crimson stain. Mattie felt Ciske's shot pass so closely, it reverberated. She smiles at Henry, and they break into the mercurial laughter of relief. The intensity of what was narrowly avoided isn't lost on anyone. Mattie hugs her brother.

"That's the second time you've saved me. Thank you!"

Hinmah swoops her twins into an unceremonious hug. Her grandchildren once again barely survive, but today, fate breaks favorably for the Wildbird clan.

Chapter 77-
LAST DANCE

DOI Secretary Mac and Adjutant General Regal Markey sit beside a large table on Air Force One. It's filled with progress reports, graphs, and charts, visually tracing each tract of land comprising the whole of the String. The president analyzes the corroborative evidence that proves each swathe, strip, and band of property is, in fact, presently owned or leased by the state of Montana.

He asks, "These so-called leases: They represent the private sector's buy-in? That makes it sounds like the farmers and ranchers approve of the String's concept."

"Yes, sir," responds Markay. "Turns out these privately leased properties prosper comparatively to those operations who simply cull wildlife. The strategy to lease back the private acreage to the original owners for the operational purpose comes at a small fee. This provides legislated tax relief on said land, and the leasebacks provide the owner additional income. FWP Director Jim Tarkio's family homestead, the Ten Lee Ranch, is both prototype and proof that stratagem works."

"Wait a minute," reacts Delahunt, "the governor's self-appointed FWP director is a String insider?

"Sir, I think we all need to steady ourselves. Today's revelations are... well... shocking. Tarkio is just the tip," continues a stunned Markay. The general reads from a list provided by Sam the Seeker's investigative team.

"There is a tactical strategist from the governor's own office and high-ranking administrative specialists inside every IT department, and that includes the lead financial Comptroller for the Department of Natural Resources. The record is lengthy. For example, the String's inner circle is aptly supported by a world-renowned Scandinavian tunnel expert. Look at these blueprints of the Bandy Hawk tunnel installations."

Markay lays the blueprints in front of the President.

"Astonishing... no wonder these eco-warriors managed to evade the National Guard," reacts Delahunt.

Amazed, the adjutant general goes on, "The entire Wildbird family is listed. A prominent Montana State University Professor, a taxidermist who specializes in robotic decoys, an expert crew of horsemen, a wildfire crew chief with plans for dual-purpose fire tunnels as demonstrated by the attached schematics. These diagrams plan ready safe zones that allow wildlife to pass through and at the same time offer emergency refuge to people.

Mac interrupts. "Do we have a complete list of all the accomplices?"

"Yes," reports the general, handing the document to Mac, who reviews the list and imperceptibly gestures to the president.

Markay continues, "The String's financial disclosures have been confirmed. It appears every penny has been accounted and credited towards the purchase of the String. There's one problem.

Since the raids began, an enormous sum of money has been contributed to the String by a variety of public and private benefactors."

Delahunt is relieved to hear the snag is a windfall.

"How much money are we talking about?"

"Let's see." The general squints through his spectacles. "Upwards of two million dollars, Sir."

Markay thumbs through the report.

"This only reinforces my theory that the String has deep roots. It seems we've merely scratched the surface. Regardless," continues Markay, "the DNRC comptroller has earmarked the excess monies to maintain and improve the ecology of the String. Her records categorically list promotional sales from various paraphernalia. Shirts, coffee mugs, insignia posters, key chains — all add to the superfluity. Apparently, even tattoo sales make contributions.

"The emblem and motto 'Join the cause before there's no cause to join' bring in a nice little sum. The inner circle's innovative use of pure donors as contributors was a stroke of genius.

"These cumulative donations prove the cause. Whoever developed the String's social media knows their stuff. I wouldn't have been surprised if the Wildbirds recruited a Madison Avenue ad agency. The record indicates a Native American woman by the name of Holdsclaw is charged with String publicity. She bled a video to cable news that flushed out the full Tully Neff embarrassment. That went viral and so did support for the raids."

"What was that reporter's name?" asks POTUS with a nearly undetectable smirk.

Mac chuckles, "Percy, Macy Percy, I think. She literally caught that poor bastard Tully with his pants down."

This rejoinder gives all three men reason to laugh.

"The Tully raid infuriated the governor. That's when he labeled the riders eco-terrorists. He claimed that these forays destroyed Montana's hunting economy. Shortly after, the ensnared Hester sisters garnered massive attention. It turns out the twins are Olympic US Equestrian Team medalists. Just imagine the Robin Hood effect. Look at this chart. Our stats show that the Hester twins played out as underdogs. The average U.S. citizen saw those young ladies as heroes."

Markay shakes his head.

"That kind of public exposure rallies even the most indolent environmentalist. Olympian role models — great! What could be better?"

The helicopter swings wide back towards Great Falls International Airport. Marine One White Hawk's first female pilot relays a radio message to DOI Secretary Reilly Geo Mac via the headset attached to the helicopter's bulkhead. He listens carefully and then heads back to his seat opposite Delahunt. Both the president and the general peer out White Hawk's windows and then back to a visibly distressed Mac.

"Sir, there has been a shooting at Bandy Hawk Lake. We don't know the specifics, but the Secret Service feels it's too dangerous to continue," reports Mac.

Markay's mind reels with tragic possibilities.

"Is anyone hurt? Do we know that much?"

More heavily invested than he realizes, Mac stammers.

"It just happened. All we know is that a National Guardsman took the shot."

Markay literally appears to shrink with the news. Calmly, the president assesses what is known.

"Mac, please tell the pilot to turn back for Bandy Hawk Lake immediately."

"But, sir, the Secret Service detail-"

Interrupting mid-sentence, Delahunt intervenes candidly.

"Well, you can tell them POTUS made this call, so they better send that Super Stallion full of Marines into the area. I don't give a damn how many helicopters they use in their shell game; this particular bird better land within twenty minutes."

The president's eyes soften.

"I gave the Wildbirds my promise. Now, get me down there, and let's find out what the hell is going on."

Chapter 78-
THE AFTERMATH

The right side of Ciske's face makes the infuriated giant's statement better than words. Sam does everything she can to stop Delsin from beating Ciske to death. At one point, the Seeker forces her handgun against Delsin's temple to prevent a deliberate homicide. With Delsin's massive hands still wrapped around Ciske's neck, Apple attempts to reason with him.

"Grandfather, please. We need this guy to tell the world what happened at Bandy Hawk. You and I both know that Crebo Lund shot Tree and Isabelle, not this sniveling piece of crap. If you want to take Lund down, we need Ciske's testimony."

Delsin's tear-stained face looks curiously innocent, even as his exposed, blood-soaked knuckles strain to keep Ciske from taking another breath. With a deep sigh, he lets go.

Seconds later, Ciske finds himself in the back of the four-wheeler. Sam and Apple glance at one another with relief before the Seeker joins Ciske in the backseat. She promptly cuffs the inert and nearly unconscious prisoner.

Apple's fear for Mattie is evident. He hastily slides in beside Delsin.

"Please, Grandfather, get us back quickly."

The trip back feels endless and is far from comfortable. Ciske moans with each bounce over the rugged terrain. The vehicle's occupants have too much time to deliberate. Has Mattie survived this latest attack on her life? Everyone but Ciske understands the importance of her survival. It's the difference between fairness and deceitfulness, justice and prejudice, bias and equality. All basic suppositions of lawfulness.

———————◆———————

The Secret Service has plans for Dennis Ciske. Little time is wasted to tender his extraction from the four-wheeler. Delsin barely stops long enough to dump the man trash. The fake National Guardsman finds himself face down in the dirt, pinned by four advanced members of the presidential bodyguard. They show little regard for previous injury. Ciske's arrest gives Garrison Colonel Clarkson a reason to place his SAT call. After his many missteps, Clarkson wants to personally inform the governor.

"Good afternoon, sir. We've made an arrest at Bandy Hawk. No, sir, the shooter isn't a National Guardsman. I'm happy to report that the counterfeit is alive. Defense officials from the FBI and Secret Service are interrogating him now. Yes, sir. Thank you, sir. I'll be sure to update you as soon as we know more."

Clarkson disconnects the satellite handheld but wonders why Lund asks if the imposter is alive. The unsuspecting Garrison Colonel shakes off the governor's strange reaction.

Chapter 79-
FATEFUL REUNION

A still-dripping Henry stands beside his twin sister inside the large cavern. Once Delsin and his passengers arrive at command, the giant literally bounds from the four-wheeler to lift a soggy but living Mattie into the air, his overt relief shared.

A drenched Henry joins the celebration, hugging his brother first and then Sam, who's secretly delighted. Apple's relief is palpable as he waits for Delsin to release Mattie. She reaches out to him and whispers an apology.

"I'm sorry I gave you the bird."

Apple smiles as maintains a protracted hold on his one genuine devotion. Finally, the Seeker steps forward.

"Dennis Ciske is in custody. The Secret Service and FBI won't take a gentle approach during his interrogation." Sam points to Apple. "That gentleman will ensure that Ciske and Lund pay for the murder of Isabelle and Tree Wildbird."

Cheers echo throughout the cave. Mattie's stature is reduced mightily as she stands next to the Seeker. The undercover agent is a good seven inches taller. The two appraise one another before Mattie uses her remaining index finger to beckon Sam in closer.

"Thank you," she shivers.

The Seeker smiles and leans into Mattie.

"The law belongs to everyone. I couldn't ignore your plea for justness."

Mattie Wildbird throws her arms around the Seeker's neck as another thunderous cheer engulfs the cave. The two rivals are forever friends.

Creekbaum is prepared. The professor turns to Gracie and Pete Holdsclaw.

"The String's a delightful story, and it's going to make a damn great movie. Let's dance, girlfriend."

Creekbaum hits the iTunes icon on the computer and tags the perfect musical refrain. The cavernous chamber rocks with the 1963 classic by the Rivington's, "The Bird Is the Word." Gracie Holdsclaw's true love drags her to the center of the command to dance as if it's their last.

A grin covers Apple's face as he grabs his girl by the hand and twirls Mattie Wildbird into the center of the celebration. Laughter reigns. Everyone joins in, including Dagmar Eiksund, who takes charge of a line dance. The party is in full swing when the president walks through the cavern's hologram.

"Man follows earth. Earth follows heaven."

Chapter 80-
SHARED INFINITY

The last group of Mattie's legendary admirers moseys up White's Pass at a pace befitting the company. No one seems in a hurry to complete this precious, yet sorrowful task. The familial company, glorious natural setting, and honorable quest fill each member with dignity. This ultimate celebration for a fabled family of determined people is a sacred event.

Everyone is in the saddle by the break of dawn to see an end to a Wildbird's mythical existence. The honor is both wonderful and regretful.

The second day's ride completely reveals the String's inner circle. Today, the funeral procession stops at each of the monumental plaques in honor of these apt environmentalists. Sam the Seeker, as orator, carefully explains why and in what order each ecological patrician is revealed.

The first plaque brandishes Dagmar Eiksund's gallant Norwegian features. His three-dimensional bronze peers out from underneath a barricaded tunnel secluded with overgrowth.

Sam dismounts here to meet Reilly Geo Mac at the base of the commemorative display. Mac opens a small but hefty metal storage box beside the plaque. The lockable cement enclosure was ordered and constructed with a presidential mandate. Sam reads aloud.

"Dagmar Eiksund, by order of the president of the United States, is bestowed the Congressional Gold Medal of Freedom for engineering feats in support of the boldest ecological advancement in modern history. You and each member of the Ink Prayer have positively impacted not only the United States of America but humankind."

Mac places the award inside the lock box as the stunned members of Mattie's procession recognize for the first time the significance of this journey. There can be no testimony more befitting the String. Tee Fairfax records everything in as much detail as possible. Now, the journalist fully comprehends the historical importance of the trip. She reels in reverence. Creating an official record of the String's vibrant path through history is more than she had hoped.

Winslow Sharp, Marley Womack, Regal Markay, James Tarkio, Gig Robbins, Greyson Chance, and Anne Creekbaum, along with Gracie and Pete Holdsclaw, are commemorated with an accompanying Medal of Freedom. These memorials are placed intermittently along the String's interior. The president's only mandate was that the many schemes used to build the String be kept secret until after his time as Commander-in-Chief. Presidential pardons might be at stake. POTUS felt the decision to exonerate the inner circle may have been condemned and possibly overturned by his political opposition. Hinmah was the first to agree that the fewer outsiders who knew, the better. Why give partisan extremists a target?

On the third day of the journey, the group passes within sight of a steep limestone escarpment known as the Chinese Wall. Sweet Brown Betty rides alongside her lifelong friend Samantha Cherchez.

"I know it's taken too long to apologize. You know, I'm sorry for the hell I put you and Beggs through during the investigation. I just got all caught up in these people's decency."

Sam the Seeker, decorous and affectionate, is quick to dismiss the breach.

"Betty, you must know that your goodness saw Beggs and me through some tough times. Your integrity protected our team's virtue. Without your principled compass and Beggs's devotion, I would've been lost."

Just then, Reilly announces the procession's arrival at the next plaque. Betty and Sam are the last to dismount. This memorial lies at the onset of the White River, drenched in sunlight and surrounded by a field of wildflowers.

Sam makes this announcement with an abundance of pride. "This is the tribute to Betty Akara-Stoltz, who is ceremoniously revered for her righteous representation of the String and its builders."

Betty cannot believe her own eyes and bellows with the sentiment. The brilliant undercover agent collapses to her knees before the three-dimensional plaque pressed into her likeness. People take turns congratulating the astonished fighter of crime and prejudice. Sam consigns the Congressional Gold Medal. Sweet Brown Betty feels its heaviness around her neck.

"Without you, the String would have perished to a blind injustice."

The bliss of this unexpected acknowledgment overwhelms Betty. She leans into her husband. The retired Sheriff Drake Scholtz supports his wife as she takes in this unexpected honor.

Chapter 81-

HUMBLE ROUNDS

The next morning, the entourage suffers from an emotional hangover. Greasy bacon and freeze-dried eggs act as medication for anyone who might have abused the drink. It's not without pain that Mattie's trailing forces saddle up. Only the magnitude of duty compels them forward.

Sphinx Mountain, the tallest in the Chinese Wall's fortress, is still covered with snow. The band heads west across rich chasms and over narrow trails blazed through the multilayered rock and slides deep within the String. Bandy Hawk is in sight now. The group rides in ever more-protected land dedicated to wildlife migration. Animals large and small take full advantage of these backcountry environs. Safeguarded from endangerment, these animals pass unimpeded by humanity's overpopulation and sprawl. Mountain lion, bear, bighorn sheep, marmot, fox, and more enjoy free passage.

It's a three-hour journey to reach the next tribute. The plaque reads "'Apple' Tamer Gray, champion to his people and land." The retired DOI deputy enjoyed thirty-two incredible years with Mattie before a heart attack leveled him along the trail to Hinmah's old cabin. Here, Apple is celebrated neither as Native American nor White, but rather as a prodigious citizen of these United States and mighty contributor to the String. His legal expertise and language finalized Hinmah's conception and dream into legitimacy. Sam spreads Mattie's ashes here, as all bow their heads in this moment of grief and reunion.

The String's circle is nearly complete. A special surprise awaits the weary travelers. Four newly placed boulders embedded with commemorative plaques stand guard before the Wildbirds' cabin homestead. The Ink Prayer's two great medicine women have a permanent home in history. Delsin and Henry's stories buttress Hinmah and Mattie's, like the fortifying roles they played in real life. The center of this boulder citadel reveals the images of two diminutive, peaceable warriors, Hinmah and Mattie Wildbird, Ink Prayer spiritualists and dreamers.

———————◆———————

Each traveler takes his or her time to set up camp and get ready for the final ceremony. The tribal council made plenty of food and drink to promote this glorious occasion.

Drake Stoltz and his crew busied themselves erecting a large white screen against the cliff walls fronting the cabin. The projector bounces historical videos of the rocky face. Cheers echo down the gorge. Betty, Reilly, and Beggs provide humorous vocals to support the mesmerizing footage created by the late Gracie Holdsclaw and her fearless devotee, Anne Creekbaum. Laughter and love mark the dedication as these three characters tease one another in front of the crowd. Sam witnesses it all and readily concedes Mattie would have treasured every moment.

Reilly and Beggs bow to one another as Cooper and Betty find a seat. Still standing before the crowd, Reilly looks to Sam for permission. She gently pounds her fist against her chest and blows him a kiss as the ceremony begins.

"Ms. Fairfax, can you come up here, please? We need a witness," requests Mac. The young journalist makes her way through the crowd.

"While you busied yourself trying to secure Mattie's story, she was doing a little research of her own," declares Reilly Geo Mac the third.

"It seems we two are related. Our shared lineage takes us all the way back to a Corporal Reilly Geo Mac of the United States Seventh Calvary. Apparently, our great-great-grandfather knew the Ink Prayer people long before we did. You'll find the corporal's remains in the Miles City Cemetery. Mattie wanted to encourage you to consider the familial connection with Corporal Reilly Geo Mac and the dynamic life he lived. She thought her own past just too boring."

The crowd roars with laughter. The shy and pleasantly surprised journalist hugs her distant cousin before returning to her seat.

"Now, in all seriousness," declares Mac, "can we get Samantha Cherchez to come forward?"

The Seeker makes her way through the throng, shaking hands and hugging many who came to commemorate Mattie's final dictum.

"I want to thank you all for coming. By now, everyone knows that Mattie left behind a letter. The contents may stun you a little. She asked me to share what she refers to as the 'real prize.'

"Secretary Geo Mac managed to secure a copy of the official document to which Mattie refers in her last letter. Mr. Geo Mac, would you please read aloud the contents of Mattie's 'real prize'?"

The laudable retired Department of the Interior director, Reilly Geo Mac, is dressed in a three-piece suit that Beggs brought from their shared Washington, D.C. home. The entire gathering is shocked to see President Andrew Delahunt emeritus appear on the screen.

"Hello, everyone. I'm sorry I couldn't make it to these festivities in person. I came to announce the completion of the final portion of my promise given to the Wildbird family. Section Two of the 1906 Antiquities Act gives the president power to protect lands owned or controlled by the government. The Great State of Montana's newly formed ecological String of Pearls is the ultimate standard for natural resource conservation and defense. From this day forward, to safeguard its purpose and future, the United States of America has officially purchased the String. It stands as the largest National Wildlife Reserve in history.

"Theodore Roosevelt himself would be proud that the String be given protective status. Not since the days he held office has such a stance been taken to protect wildlife.

"Like Roosevelt's declaration of Yellowstone, I, as president of these United States, stand tall in my pronouncement. Let it be known that all who fostered and encouraged the development of the String are now properly acknowledged, this by my order, signed by the president of these United States. With that, I send my highest regards. Enjoy the celebration and have a cold one for me."

The white screen goes blank. Stillness prevails. It's as though if anyone in the crowd breathes, it might adversely affect the conclusion. Sam stands before the gathering.

"Ladies and gentlemen," offers Sam.

"The federal government purchased the String several decades ago. It has been controlled and cared for by the United States Forest Service. That first step was a victory unto itself. Today, as per a past agreement, Andrew Delahunt's word is made right: The String is an official national monument."

A happily spontaneous eruption reminds Sam of the Super Moon celebration. She revels in its reverberation, waiting patiently before she continues.

"You already know that Dennis Ciske admitted a drunken Crebo Lund shot Tree and Isabelle Wildbird. That particular score was settled the day Ciske confessed to taking a second shot at Mattie."

Sam turns to look at Bandy Hawk lake, remembering the terror of that moment as history nearly repeated itself.

She continues.

"The FBI's interrogation and Ciske's confession made it apparent to the governor that it was only a matter of time until he'd pay for his crimes. You may have read of Crebo Lund's suicide those many years ago. While the score has been settled, nothing can ever compensate for the Wildbirds' misery. It's my considered opinion that Hinmah's self-proclaimed insanity and Mattie's resilience made the String possible. Thank you, President Delahunt. Your pledge that the String be identified as a national monument has been upheld."

Joyful adulation, tears of gratitude, and simple displays of disbelief grip the crowd. A buzz of excitement floats down the canyon and across the lake as the old medicine woman's cabin settles into Sam's peripheral vision. Lost in her own memories, the Seeker listens again to the children laughing as Hinmah makes fun of the extravagant and unscrupulous Sir George Gore.

Behind the crowd, Drake Stoltz shyly introduces himself as he points a projector at the rocky ledge covered with a white screen. Playful celebration lingers as Gracie Holdsclaw's original footage plays off the mountainside. The inventive inner circle can be heard conversing in the background as they react to each National Guard response, tactical warfare at its finest.

Sam the Seeker stands in the foreground as Virtuoso and Mattie glide by in a race to the plateau's edge. The String's riders split off in groups of threes, until Mattie and her beloved steed are left alone, fluttering towards the rising sun. The film pulsates as the enchanting Virtuoso dances and weaves in a tight circle. Mattie smiles at the heavens. A final wave of light follows her and Virtuoso over the plateau's edge into the archives of history.

-THE END-